Who's Killing All the Lawyers?

A. G. Hayes

Savant Books
Honolulu, HI, USA
2011

Published in the USA by Savant Books and Publications
2630 Kapiolani Blvd #1601
Honolulu, HI 96826
http://www.savantbooksandpublications.com

Printed in the USA

Edited by Mary Yamin-Garone
Cover by Christie Ussher. Image created from public domain base
images "sword of justice" and "old style arrow" clipart by OCAL at
Clker.com.

13 digit ISBN: 978-0-9832861-2-7
10-digit ISBN: 0983286124

Dedication

To my wife Connie and family, Michael, Patricia and Christopher, who encouraged me in so many ways to enable this story to see the light of day.

Acknowledgements

To author and poet Maggie Roth for her tireless advice and encouragement. My special thanks to Hollywood writer Lea Andrews and the Hungarian Grammarians and my agents, Gloria Koehler and Donna Eastman at Parkeast Literary Agency. Without them I still would be collecting rejection slips. Finally, special thanks to my editor, Mary Yamin-Garone, and her sharp eye for a comma being placed before a conjunction introducing an independent clause and my publisher, Daniel Janik, the "Man Behind the Curtain" I *did* listen to.

Who's Killing All the Lawyers?

Chapter 1

The man in the tuxedo had an arrow buried almost to the fledge jutting from the left front of his white starched shirt. His right fist, crusted with dried blood, was clamped around the arrow below the flight, indicating he never knew what hit him.

In mortal pain, his instinct was to attempt to withdraw the foreign object he suddenly found embedded in his chest. Because an Indian arrowhead is perfectly configured to enter freely but not exit easily, that struggle merely served to rip his organs more severely as he endeavored to extract it. Flat on his back, the deceased lay in an old, wooden, cattle chute just off Centerville, a lonely road in Gardnerville, Nevada.

Special Agent Joseph Falk parked his World War II jeep just off the pavement on Centerville, killed the engine and slid from the vehicle. Falk was a handsome, chestnut-haired man in his thirties.

The collar of his deer-hide jacket was turned up to merge with the rim of a woolen cap that covered his ears. Together the garments sealed off the cold wind that rustled the sagebrush of Job's Peak, a jagged pinnacle of the Sierra Nevada Mountains that overlooked Lake Tahoe to the west and Douglas County to the east.

The moon was low, casting geodesic light across the sloping countryside. Falk mumbled to himself as he strode toward the Douglas

County patrol car and the deputy sheriff. The lawman was one of three individuals who had preceded him to the location, evidenced by an old Plymouth sedan and a Cherokee parked alongside the highway, their engines still crackling as they cooled.

Falk had no idea why he was called to this crime scene. He was Reno FBI, Rover Division. This investigation was not his and he wasn't going to let it become his. The body was on Nevada Bureau of Land Management property. Being involved meant working with BLM agents and working with *anyone* right now flew in the face of Falk's brooding, fiercely solitary nature. He still was chewing on his wife's death.

"Morning," he mumbled to the deputy, introducing himself.

"Five-thirty," the man said with a sigh made visible by the cold air. "Thirty minutes to my official quitting time." He kicked idly at a rock and told Falk what Falk already knew. "This stiff is on BLM property, making this a federal case, which means a shitload of reports and red tape." He leaned against the door of his cruiser, arms folded over a paunch Falk guessed he'd been working on for fifty years. "I'll be lucky if I get off the job by noon."

Concluding that the man already had been at his job for too many years, Falk didn't offer so much as a shrug. "Who called it in?"

"Mr. Anonymous, about forty minutes ago from a pay phone up at the lake. Caller's probably seen too many TV shows depicting the person who finds the vic as the *numero uno* suspect."

Falk left the highway and scrambled through a gate, inhaling fresh, grassy aromas of pastureland. He climbed up the side of another cattle chute a dozen yards from the highway. Portable lights the deputy had strung along a fence separating the field from the pavement illuminated it.

2

"Good morning," Falk felt obliged to say to a woman he had never met but knew to be the Carson City Medical Examiner. It seemed she already had examined the body. She stood, nodded and pulled off her heavy latex gloves. "I'm Joseph Falk, FBI," he added. Under the glare of the bare bulbs, she looked thirtyish, beautiful but tired. Medium height and slim build, she wore a thick merino wool coat and a watch cap. Her dark skin was smoky in the early morning light.

She shot Falk a quick, absorbing look. "Millicent Maxwell, ME."

Standing beside her, a tall, rangy blond in his early thirties offered a nod in Falk's direction. "Wes Webster, BLM."

Falk had a preformed opinion of BLM agents in general. He mostly thought they could phone in the type of jobs they did.

"Don't see many killed that way," Webster said, nodding toward the arrow jutting from the dead man's chest.

Maxwell scribbled in her notebook and then looked up at Webster with a straight, brown-eyed gaze that didn't miss anything. "Right, not much doubt as to cause of death. He's been dead about forty-eight hours."

Falk leaned forward for a closer look. "Certainly not your regular, garden variety arrow."

"Also right." Maxwell pointed with her pencil. "In essence, a radio-controlled missile; the flight is thin, pressed aluminium."

Falk nodded. "Really?" He didn't attempt to disguise his surprise at Maxwell's apparent knowledge of an extremely unusual weapon.

She continued while Falk scrutinized the arrow. "You probably already noticed there's a fiber optic wire protruding from the end of the shaft, attached to a dime-sized disk. It's curved and fashioned to retain its aerodynamic shape."

Falk's eyebrows wrinkled upward. The woman had a keen eye for details. "You sound like a weapons expert."

He thought she might imagine that her quick assessment intimidated him; bruised his male ego. A black, female medical examiner was not such a novelty anymore but her cool expertise probably ran up against its own prejudice in some quarters. Right now, he wasn't of a mind to care what she thought.

As if offering him a gracious out, she said, "In all honesty, I've seen one of these before…had a chance to study one."

"Where was that?"

"I can't disclose that information."

Falk stretched into a standing position, his large, slender hands resting lightly on his hips. He *did* have a prejudice against uncooperative, smartass medical examiners. "Pardon me?"

"Try the Carson City DA's office." She snapped her bag shut. "Nice meeting you, Agent Falk, Agent Webster."

Falk watched her nimbly climb down from the chute, seemingly unencumbered by her heavy coat. She got into the Plymouth sedan and drove off.

"She's new," Webster said. "Only been with the department a couple of months, I understand. From back east; Chicago I think."

Falk shrugged. He returned his attention to the body. "She call the coroner's wagon?"

"Should be here any minute." He watched Falk go through the man's pockets. "How the hell does a man in a tux end up in a cattle chute out here in the boonies with a high-tech arrow through his heart?"

Falk had just asked himself the same question. He reached into the inside pocket of the tuxedo jacket and removed a slim leather wallet, flipped it open and checked the driver's license. The photograph was indeed that of the dead man, Howard L. Kiley. The address, an expensive area in Incline Village, Lake Tahoe, was consistent with the tux and Rolex on his wrist. Robbery was not the motive. In addition to the Rolex, credit cards and cash were still in his wallet. His business card indicated that he was an attorney-at-law.

Falk folded and replaced the wallet and continued his examination. The only dirt on the victim's clothes was on his back, acquired when his body landed in the chute. The soles of his shoes were clean. Falk silently wondered if Webster had come to the same conclusion he had when Webster answered the unasked question.

"This is a dump job."

"Right," Falk mumbled. "Howard Kiley was nowhere near a cattle chute when the arrow pierced his heart."

Why was he killed this way and dumped here? Was he killed by Indians? He knew today's Native Americans were certainly more sophisticated than they were in the last century. Was it possible that they had created smart arrows and were killing people with them?

On the other hand, did someone simply want it to appear that way, to implicate Native Americans, at least symbolically? Falk was certain about one thing: whoever reported it did so to be sure the body was found. Another few hours and it would be road kill for carnivorous wildlife.

A BLM vehicle that arrived without sirens or flashing lights interrupted Falk's thoughts. The deputy's harsh voice immediately drifted up to Falk and Webster. "Your crew's here, Webster. You don't need me any longer. I'll have the lights collected later; almost daylight anyway."

"Thanks, you can go," Webster shouted. "I'll release the body soon as I'm through and stop by your office for the paperwork."

Falk watched the deputy wave and head back to his cruiser, no doubt thinking of the large breakfast he would soon devour at Sharkey's, where most locals went for good food and coffee. Falk climbed up the wooden slats to exit the chute. "Yes, it's your homicide, Webster. Body's on BLM land."

Webster nodded in the direction of the occupants of the BLM vehicle who got out and started toward them. "I've asked for video and still pictures."

A gray-haired man wearing a size 2X parka puffed up to the cattle chute, photographic equipment hanging from his shoulders like loose reins on a carthorse. Not long from retirement, Falk judged.

"Alex Spade," Webster said to the rotund man, "this is Special Agent Joseph Falk, FBI."

When Spade's eyebrows shot up, Falk said, "I'm not here officially." It was a wish and a statement. Falk was here because Tom Stewart ordered him to be. Stewart was his contact in Cerberus, a covert federal agency that employed Falk's skills and, to a particular, mentally well-defined degree, enjoyed his loyalty.

Stewart had called him at 4:15 that morning, apprising Falk of the attorney's body in the chute. It was the latest in a recent string of similar lawyers' deaths in Nevada and California.

"Check out the scene on Centerville Road," Stewart had said, "and meet me at the usual place at seven."

Falk left his apartment in Reno and headed south on I-395, through Carson City and to rural Centerville Road. He hoped checking out the body would be the extent of his participation but a hunch nagged at his heretofore impeccable intuition.

"Spade's a still expert," Falk heard Webster say. "He's been shooting crime scenes since they used Speed Graphics."

Falk noticed that Spade wielded a digital, strobe-equipped Nikon that he unslung then started shooting film. The camera snapped and whirred as he deftly captured all angles of the victim's deathly repose.

"Is Koski with you?" Webster asked.

Spade jerked his thumb over his shoulder. "Yeah, moving slowly. She's no morning person."

Later Falk remembered that assessment and added that Susan Koski did not appear to be an afternoon or evening person. In fact, his observations concluded she seemed to be merely going through the motions of living.

Koski looked like a teenager but was probably in her late twenties, dressed in a bulky snowsuit and baseball cap turned backwards. She casually approached the chute, hardly acknowledging Webster's introduction of Falk.

Koski was about five-one. She looked like a person whose bathroom scale didn't need to register a hundred pounds. She had short, raked-back, ash blonde hair, full pouty lips and was pretty in a natural, no-fuss way. Falk later learned she recently had engineered a lateral transfer to BLM from Las Vegas PD and that she did her job well. She may be the best videographer in the district. Due to a particular circumstance in her not-too-distant personal past, she vacillated between numbness and rage.

"Koski, go over everything, too, inch by inch," Webster instructed. "Cover the area around the chute first. Come up here when Alex is through. I'm pretty sure the body was dumped."

"Okay," she said in a disinterested, husky voice.

Falk watched for several more minutes as Koski silently obeyed, shooting with her digital Sony camcorder. She used her equipment with practiced ease, one eye at the eyepiece while the other seemed to be seeking out the next frame. He noticed her eyes, sea green, and the sort in which ships were wrecked.

A siren wail began in the distance and grew steadily.

"The morgue wagon," Webster advised. "They like to arrive in style."

Falk turned and walked to his jeep. He did not envy Webster. He seemed like a regular, possibly too youthful guy, having to work with a know-it-all medical examiner, a fat man salivating for retirement and a young, zombie-like videographer who probably couldn't be goosed into an emotion.

Falk looked at the clouds that snaked around the mountaintops. Not yet winter and the Sierra already had gathered weather that boded a harsh season to come.

Chapter 2

Yesterday Falk was in his element; seven thousand feet in the Sierra Nevada Mountains on an assignment for the Bureau's Rover Division. His jeep had churned its way over a rock-strewn trail, the purr of its well-tuned engine belying its appearance. Splotches of gray primer mingled with faded khaki paint made the vehicle difficult to see in the surrounding terrain.

That was how Falk preferred to work: alone, blending into twisted scrub, pitchy pines and craggy mountain outcroppings. He was a deep cover, roving agent for the little-known Rover Division, established after the government's 1993 debacle in Waco, Texas. Falk was a self-contained man, not unlike the OSS agents dropped behind enemy lines in Europe during World War II or today's Special Ops troops.

The federal government finally had become aware of its need to improve covert observation and control over potential terrorists and rogue paramilitary groups. As a rover, Falk's job was to infiltrate such fringe assemblages all over the western states. His aim was to be accepted among the ranks of such factions, keep to himself and report whatever useful information came into his possession to the Bureau.

Today, Falk had been ready to head for Reno HQ to file just such a report when the global system mobile phone in his jeep rang. If not for the damned GSM phone that employed a Cerberus satellite and was used by Cerberus agents worldwide, he would be unreachable here in the mountains. "Falk," he growled into the receiver.

"Joe, Stewart here. We need to talk."

Tom Stewart was not only Falk's primary contact but also director of Cerberus, a federal government agency so top secret that few in the Bureau, CIA, NSA and even Homeland Security knew it existed. Stewart never called him unless it was important.

"Okay, Tom, what's happening?"

Stewart had scheduled a meeting with him for later today but he called this morning to inform Falk of the corpse in the cattle chute and changed their meeting to six a.m.

It was precisely six and still dark when Falk turned off the highway. Three letters in the flickering neon sign were out, leaving the stuttering message in garish pink to read: VA ANCY. CABI S WITH KITCHE S. Falk passed the pink anagram, bumped across the potholed parking lot and proceeded to motel cabin number eight. It was the last in a row of wooden cabins built when they were known as motor courts. He snapped off the headlights and eased from the jeep. As he neared the cabin door, it opened. No lights glowed from within.

"Come in," a deep, familiar voice said.

Falk entered and the door closed behind him. A second later, a low wattage table lamp came on, weakly illuminating the shabby two-room cabin. He crossed to a wooden table, pulled out a chair and eased his one hundred and seventy-eight pounds onto it.

Tom Stewart was a white-haired man in his late fifties, tanned and trim. He went to a gas burner and removed a coffee pot. "Coffee?"

"How long's it been brewing?"

"Long enough." Falk raised an eyebrow and Stewart caught his meaning, adding, "But not *too* long." He filled two tin mugs and handed one to Falk.

"What's the problem, Tom?"

Stewart lowered himself into a sagging easy chair. "I couldn't tell you on the phone yesterday but I got word that the Bureau is putting together an investigative team to look into what has now become the serial killing of lawyers. They want you to head it up."

He hurried on before Falk could protest. "This will be a new gig for you; not Quantico-controlled as you once were and not a solitary Rover Division agent. You will be out in the field and responsible for clearing up this mess. I wanted to give you as much of a heads-up as possible."

Falk set down his mug. "Why are they tapping *me* for this? I want to continue what I'm doing."

"They need the best and that's you. It's that simple. Yours was the first name that came up at the bureau chiefs' meeting yesterday."

Falk shook his head. "It figures they'd choose the one person who doesn't want the job." He paused and studied Stewart. "As always, I'm amazed at how much you know about what's happening at the Bureau."

Stewart grinned. "My ESP and I have a friend at Covert Transmissions, Domestic, both reliable sources."

Falk watched the play of humor on the man's face. Freshly open and honest one moment, Stewart's expression could evoke images of unfathomable darkness in the next.

The two men had met several years ago when Stewart recruited Falk for Cerberus. The name *Cerberus* was derived from the dog of Greek mythology said to have three heads and designated as keeper of the entrance to the infernal regions where the gods resided.

11

Those in the present-day organization who adopted the name believed it was their duty to see that America was protected from domestic insurgence, to sniff out foreign terrorists and to respond to any threatening intruder, internal or otherwise, with ferocity. Falk initially resisted initiation into Cerberus but ultimately he acknowledged the need for an organization that covertly supported America's security.

Falk's membership in the Rover Division was an added bonus to his recruitment and, in turn, he felt honored to lend his expertise to what he now believed was a vital tool in the future security of the country.

"Your Bureau control will call and give you the details of this assignment," Stewart went on, "but let me fill you in on what we know. You're not going to like it."

Falk resignedly tipped his chair back. "Okay, Tom, spit it out."

"You said you'd heard about the recent murders of California and Nevada lawyers so you know that, like the man in the cattle chute, all were killed by arrows to the heart."

Falk sighed. "You think the government believes Indians are to blame. So-called arrows are killing lawyers at a time when various Native American tribes are exercising their sovereign rights to open more casinos in the interest of self-improvement." He shook his head. "I'm not altogether convinced. You know these are not conventional arrows. They're more like guided missiles designed to look like arrows."

Stewart eyed Falk over the rim of his coffee mug. "Didn't you recently disclose that there have been reports of Indian militia maneuvers?"

"What I reported were scattered, disorganized, half-ass military-type maneuvers by some members of the tribes...more like bonding excursions, nothing menacing."

"But with the potential to organize, right?"

"Do we even have a *clue* Indians are killing the lawyers—any real evidence?" Falk gave him a skeptical glance and a slightly impatient gesture that indicated he still awaited the bottom line.

"So," Stewart said, "maybe the tribes have decided that no one is paying enough attention to them. Maybe they've decided to kick the pressure up a notch. Emboldened by economic security from their casinos, maybe to expand their gaming rights and thus obtain privileges they believe are due them."

He finished his coffee and set the mug down. "You may find it difficult to imagine a full-scale Indian uprising in this country in the 21st century, Joe, but I believe it's a distinct possibility." He leaned forward. "I don't know about you but that thought scares the hell out of me."

Falk let his chair return to all fours. "I don't know, Tom...all of this because of a few more casinos..."

"Casinos translate into money, Joe, which translates into power —power to negotiate for...whatever..."

Falk got up and headed for the coffee pot. "Try this, Tom. What if it's not the Indians? What if it's somebody who wants us to *think* it is?"

"Okay, who then and why?"

"Well, the Nevada gambling cartel for one. They're dead set against any increased Indian gambling in California." He signalled with the pot but Stewart declined. Returning to his chair, Falk continued his thought. "The Nevada Mafia could have chosen this reign of terror against lawyers to scare the public into anti-Indian sentiments. The mob feels the pinch every time a Californian fails to cross the state line to gamble in Nevada. If they succeeded, it would keep millions in Nevada gaming and resorts."

Stewart seemed convinced of his initial argument. "From all accounts, the murdered lawyers were working *against* Indian gambling. That would put them and the Mafia on the same side."

Falk nodded. "That's the one thing that doesn't make sense. Then again, it's possible we're not dealing with an American Indian or a Michael Corleone. Maybe it's just one crazy son of a bitch who majored in archery and simply hates attorneys."

Stewart seemed to go along. "Or perhaps the killers are foreign terrorists with their own reasons."

Falk gave him a cynical stare. "You're pumping sunshine up my butt. You've already made up your mind as to who you think is responsible."

Stewart's lips turned into the bemused grin with which Falk had become familiar.

"In any case," he said, "the governor of Nevada has agreed to let the feds help solve this quickly. He wants to avoid using high profile agents in logo jackets. Naturally, local police are investigating. We and the Bureau trust their ability about as much as we trusted LAPD to nail O.J. or the Boulder police to arrest the person we all know killed JonBenet Ramsey.

"Moreover, if there's inside involvement the locals could be suspect. So, they're counting on you and a small, elite team to do the leg work…get the facts from the bottom up."

Falk rose and stretched. "When does this assignment begin?"

"You'll hear from Lester Carter at the Bureau tomorrow."

"I'll check in with you from time to time."

"No need. I'll know where to find you."

Falk had a few more questions. "Tom, how and why is Cerberus involved in this?"

Stewart stood and ran a hand through his thick white hair. "We're not actually involved at this point but as a Cerberus member, you know it's our responsibility to always be acutely aware of the balance of domestic power and any possible shifts in that power. Let's just say that the economy's suffering enough. We don't want to be surprised by an economic earthquake."

Falk generally felt Stewart had a habit of speaking in riddles, like a baseball club's general manager dancing around the subject of trading an iffy pitcher. This seemed to be one of those occasions. Rather than try to decode the man's thoughts, and since that seemed to be the extent to which Stewart was prepared to explain, Falk nodded and started for the door. "What do you know about this so-called elite team I'm supposed to get? Bureau agents or local?"

Stewart's eyes flickered as he went to the door and opened it for Falk to exit. "I don't know for sure but if what I'm hearing is correct, as I said, you're not going to like it."

Attorney Mark Sharpe stood on the balcony of his lakeside home, smoking an expensive cigar. Six feet tall, almost two hundred pounds, the counsellor was as imposing a figure at home as he was in the courtroom. Clothed in a heavy brocade dressing gown, he gazed across Lake Tahoe, which shimmered in autumn's early morning light. Snow dusted the mountains rimming the lake. This was a dream location, his third residence and, unless the feds raised interest rates and the NASDAQ dropped even further, soon he would consider a fourth.

His wife called from inside the house, "Coffee's ready. Breakfast in five minutes."

Sharpe blew a smoke stream and watched as a light wind swirled it for a moment before it vanished. He entered the bedroom and was halfway across the room when something made him stop and return to the balcony. There was a cough of smoke from his last inhalation when the arrow thudded into his chest. He fell back against the wall. His knees buckled and he slowly slid to a sitting position on the balcony floor, a vivid, vertical track of blood tracing his descent.

Chapter 3

That night Falk's mind dwelt heavily on the moment of physical impact that each of the lawyers must have experienced in their deaths. The terrifying human condition of being unexpectedly hit by a lethal projectile. Then, in the wolf hours of the next morning, from nowhere, Falk heard not the twang of a bow string, but the sharp, deadly crack of a rifle. A bullet speeding in slow motion travelled inexorably in his direction. He was in a dense, surreal forest yet the bullet—red with a shine like dripping lacquer—kept to its steady trajectory. It didn't strike anything directly in its path despite trees that grew so closely together they seemed to inhabit the same piece of landscape.

Falk sat in the passenger seat of his Toyota and stared straight ahead through the windshield. He still saw the lethal bullet homing through the woods to his right, flashing in a beeline for his right temple. While he expected its arrival, he also was powerless to escape it. When it hit him, he felt a knife-like incision in the right side of his head and the world exploded.

He awoke.

He sat upright in his bed, perspiration weeping from his body, the sheets over and beneath him sodden with sweat. He turned and let his feet slide to the floor. He'd had the same dream many times in the past two years yet it was *not* his nightmare; it was Meg's.

17

He looked at the red glowing digital figures of the black square on his nightstand—four o'clock. He stood and ripped the soaking sheets from the bed. You could make soup with them! He threw them toward an overflowing hamper in the corner of the bedroom and grabbed his robe.

Over his usual weak coffee, he reminded himself of what the therapist, with whom he kept only three appointments after Meg's death, said: "It wasn't your fault your wife was killed."

Wasn't it?

They were returning from a day in the backcountry in their four-wheel drive Toyota when the engine quit. Despite his best efforts, he could not get the damn thing started. It was late afternoon and without a cell phone he had no choice but to walk to get help. Meg wanted to go with him but she had turned her ankle when hiking earlier in the day. Not a sprain but it was painful. There was no way she could walk the rough terrain.

Falk always carried emergency blankets, flashlights and the like so he made her comfortable and promised to return as soon as possible. He never saw her alive again. When he returned two hours later, she was dead; shot once through the head. The police were unsuccessful in determining who was responsible for what was ruled "death by misadventure." Whoever fired the shot most likely never knew they killed someone. The theory was that the shooter, using a high power Winchester, could have been a mile away when he fired, missed the intended wild animal target, and the bullet continued traveling until it struck Meg.

She'd been sitting in the passenger seat with the window open a few inches to allow fresh air in. When the bullet reached the Toyota, it had enough speed left to kill her, striking her right temple. The irony was that had the window been shut, the bullet, nearly spent, would merely have struck the glass, possibly cracking it but not with enough power to break it.

Falk headed for the shower. Going over it again did no good. He had to clear his mind. Lester Carter of the Bureau would call any minute to inform him of the assignment Stewart had generally outlined yesterday. In a cynical moment, he thought of the stinging lawyer jokes he had heard or read on the Internet and wondered if someone had really taken the quote from Shakespeare's Henry V1 seriously; "The first thing we do, let's kill all the lawyers."

As hot water cascaded down his body and attuned him to the day, he thought about the team to which he was assigned. He hoped they were a bright, dedicated group.

Who's Killing All the Lawyers?

Chapter 4

In less than two hours Falk received messengered papers confirming his temporary transfer out of Rover Division to FBI headquarters in Reno. Carter, his bureau chief, had called briefly but had no details. He only informed him that Nevada State Attorney General Donald Lovesy would be arriving at Reno HQ to meet with Falk and his team at three p.m.

Shortly before three Falk joined Lovesy and his two aides in a secure room on the second floor. The building supposedly was constructed to preclude any possible listening devices. Falk stopped before an eight foot square Plexiglas map of the United States that seemed portable and hung with temporary hooks. Lovesy faced a computer monitor, keyboard and printer on the table beneath the map.

"Marvelous device," Lovesy said to Falk, who watched as he tapped in the name Mark Sharpe and a code number two, both of which came up on the monitor. Simultaneously, the number two glowed blue on the black and white map in the area of Lake Tahoe, which was lit up in red, in the yellow-colored state of Nevada, where Sharpe met his demise.

"Marvelous device," Lovesy repeated. He hit one of the keys and the map went dark, then he tapped a button on the printer. A color printout of the previously lit section of the map highlighting the locations of all the recent lawyers' deaths slid out of the machine into his waiting hand.

Lovesy seated himself at the head of the table. Falk took the seat to his left just as the door opened and three individuals Falk recognized entered the room.

"I believe you all know each other," Lovesy said, waving a hand in the air.

Falk attempted to keep the sinking feeling he felt in his heart from showing on his face as he nodded to each of them.

The slim, stunning, African-American medical examiner was dressed in black linen overalls over a beige crewneck and a black Georgio Armani blazer. Gold chains adorned her neck and wrists and various rings brightened all but her ring finger.

BLM's Wes Webster's most involved assignment before now was probably hunting for a mountain lion that had killed a dog, some sheep and a nine-point buck out of season. Alex Spade, gray-haired and overweight, wore a permanently disheveled suit, his soon-to-be-retired Nikon hanging from his neck.

Then all heads turned as the aide who had stationed himself near the door responded to an exterior sound. He opened the door to admit the fourth member of what Falk now knew was to be his "elite" team. It also was the reason Stewart had warned, "You're not going to like it."

Susan Koski, the petite, slow, sauntering sensational blonde, wore black slacks, an oversized hand-knit turtleneck sweater with a mosaic design and black boots. Her eyes reflected a distracted Twiggy look. She slid into a chair next to Spade, set her camcorder on the floor and leaned back, crossing her hands on her lap as if waiting to be entertained.

Lovesy did not seem the least bothered by her late arrival but Falk remembered Spade saying that Koski was not a morning person. It was six minutes after three.

"Ah," Lovesy said, "so glad you all could join me." He gestured and one of the aides approached him with a sheaf of papers. "These two gentlemen are part of my staff," Lovesy said. It was clear that he did not intend to introduce them.

Portly Donald Lovesy, middle-aged, with a large, square mouth and a smile like a toothache, wore a too-tight suit, the jacket of which he alternately unbuttoned and buttoned, straightening and sucking in his girth on each occasion.

"Shall we begin," he said, aware that none believed it to be a question. "Needless to say, the governor is more than anxious to complete this investigation *yesterday* and to foil the media circus that can possibly result from it. As you know, the recent murders in Nevada and California were all committed with the same kind of weapon and each victim was a lawyer.

"The homicide investigation you are being asked to conduct will be quite visible, followed closely by print and broadcast media, an unfortunate and unpleasant fact. You are authorized to tell them nothing."

He paused and pursed his thick lips as he repeated, "*No thing.* Whatever you uncover is hereby classified top secret. *I* am the only one who gets a copy of whatever documents flow from this endeavor."

He paused again, quickly glancing around the table. "No doubt you've all heard rumors about who is responsible for these killings— the American Indians, the Mafia, radical Islamic militants, the Iraqis, the Russians, the Chinese…"

He waved a hand and let his voice trail off as he straightened and slipped the middle button of his jacket from its hole. "Whoever—we need to know the truth ASAP." He turned to Falk. "We'd like to see a thorough and timely 24/7 probe. You'll report the results directly to my office or to a contact Washington has assigned us—a man in the National Security Agency whose name and phone number you'll be provided with."

He pulled himself up in his chair and re-buttoned his jacket. "Questions?"

Maxwell said, "I understand the importance of the assignment, sir, and I'd be honored to serve. I'm a medical examiner, not an investigator. I'm not sure what expertise I could bring to such a team."

"My intelligence sources tell me that you're uniquely familiar with this type of arrow, that you have studied several…"

"Well, yes, extensively, in fact, but—"

"That fact, in addition to our desire to confine the team to those already involved in some way, makes you an ideal person to be pressed into service for your country in its hour of need."

Maxwell could only nod as the AG went on addressing Falk. "You will have full access to all files on the murders—electronic and otherwise." He squared the edges of a stack of papers in front of him. "Including those in California."

He deliberately stared at each person. "You will be under FBI jurisdiction until otherwise notified. Bear in mind the governor's insistence that this remain a top secret operation until brought to a swift and satisfactory conclusion. Do I make myself clear?"

A murmur of agreement echoed around the table. "Very well, now you will sign documents to that effect."

He handed boilerplate forms to each of them. "Read and sign

these, please." As he collected the signed forms he said, "You will be given all the support you need from any state or federal agency that can be of assistance, including the Office of Homeland Security."

Handing out cards, he advised, "One number on this list, the NSA contact I mentioned—Samuel Ryland—you should have with you at all times. Washington has assigned him to oversee your investigation."

This was the first Falk had heard of Ryland. "Sir, does that mean we *report* to him?"

Lovesy unbuttoned. "No, not at all. I understand that Samuel's a busy man. He'll be around if you need him. If I need an update I'll call him. He'll be on the periphery.

"Well," he pushed back his chair and buttoned up again, "I'm sure you five will work well together. Thank you for your service."

The closest aide opened an attaché case and extracted a thick stack of files that he deposited on the table. Falk noticed they were stamped in red: AG Channels Only. "These are top secret." Gesturing to the computer, he added, "E-files are at your disposal." Then, with the two aides at his heels, Lovesy left the room.

Falk jammed his hands into his pants pockets and walked to the window. He felt uncomfortable for several reasons. For one, he was dressed in a suit and he was a man who looked and felt better in a sweater and jeans. For another, he had a question he decided to keep to himself. With his team being so "visible," as Lovesy put it, the media was bound to get interested and ask questions.

Yet he was under orders not to give them any information. If the fourth estate did not get answers in one quarter, they were motivated to query another. It was almost as if the reporters were being set up. Teased to ask yet denied access to answers, forced to dig deeper—

why? He'd have to see how it played out.

Not speaking to the media or anyone else for that matter was okay with him.

He thought about what he knew of Lovesy. When the AG last ran for office he'd won by smearing his opponent at every opportunity. Now, Falk had to take orders from the man he considered an unprincipled politician.

It was a typical aspect of FBI employment that made Falk glad he belonged to Cerberus. It was an outlet for the frustration he sometimes felt over the tactics of the too-often bungling Bureau.

Falk stared down at the rooftops of Reno and sighed. That brought him back to his present problem, the four albatrosses Lovesy had hung around his neck.

Koski muttered in her disarmingly husky voice, "I suppose that once we've looked at these files we have to eat them," referring, Falk supposed, to the AG's remark regarding them.

Maxwell grinned but one glance at Falk sobered her.

"Damn," Spade groaned, getting up from the table. "I don't know what *I'm* doing here. Has anyone stopped to realize that I'm only days from retirement?"

Falk looked from Spade to Maxwell to Koski then to the tall, quiet BLM agent. "What about you, Webster? You got anything you want to gripe about?"

Webster looked around with a surprised expression and shrugged. "I'm cool."

"Good, because anybody who has anything negative to say about this assignment and who isn't ready to totally commit to it can get the fuck out!"

There was silence while Falk waited. Nobody moved. "Look, I

didn't ask for you—any of you—but I've got you and we've been given a job to do." He returned to the table and sat down. "Let's begin by going over these files, shall we."

Three hours later Chinese take-out food containers were scattered on the table. Falk rubbed his forehead and gazed at the slumping assembly. "Okay, I think we've learned all we can from these and the computer files. We'll meet here in the morning, at which time I'll have worked out our first course of action."

"What if I'm needed in my department? Has anyone been assigned to take over for me in Carson City?" Maxwell questioned.

Falk opened up a file marked for his eyes only. "Yes. As of now, you'll be staying at a hotel in town. Some of your clothing already has been transferred by a female agent." He closed the file. "I'll have a car take you there." He noticed that she seemed disconcerted that someone had gone through her personal belongings but he made a mental note that rather than complain, she opted for irony.

"Oh, a *female* agent," she quipped, "that makes it all okay."

Falk got up. "Okay, people, tomorrow morning, here, at nine sharp." He flipped open his cell phone. "I'll get your transportation, Maxwell."

Before he could dial, the phone rang. "Falk," he snapped. After a few moments he said, "Thanks" and disconnected.

He punched in a number and while it rang he informed his four hangers-on, "The Douglas County Sheriff's Office reports that, as with the others, the Centerville arrow contained no prints." He'd been hoping for a positive break but no such luck.

Falk stopped at a convenience store on his way home. When he returned to his jeep, a deep, familiar voice pronounced his name from the dark Lexus perfectly parked beside his vehicle. He turned and saw

Tom Stewart at the wheel.

"Got a minute," Stewart said casually.

Falk rounded the back of the Lexus and slid into the passenger seat. "Tom, how in hell do you always know where to find me?"

Stewart offered his characteristic grin. "ESP and—"

Falk interrupted. "I know. I know—you have a friend at Covert Transmissions, Domestic, both reliable sources."

"You're going to want to know this." Stewart's head often moved from side to side as he spoke, his eyes alert to any movement near the two automobiles. "I just got word that a man who has been known to be connected to various nefarious activities in Nevada—nothing that can be proved, mind you—may be a mediator involved in the deaths you and your A-Team are investigating." He paused.

"Oh," Falk said coolly.

"He's known only as The Fox."

"The Fox? Aren't we cute."

"I know, conjures up old cloak and dagger images. If he's in any way involved in this business, however, he could be a formidable player."

Falk frowned. "Hold on a second. I've heard that name before."

His eyes went abstract as he related a chance encounter he had some time ago with an old trapper who had retired from his job at a mine up in the Sierra near Bowman Lake.

"I'd been hunting in the area and came across this guy and we shared a fresh trout dinner at his camp. This geezer told me that one day when he was still working at the mine, he overheard a guy talking on a cell phone as he sat in his car in the parking lot. The old guy remembered very clearly the words he heard the man say because, as he put it, 'They gave me the shivers.' The man on the phone said, 'This is The Fox. Kill our target.'"

"Did he see the man?" Stewart asked.

Falk shook his head. "I asked the same question. He said he only saw the back of his head—dark hair—as he drove away in a nondescript compact."

"Did he notify the police?"

Falk shrugged. "Said he thought about it and decided he might have misunderstood…that the guy may have been talking about an animal…about killing a fox…I don't know. I guess, finally, he figured he might have imagined it. Still, he never forgot it."

Stewart sighed. "Well, if there's anything to the old man's tale, all the more reason why you should be aware that this chap is out there."

Falk slid the information to one of the back burners of his mind. "Thanks. Anything else?"

Stewart put the key into the ignition and the expensive engine purred to life. "Just good luck."

As Falk climbed out of the vehicle, he thought about his A-Team and mumbled, "I'll need it."

Who's Killing All the Lawyers?

Chapter 5

Nine o'clock the next morning, Falk silently pushed through a wave of print and electronic media reporters gathered outside the Reno office.

He entered the conference room, carrying a cup of coffee, and sat down. Webster was seated, reading the *Reno Gazette-Journal*. He lowered the paper, "Morning."

"Morning," Falk answered. He sipped his coffee and looked toward the door as Maxwell entered, followed by Spade. Falk turned to Webster. "I did say nine o'clock. Where's Koski?"

Spade wheezed as he lowered himself into a chair. "She sometimes has trouble with her car…and she's not a morning person."

"You said that yesterday," Falk snapped. From what he had learned about Susan Koski since their meeting last night, she may not give a damn. He was stuck with her, at least for now.

He needed a top-notch videographer on this assignment. He would try to be patient.

Falk was already feeling the smothering sense of company. He was doing exactly what he did not want to do: babysit this BLM bunch. He was antsy to get this assignment over with. He wanted to get back into the field, where he was alone, where he was most dangerous and where the eternal distance between Meg and him lay lightest on his heart.

He looked around the room. He hated small talk but information collecting about those you had to work with was never a waste of time, even if it seemed trivial.

He'd read the bios on each team member that Lovesy supplied. At some point in the near future, Falk's life might depend on these individuals. He needed to know what was *not* in their files. He turned to Maxwell, whom he learned was single with only one living relative —a father in Chicago, an ex-cop to whom she never spoke or corresponded.

"Everything to your liking at the hotel?"

"It's okay. It's a hotel." She sipped a strong Latte Grande that she held in both hands for warmth.

"I understand you work with Police Chief Bud Vigo in Carson City. What's he like?"

"In his fifties, about five-seven, dark hair with a stupid bowl haircut and blue eyes that are so light you sometimes think he has no eyeballs."

Falk smiled inwardly. He got the smart-ass answer he expected but ignored it. "I mean what's he *really* like? They say he's tough."

Maxwell took another sip of coffee and seemed to relax somewhat, sensing what appeared to be a sympathetic ear.

"In truth, he's a bit obsessive—drinks, smokes and like so many Nevada natives who insist they never gamble—can't resist testing any slot machine he comes across."

Falk shook his head. "Smokes…that's really bad."

"And he smokes unfiltered cigarettes!" Her eyes rolled. "He says it's the chemicals in the filter tips that kill you." It was her turn to shake her head. "Regarding working with him, yes, he's tough. It took me a half hour yesterday to convince him to let his pilot and his precious department helicopter fly me to Reno for our meeting with Lovesy."

"Seems unreasonable."

She was back in the emotion she felt twenty-four hours earlier. "I made the point that it would give the chopper crew a break from nailing tourists on I-395 but he insisted he wasn't running a taxi service." She paused. "He finally acquiesced."

Falk glanced at his watch; five minutes past nine. "Why do you think he was so reluctant?"

She shrugged. "He's just naturally surly. It's as if something's always eating at him."

"Or maybe he wasn't thrilled that you were invited to that meeting and not him. Could be just plain professional jealousy."

She looked up at the clock on the wall. "Maybe."

Falk got the feeling that she felt she might have said more than she meant to.

"How long do you think this investigation will take?"

He sighed in sudden irritation and couldn't resist voicing the source of that emotion. "Depends on how soon her highness gets here and we get started."

At that moment, the door opened slowly and Koski entered nonchalantly. Her video camera was slung over her left shoulder. She held a Styrofoam cup of coffee in one hand. On her head was a soft white polar fleece snowdrop hat that framed her brooding face with a '20s flair. She carried a snow jacket and wore a long, heavy, natural-cotton turtleneck sweater that covered all but the legs of dark sweat pants.

In her quiet, inflectionless voice, as if she was offering no apology at all, she said, "Sorry to be late." Distracted, she rummaged in the purse that hung over her right shoulder. "I had car trouble."

Falk noticed Maxwell give Koski a lower-over-upper-lip smile. He made a mental note that the medical examiner either was the compassionate type or was good at faking it.

"We know you're not a morning person," Falk said, hoping the sarcasm he oozed punctuated his frustration. He glanced quickly around without making eye contact with anyone.

"I'll say this slowly." He didn't care that it sounded condescending. "It's important that you all fully understand my expectations for you as members of this team. Each of you has various skills and training. It's my job to see that you and I use those skills to maximum effect."

He turned to Maxwell. "Your medical training, familiarity with police procedures and knowledge of the arrows should prove invaluable."

Webster paid wide-eyed attention as Falk addressed him. "You'll be second-in-command in the event of my absence or incapacity. You're seasoned in various facets of criminal justice and have had hands-on confrontations with criminals at all levels in rural and urban settings."

Out in the air, those words sounded over-generous but surprisingly, Webster's file had impressed Falk. The Bureau of Land Management was an agency of the U.S. Department of Interior, managing 1.5 million acres in Northwest Nevada. Webster was responsible for a good portion of it.

"Spade and Koski, as photographers you're going to be very busy. I'll want a lot of video and digitals for every situation in which we're involved."

Spade suddenly cleared his throat for attention. "I don't mean to sound...unpatriotic..." He paused and seemed to choose his words deliberately, a fact not lost on Falk. "I wonder if you have any specific idea as to how long this investigation will take. Due to my pending retirement, I mean...my wife and I having made plans to drive to Arkansas to visit her sister and all...The RV's ready to go." He laughed nervously and his round, chubby face reddened. "In two weeks I'm scheduled to be a senior citizen holding up traffic from here to Little Rock."

Falk managed a thin smile through gnashed teeth. "If all goes as I anticipate, Spade, we should all be back to our normal pursuits in a couple of weeks." Almost inaudibly, he added, "God knows, I hope so."

He glanced around the table. "Any more questions?" When there was none, he continued. "First, bad news. I got word earlier that a hang-glider pilot was found dead this morning near Spooner Summit close to Spooner Lake. It appeared to be an accident; he crashed into a tree. When rescue personnel got him down, however, they discovered he'd taken an arrow in the chest before he hit the tree. He was a corporate attorney moonlighting for a Vegas hotel against expanded Indian gambling."

Falk paused long enough for the others to assimilate the news. "Now, just because we'll be watched by the media and our movements reported doesn't mean we won't try to stick to standard investigative procedures.

"This morning we'll check out the locations of two killings. Webster, you take Maxwell and Spade and go to Spooner Summit." He handed Webster a map with the marked area. "Scrutinize the terrain up there, particularly any spot that offers cover from which to fire an arrow. Spade, I want extensive digital photos. Koski and her equipment will go with me to the house at Lake Tahoe where…," he checked his notes, "Mark Sharpe was killed."

As she had in the Lovesy meeting, Koski sat silently, seeming to listen at times, distracted and aloof at others. In any case, Falk already had set a mental limit on how much time he'd give her to snap out of it.

"We should be at our initial destinations between eleven thirty and noon."

He reached into a case on the floor beside him, removed one of two phones and slid it down the table to Webster. He took out the second phone and placed it on the table in front of him.

"These have a closed frequency. Although they're cellular, they're the closest thing we have to a secure line with the ability to send and receive while scrambling and decoding."

Falk felt the need to translate for his BLM charges. "Meaning that when I transmit, it goes out scrambled, cutting down on the chances of a spurious signal being picked up by someone else. When you receive my message, your phone will automatically decode. Any questions?"

Koski chose this moment to offer sardonic appraisal. "Those Chinese are amazing."

"Made by Motorola, Koski, right here in the U.S. of A." He turned back to Webster. "I'll have Koski call you when we're done at the lake, then we'll switch locations. You'll examine the Sharpe crime scene while Koski and I check out the Spooner location. This way, if one of us misses something, hopefully the other will catch it."

He stood and finished packing his case. "We'll leave by the back door. Despite what Attorney General Lovesy said about our being visible, I'm not ready for the media sharks out front."

"Do we have any leads on perps yet?" Webster asked.

"Nothing," Falk said, "but that's what we're here for."

When the four walked out, Falk noticed that Maxwell initiated a conversation with Koski, the latter seeming to be hard pressed to hold up her end of the discussion. Webster had to slow down for the lumbering Spade. Frank wondered how in hell he was supposed to pull these dilettanti together into an efficient team.

The Kingsbury grade is a twisting highway out of the Carson Valley to Lake Tahoe. Cut through steep granite hills covered in pine and jagged rocks, it was an engineering masterpiece. Falk silently concentrated on the tortured curves while, beside him, Koski sustained a drum beat on her knees, as if listening to an inner rhythm.

"Why didn't you take Spooner Pass to the lake?" Koski suddenly asked. "Would have been quicker."

Up to this point she had said nothing. Falk actually preferred it that way. If he had to wet nurse a prima donna he'd just as soon do it in silence. "We'll go down Spooner on our way back," he snapped.

Koski mentally sang along with Carole King's "Tapestry" and tried not to think about what this guy's problem was. It was obvious he wanted her here about as much as she wanted to *be* here. She leaned back and closed her eyes.

When she had transferred to BLM eight months ago from Las Vegas PD after David went to prison, she felt sure that work would resurrect her from the walking dead. She found that she was unable to throw herself into her job as she once did, still stinging from the sadness and bewilderment of suddenly being alone after two intensely happy years with David. She wondered if the emptiness in her would fill up again.

David had not come to her as a knight in shining armor. She never wanted that. She wanted someone interesting, intelligent, kind and exciting. That David was all of that and more—tall, handsome with a disarming smile and explosive to an acceptable, intoxicating degree—was magnetic to her.

He was born in Tel Aviv in 1963 and trained to shoot and in the use and care of various weapons. When he was eighteen, his two older brothers serving with the army were killed in a skirmish in the Golan Heights. David and his parents immigrated to America where he drifted into law enforcement.

He was with Las Vegas Vice when Koski met him. She often speculated that maybe it wasn't something in his distant past that turned him—maybe it was his job. Dealing with those who fed on the warm rot at the bottom of society's slimy underbelly every day probably took its toll. Nevertheless, the true puzzle was in her. When she met David, she was on good terms with her instincts. She had complete faith in David's goodness and trustworthiness. No doubt she was wrong.

"Damn tourists! They don't bother reading the signs," Falk snapped, "and then they wonder why so many of them run off the highway."

The RV made it around the bend but the driver probably wished he had slowed down. As Falk reached the crest and began the downhill toward Highway 50 and Lake Tahoe, he intermittently glimpsed the lake; a cold blue gem.

He was bored, noting how telephone poles seemed to count their passing, and decided to try to gather a little information. "You get a chance to speak to Maxwell yesterday when we finished for the day?"

"Not really. We merely exchanged a few words as we collected our stuff. Why?"

"She told me she saw another arrow similar to the one we checked out in Centerville but she didn't say where. Did she tell you?"

There was more traffic now as they neared Incline Village. Koski cranked down the window. "No." When she offered nothing beyond the one word, he lost the impetus to inquire further. He glanced at the clock on the dashboard. "Better check out your equipment. We'll be there soon."

"Okay," she said but he noticed she made no movement to follow through.

"Uh...?" raising his eyebrows questioningly in her direction.

"It's already done. My car might break down now and then but my gear is always ready to go." She restarted the drum beat on her knees and added, "So, if we count her arrow—which we can assume is tied to a murder—plus the one in the cattle chute on Centerville, the hang-gliding lawyer at Spooner, Sharpe at the house at the lake and the killings Lovesy told us about...that makes seven."

"Yes," he said in a businesslike tone, "it seems someone's taking all those lawyer jokes to heart." He slowed as a couple of teenagers carrying a canoe sprinted across the highway, dodging traffic in their eagerness to get to the water. "Keep your eyes peeled for the address. It should be a right turn."

They fell silent again and Falk was content to return to his own thoughts. They'd managed a little conversation but it was filler. He could not imagine himself ever having a protracted, give-and-take discussion with the woman.

Nonetheless, he did wonder about her. She was an enigma. He'd read her bio, knew that her parents were deceased and she had no siblings. She'd left LVPD to work for BLM nearly a year ago and held a BA in criminal science. She'd expressed her interest in BLM's Video Division and trained in videography at the FBI Academy in Quantico.

Koski was twenty-eight years old, unmarried, five-one, a little under a hundred pounds of perfect physical condition, with intelligence that would have allowed her into MENSA with IQ to spare. He also read her file from Quantico. The FBI attempted to recruit her on the spot but she refused, saying she enjoyed the wide open spaces. So did he but he couldn't think of another thing they had in common.

"There," she said, pointing, "second road coming up on the right."

He passed the first turn, checking the sign. "Mountain Mist Drive."

"Ours is Vista Point Drive," Koski said.

"Those colorful names add to the price of the homes," he said as he hung a sharp right and started up a steep hill lined with stately pines. The address they sought was the last house, almost at the top of the ridge. The slate driveway twisted like a gray snake toward the entrance.

He parked in sight of the front door and glanced back toward the lake. "Great view, like sitting in the treetops."

Shallow steps ran up to a double front entry flanked by plants and blooms positioned to give the entrance the ambiance of a cool grotto. Falk took in the gracious two-story house of rock and timber. "This place must be four thousand square feet if it's an inch." His words hung in the air while his disinterested companion chose not to comment.

As Falk and Koski entered the home on Vista Point Drive, Webster, Maxwell and Spade tramped through brush and climbed over rocks until they reached the area where the hang-gliding victim had died. Familiar yellow tape hung from the surrounding trees and bushes.

"I'm not sure exactly what we're looking for, Webster," Maxwell said. "Obviously, the police have already investigated this scene. We know he was hit with an arrow before he crashed into the trees. I'm not sure what else we can learn."

Webster leaned against a tree, loosening his tie. "Well, Falk apparently wants us to see—to *realize*—both the scenes, get a fresh perspective. You're a medical examiner. You know that details are important."

Spade sat on a flat rock in a tangle of cameras. He waved a pudgy arm at the surrounding trees.

"You want me to take pictures of...what?"

Webster moved toward two pines, pointing upward. "The vic apparently hit the top of these trees...note the broken branches there... and his chute must have tangled near the top. Falk said the sheriff's men had to pull the body down...probably about here."

He ground the heel of his shoe into the earth, which was carpeted with pine cones and needles. Spade joined him then, snapping shots of the area and the cathedral of branches overhead.

Maxwell approached the spot. "This crime scene has been trampled so badly that it's useless."

"There," Webster said, pointing to the disturbed bark on one of the pines, "investigating officers blazed the tree to mark the spot."

Gesturing in the direction of the dense forest beyond the partial clearing where he stood, Webster said, "The killer had to have been in there somewhere."

Maxwell followed his line of sight, standing pensively for a long beat, her natural curiosity involving her more in the details with each passing moment. "One would need to be quite adept just to navigate that dense area, let alone get off a good shot with a bow and arrow from there."

Spade let his Nikon slide to his side and he, too, appraised the surrounding woods. "What did the officers at the scene say about the trajectory of the arrow they dug out of the hang-glider pilot's body?"

"Nearly straight on," Webster replied.

"Straight on!" Maxwell exclaimed. "That would indicate the killer was on a level with the vic, like up in a tree when he shot the arrow." She shook her head. "This means we're dealing with an extremely powerful archer. Just to get his or her tackle—which we have concluded from the type of arrow must include some kind of sophisticated propelling device—up in those trees takes a lot of effort…and maneuvering a bow in such tight quarters…" She carefully picked her way as far as possible into the dense woods, dodging branches and strands of dead moss that hung from the trees, while Spade followed with his camera ready.

When they rejoined Webster, Maxwell said, "Of course, I'm more accustomed to examining corpses than forests but if you ask me, something's wrong with this picture. If an archer was up in those trees they must be some kind of contortionist. They didn't disturb a single pine needle."

Chapter 6

As they covered the crime scene, Falk was impressed at how efficient and professional Koski was once she actually became involved in her work; intuitively knowing which areas and items Falk wanted videotaped before he pointed them out. This did not make her a necessary asset, just an unavoidable one.

Now he stood on the balcony, scanning the view through a pair of powerful binoculars, searching for a likely spot from which an archer could perform with stability. "The killer had to be close enough and accurate enough to hit Sharpe in the chest first shot out," he speculated aloud. Koski, meanwhile, had switched off her recorder and stood by silently.

Continuing his magnified search of the trees, rooftop and surrounding area, he focused on a house on the opposite side of the hill, its red tile roof visible above the treetops.

"Ever shoot arrows?" he asked directly.

"Yes, when I was younger."

It did not surprise him that she was not curious about his query. "I was on an archery team in college. We almost won a trophy."

He lowered the binoculars and squinted at the red roof, wondering if it was too far away to accommodate the accuracy needed to kill with one shot.

"I say 'almost' because we had a hard night before the competition."

"Studying for finals?"

"No, we were so sure we'd win that we went out and partied all night."

Then the cell phone rang, its tone muffled from inside Koski's jacket. She produced it and flipped it open. "Koski here."

Webster's voice was tinny and loud and Falk could hear it as he stood beside her.

"We're ready to leave our location now," Webster said.

Koski looked at Falk, who nodded. "Falk says okay."

"We'll arrive there in the next half hour. This is an isolated spot to find. When you proceed toward Spooner you'll see a sheriff's deputy waiting in his car as you turn right out of Vista Point Drive. I've instructed him to direct you to the scene." The phone clicked off.

"That yokel," Falk sighed heavily. "He thinks *I* need help finding the location."

Koski shrugged defensively. "He probably just thought…in the interest of saving time…"

Oh, now she's quick to remark. Falk turned back to the rooftops fronting the balcony and pointed. "Pan across that ridge, a long, slow pan starting at the right. When you see the lake, come down until you get to that pink house, far left. See it?"

"Of course."

"At that point, shift to a close-up, retrace the pan back to the red tile roof and give me a one minute focused hold on the roof before you adjust to normal and fade."

"A full sixty-second hold on the roof will seem like an hour on tape. Sure you need that long?"

He took a deep breath. "I'm sure."

She positioned the camera, ready to begin.

"No," he said, "here…stand right *here.*" He tapped the rail and moved aside until she was in the approximate spot he had vacated. She turned, assessing the terrain he indicated. Looking over her shoulder, he took her arm and quickly moved her one inch to the left.

He felt an ephemeral shock that stung the hand that touched her and reverberated to other parts of his body. Quickly moving away, he said more gruffly than he had spoken to her before, "Start shooting."

Webster's car made its way around the lake. Spade sat in the back seat with his camera gear. Maxwell was in the passenger seat beside Webster.

Maxwell stared blankly at the passing rural scene, her mind going back to the time, less than two weeks ago, when she'd seen the first of the high-tech arrows. A hiker had found it embedded in a tree trunk in the hills near Wally's Hot Springs when his dog ran into the brush and he went after it. He noticed it looked different so he stuck it in his backpack and finished his hike. It was later, when he arrived home and was unpacking, that he examined the arrow more closely, noting the tail fin and electronic contacts. He was afraid that the arrow was an explosive device. Being civic minded he took it to the Carson City Sheriff's Office.

Maxwell, along with her boss, Police Chief Bud Vigo, and others at the office, examined the arrow. It was sealed in a plastic bag and placed in the evidence cage.

Maxwell shuddered and pulled the collar of her coat around her neck.

Webster glanced her way. "Too cold for you, Doc? I can roll up the window."

"No, I'm fine." It was not the cold air of late autumn. It was the fact that she knew the arrow had vanished from the sheriff's evidence cage without a clue.

Before that, she considered evidence bags as sacrosanct. Untouchable. Then one day, entering the caged room at the rear of the department, she noticed that the tagged plastic evidence bag containing the arrow was gone.

She reported it. She and Chief Vigo looked everywhere, questioned everyone but it was never found. After that, even when she was not at the office, she often wondered if someone was there, breaking in, absconding with other evidence.

"Almost there." Webster flipped on the turn indicator and eased into the left lane, approaching Vista Point Drive.

As Webster was making his left turn, Falk and Koski, having followed the squad car Webster had provided, turned off the main road onto a dirt trail running into a grove of trees near Spooner Summit. The deputy stopped and climbed out. He was thirtyish with a tired, weathered face and gray eyes that lacked any semblance of humor.

Falk nodded to Koski and they both got out from the car and joined the deputy. The deputy hooked his thumbs into his well-worn leather gun belt, turned his head to the left and shot a stream of tobacco juice into a clump of grass three feet away. "I was told to meet Falk and Koski," he mumbled. "That you?"

Falk nodded and the man said, "C'mon, I'll show you where they found the hang-glider." He walked away.

Koski was twenty feet behind Falk as they followed the man into the heavily wooded area. Koski said, "If I'd known this was going to be a trek, I'd have asked that we stop for something to eat first."

The deputy continued for several more minutes before he

stopped and jerked a thumb over his shoulder. "She should walk into the clearing where the victim was removed from the trees. She can shoot the video at the same time. It will produce a more thorough picture. Then you, Agent Falk, can move in and she can pan your entrance from that angle to complete the shot."

Falk blinked deliberately. "Who does she look like? Steven Spielberg? This is not a movie we're shooting here, deputy."

Koski shot him an irritated look. "It is sometimes helpful later if you set up the scene, Falk."

Falk shrugged. "Go ahead. I'll wait here. Let me know when you're ready for my close-up."

Falk waited, expecting the deputy and Koski to walk no more than a hundred yards ahead. Soon they disappeared into the trees. Alone, he began to absorb the surroundings but a chill soon nudged him forward, straining to see where they were. He had gone about two hundred feet when he saw them.

Koski was on one knee, panning the ground with her camcorder, the sheriff standing behind her. The hair on the back of Falk's neck rose as if attracted by a magnet. Unaware of Falk's presence, the deputy removed an automatic from the inside pocket of his jacket and Falk saw the ugly shape of a silencer...

"Look out," Falk shouted and burst forward, his own weapon clearing leather.

Koski instinctively whirled as the deputy turned, surprised by Falk's yell. She rolled onto her side, kicking, knocking the deputy off balance. The pistol flew from his grip and Koski was on him, rolling with him across the ground.

In the next instant, they were up and the deputy swung a beefy fist, a glancing blow on her cheek. He plunged his knee into her ribs with a crack that sounded like splintering bone. Koski bent double, groaned and sank to the earth.

Now that the two were separated, the deputy pulled his service revolver from its holster but Falk got off a shot and the side of the man's head was blown away in a pink mist. He spun and staggered before his legs folded. He collapsed without a sound, the revolver still clutched in his hand. As Falk approached the grotesquely twisted figure with arms splayed on a blanket of pine needles, the man's left foot kicked twice in a final spasm.

Koski rose slowly, brushing earth and leaves from her clothes. "At Quantico," she said breathlessly, "we were taught that being in law enforcement and dealing with criminals didn't require any special talent. You simply had to understand how to handle fear." She picked up her cap that had spiralled from her head in the fight. "I guess I didn't learn that lesson very well."

Falk wiped the back of his hand across his sweaty upper lip. "Meaning you were afraid just now?"

"Terrified."

"Welcome to the club." He suddenly remembered the blow to her ribs and studied her face for signs of the pain he imagined she felt. "I thought I heard…your ribs?"

She reached inside her jacket and pulled out the broken cell phone. "You heard this crack." When Falk smiled, she added, "I know, made in the U.S. of A." She tossed it aside.

He leaned down, forced the revolver from the dead man's fingers and handed it to her. "Keep this. We're going to need all the help we can get." He looked down at the would-be killer one more time. "I knew there was something odd about this guy." He pointed toward the man's feet. She glanced down as Falk indicated that a man in a black sheriff's uniform wearing brown shoes and white socks should be suspect. "We've got to move fast before they try again."

"Before who tries again?"

"I have no idea but we can't go back to the office."

"Can't—why not?"

"Look, someone tried to *kill* us!"

"Why does that mean we can't go back to the office?"

Falk grunted. "The fewer people who know where we are the better."

"I know Webster arranged for this so-called deputy to meet us," Koski replied, "but surely you don't suspect Webster...or Maxwell or Spade for that matter."

"Not at this point. I'm sure Webster talked to the real deputy, who most likely was intercepted, maybe killed."

"What do we do now?"

Before Falk could answer, a voice behind them said, "You come with me."

They spun in unison and faced a tall bearded man holding an AK-47 at waist height. "Throw your guns into the middle of the clearing."

Falk tossed his automatic, nodding to Koski to do the same with the dead man's gun. He watched the man as he walked toward them. He had slick black hair, a compact build and looked fit and agile.

"This yours?" the man asked, picking up Koski's video equipment. When she nodded, he slung it onto his shoulder. Gesturing with the assault rifle, he commanded, "Keep your hands on top of your heads and walk ahead of me." As they obeyed, he looked back at the dead man and growled, "You'd never have been able to take him if I hadn't had to take a piss when I did."

49

A half a mile later, they came to a battered, grimy Chevy parked beneath the branches of a drooping pine. It was the kind of car you could leave on the street overnight with the keys in the ignition and no one would bother it.

The man gestured toward Koski with the Kalashnikov. "Open the trunk." He removed a silenced automatic from his jacket and held it to her head. He lowered the AK-47 and her video equipment into the trunk and covered them with a blanket, slamming the lid shut. "You drive," he told Falk, tossing him the key. "We'll sit in back. Don't try any heroics, Falk, or you'll lose your friend here. Understand?"

"Absolutely."

"Fine. Now listen up. Ahead, on your right, you'll see an old logging trail that exits onto Highway 50. When it does, turn right and head toward Virginia City. Move out."

Falk gripped the steering wheel and stared ahead, his mind chewing on the realization that he was what he swore he'd never be again: helpless—as he was helpless to save his wife's life. Meg's ghost was with him every morning when he looked in the mirror. Glancing in the rear view now, he doubled his fists, seeing their captor holding a gun to Koski's ear. The man returned his gaze maliciously, raising both eyebrows. Falk turned the key in the ignition and the engine rumbled to life. His hands on the wheel gave him hope, a sense of power, which, somehow, he'd turn to his advantage.

Chapter 7

Spade reloaded his Nikon. "I've shot a total of seventy-two pictures at Spooner and here. That enough?"

"That should be fine." Webster walked from the balcony back into the late Mark Sharpe's bedroom, sat on the edge of the bed and removed the Motorola phone from his pocket. Tapping out a number, he spoke as he waited for the ring. "We could get a late lunch. I know a little place on the side of the lake not far from here. Falk and Koski can meet us…" He paused and tapped out the number again. "Funny, I don't get a ring on his end."

Maxwell came into the room and began to pace. "Perhaps we should have purchased a Chinese model after all."

Webster flipped the phone shut. "We'll try him again from the restaurant. Let's go eat."

As they drove away from the location, a TV news van drove up the hill like a bloodhound following its relentless nose to the dead lawyer's lakeside home.

They were halfway through dessert when Webster looked up and saw a couple of deputies moving toward them between tables.

"Sorry to interrupt your lunch, Agent Webster," one of the men said as he stopped beside him, "but we need you to step outside with us." Maxwell and Spade exchanged glances.

"What's the problem?" Webster asked.

"We need to be outside, sir."

Webster pushed his chair back. "Wait here."

"Now what?" Spade grumbled as he watched Webster follow the two men from the restaurant, then returned to his apple pie.

Maxwell sipped her coffee. Instinct told her that this visit by the sheriff's department could be connected to their inability to reach Falk. Were he and Koski okay?

Spade was scraping his plate so as not to miss a crumb of crust when Webster returned.

"Bad news. They've just discovered the deputy I assigned to show Falk and Koski the hang-glider location—dead; locked in the trunk of his patrol car up at Spooner. Falk's jeep was parked nearby but no sign of him or Koski." Spade and Maxwell pushed their plates aside and rose. "There's a search party going over the area right now," Webster added. "Let's go."

When they arrived at the scene, local television and press were already nosing around. Spade and Maxwell followed Webster as he silently shoved through the crowd among shouted questions.

"The incident officer will issue a statement later," Webster said in the reporters' general direction, flashing his badge to a deputy who waved the three into the area.

Maxwell ducked under the line of police tape that cordoned off the squad car and surrounding area. She could see the trunk was open and a CSI photographer was preserving the dead body on film.

"How was he killed?" Webster asked the deputy.

"One shot to the head at close range." He shook his head. "Poor bastard was just doing his job…never had a chance."

Maxwell watched in silence as the crime scene investigators

worked around and in the squad car. She had worked with CSI people and knew how determined they were in digging up clues that might otherwise be trampled on and lost. They were meticulous, able to coax a clue from the seemingly most insignificant evidence, painstakingly measuring minute distances and trajectories, utilizing everything from high-tech equipment to Q-tips.

She thought about how far the science of criminology had come since her father was a police officer in the '60s. As a child, she could sit and listen for hours as he related events of his days on the force. Forensics amazed him.

"I'm only a beat cop," he'd say. "What do I know? I don't even understand how those people in the lab can figure out what *type* blood it is let alone whether a blood spot on an object is old or recent, the angle at which the blood hit the object, the velocity of the blood as it hit the object..." He shook his head and added brightly, "Pretty soon the perps won't stand a chance."

As she followed the deputy through the trees, Maxwell thought cynically that perps will always stand a chance and wondered if her father was still alive.

The reason she had not spoken to him in years flooded not only her mind but all her senses, stirring the old animosity. It was the killing of her best friend's father by her own father when Maxwell was a teenager. Her mind blinked at the thought and she managed to push away the chill of memory.

Suddenly Spade was at Maxwell's side. "They've unearthed another body a hundred yards away. We'd better take a look."

She shuddered, dreading taking that look, knowing that Falk and Koski had been in the area but she breathed a sigh of relief when she saw the dead man. Half his face was blown away but it was plainly not Falk. The corpse was dressed as a deputy but wore white socks and brown shoes.

"A couple of usable footprints here," Webster said to the deputy. "One set small enough to be a woman's. You took casts?"

The officer shook his head. "Not deep enough. Maybe CSI can work up something."

A member of the search party ran back into the clearing and reported tire marks indicating that a vehicle had driven through the woods and departed by an old logging road nearby.

Maxwell, Webster and Spade turned from the scene and headed for their sedan but not before a covey of men and women who incessantly cackled questions approached. Maxwell blinked to dispel the red dots that swirled in her vision as the reporters and TV news crews surrounded them, making their departure a flash bulb event. Now and then, one shouted question managed to isolate itself from the others.

"Doctor Maxwell, do you have any idea who is responsible for these murders?" a loud, deep baritone from the *Reno Gazette-Journal* wanted to know.

"Not yet," she said as she kept walking. "We'll let you know when we do."

"Do you suspect Native Americans?" the deep baritone persisted.

Maxwell crinkled her brow. "No."

"So, you're saying that other than Native Americans are responsible?"

"No, I'm saying…" Another flash went off in her face and she realized that a photographer had caught her mid-sentence. "I'm saying that we don't know yet."

"Highly placed sources say that the Nevada Mafia has hired a team of terrorists to kill all who oppose the spread of Indian gaming," a female reporter insisted, pushing a microphone at Maxwell. "Can you confirm that?"

"No."

"Then you're saying that the Mafia is *not* responsible?"

Webster suddenly swept an arm in front of Maxwell, creating a path for her. "She said we don't have any information we can give you yet," he shouted in an authoritative voice Maxwell never heard him use before.

She turned up the collar of her heavy coat and buried her hands deep into the pockets as she, Spade and Webster climbed into their vehicle, wondering about the fate of their two companions.

Who's Killing All the Lawyers?

Chapter 8

"Keep your eyes on the road," the man in the back seat growled at Falk. "We don't want any accidents."

Falk drove Highway 50, which wound down the wide sweeps and curves descending into the Carson Valley. They were more than thirty-five miles from Virginia City. As long as he followed orders he and Koski would stay alive.

He glanced in the rear view mirror and caught Koski's vision riveted to the same reflective rectangle. He tried to read her eyes and realized that neither fear nor terror resided there. Her eyes were smoking; her lips pressed tightly together. She wasn't afraid. She was pissed off.

He slowed for the traffic light at 395. A couple more miles and they'd pass through Carson City. The light changed and he moved forward.

"As we go through Carson," the man said, "stay within the speed limit. Keep to the right and let anyone who wants to pass go ahead. Got it?"

"No problem," Falk muttered and in the next instant caught Koski's vision again. Her eyes rolled skyward in apparent frustration. What was the woman thinking? What would she have him do?

Koski silently steamed. When she started this assignment, she had been…well, she had overheard Spade call her "beautifully indifferent." Perhaps she *had* been apathetic. Nevertheless, she was involved now and wanted to get this situation over with—offensively and quickly. Falk liked to appear self-sufficient so why wasn't there some FBI magic he could pull out of a hat? They had come all this way and he had done nothing but obey the scumbag beside her.

Periodically throughout the journey the man pulled his gun away from the side of her head and rested it on his knee, always keeping it aimed directly at her. It was beginning to look as if deliverance was going to be up to her. She had to figure a way to get hold of that gun.

"What do you want from us?" Falk suddenly asked, moving his head slightly so he could see the man's face in the mirror.

"Doing my job."

"Does that include killing us like the real deputy your friend impersonated? Why didn't you just kill us back there?"

"Too many shots fired in those parts. We're going to Virginia City as ordered. A quiet town…a good place to…" his voice trailed off.

Falk shifted into low gear for the steep, winding hill that signaled the approach to Virginia City.

"Okay," the man said, "there's a side road coming up about a quarter of a mile on the right, turn in there."

Falk knew at once if he made the transfer to a deserted rural trail their situation would worsen. At least here, near the city, small as it was, there was the potential for help. The car suddenly gave a lurch as it jolted across a pothole. Falk glanced back and saw that both passengers had their seat belts fastened. The realization spawned an idea.

The highway dipped at an angle at the turn and the shoulder fell away to a deep trench on the right side of the road. Letting up off the gas, Falk immediately hit the accelerator, repeating this pattern several times. The old Chevy shuddered and jerked, stuttering forward.

"The engine's about to quit," Falk shouted. "According to the gauge, we're not out of gas. We've got a problem." He knew oncoming darkness made it difficult for the man behind him to see his feet and the situation he was creating. "You want me to stop?" he asked, his voice quivering with each alternate rev and sputter of the automobile.

Startled and aggravated by the sudden lurches, Falk's captor unhooked his seat belt and leaned forward, attempting to examine the dashboard for possible red lights that might indicate the cause of the trouble. Yanking hard on the steering wheel, Falk jammed the gas pedal to the floor in the same instant. The car lurched violently from the sudden acceleration and powered into a nosedive over the shoulder and into the ditch. The man's head was slammed against the window frame with a sickening crunch then whipped back and smashed against the doorpost.

Koski, still strapped within the security of her seat belt, reacted instinctively and grabbed the gun.

The tortured engine stalled and Falk turned and looked back. Their companion was out cold. Koski seemed shaken but unhurt. "You okay?" he asked.

She followed him from the wreck, the automatic in her hand. "You don't give a damn if I'm okay or not!"

Falk was stunned by her words.

She stopped and rotated her head and shoulders to relieve the tension in her neck. "Jesus," she went on derisively, "I was beginning to think you were *never* going to make a move."

They were back to square one in their relationship. "You're serious, aren't you?" Falk asked. "Did you forget what they teach at

Quantico about hostage situations? Remain calm. Do not jump into actions that are not well thought out. Choose your moment carefully... Did you forget that?"

"I *never* forget—anything."

"Don't take everything so personally, Koski."

She reacted as if she had been slapped.

Falk didn't believe they were having this absurd conversation. All he could do was move on quickly. "Look," he said, keeping his voice under control, "let's both shut up and do what we have to do here."

He climbed out and headed for the trunk. "We're going to tie up our *faux* deputy and stuff him in the trunk." He lifted the lid. "You'll wait in the front of the car for the first vehicle that comes along. Tell them to take this guy to FBI Reno and they can take you back to whatever cave you hang upside down in each night."

He regretted it as soon as he said it.

In the gathering darkness and silhouetted by a faint glimmer of moonlight, Koski had what looked like smoke coming from her ears. It was only her warm breath in the cold air.

"Now *you* listen," she said, her voice low but more bitter than the wind. "I didn't ask to be put on this fucking assignment with you. It was thrust upon me. It's my job, which I happen to need right now but you wouldn't understand that. All you understand is your crippling, neurotic obsession with solitude. You exude it. I consider being able to read people to be part of my job and mister, you're an open book. Whether you like it or not, I'm in this now and I'm going to stay until we find out who's killing lawyers and why."

She paused and stood unmoving, the outburst having left her drained. "So, we're going to tie and gag this guy, leave him by the side of the highway with a note for whoever finds him, get this car out of the ditch and get back to Reno to connect with the other members of this so-called team."

Falk realized his mouth was open. It not only was what Koski had said, although it made sense on a level he'd explore later, but what he had been thinking. Preparing to leave this woman in the car. Of course, she would not have been alone but—worse—she would have been in the car with a would-be killer! If somehow he managed to—.

He took several deep breaths and then shrugged in a conciliatory way. She had him pegged but he, too, had been right. She was fighting a war with something, a war that probably would not end until she got something...or maybe until she gave something.

His dark brows arched mischievously. "Is there any truth to the rumor that a poor sucker in the Las Vegas PD put the moves on you too heavily and you yanked his balls off?"

Koski was silent before finally, striking a mental balance, she dropped her arms by her side and replied offhandedly, "Ask "her.""

Falk grinned. "Okay, we'll leave him here with a note." He took a sheet from a pocket organizer and began to write. "We can't get this car out of the ditch ourselves. It'll require a tow truck."

"You're right." She grabbed the assault weapon and her equipment from the trunk.

"What else is in that trunk?" he asked as he continued writing.

She rummaged around. "A rusty jack, jumper cables, chains, an old blanket. That's about it."

"Take the blanket," he said. "We might need it."

She did a double take. "An old blanket?"

He finished writing the note. "Help me get him back here."

Once the semi-conscious man was stuffed into the trunk, Falk made a slit in one corner of the note with a fingernail and forced the paper over the button of the man's shirt. It read: CALL FBI RENO. THIS MAN KILLED A DEPUTY SHERIFF. AGENT FALK, FBI.

Falk caught sight of a leather bag in the corner of the trunk. "Bingo! An *old* cell phone, the kind that rings, operated by battery or from the cigarette lighter in a car." He hung the bag around his neck, wrapped the AK-47 in the blanket and slung it over his shoulder.

As Koski gathered up her video equipment, Falk thought he was beginning to like the pint-sized pain in the ass but as for someone to rely on as a partner? She'd missed the cell phone and had not thought of using the blanket to conceal the rifle. As always, the only one he could truly rely on was himself. They started walking back to Highway 50.

Suddenly he grabbed her arm, pulling her deep into the shadows at the side of the road as a car approached. The evening was dark enough for the vehicle to require headlights, which swept a bright arc as it passed.

"Why'd you do that?" Koski asked, pulling her arm free from his grasp. "We've got to flag a ride to Reno and there's little enough traffic on this road."

Falk returned to the side of the highway and she followed. "Koski, hasn't it occurred to you that somebody knew that Webster arranged for a deputy to escort us to Spooner and that same somebody probably arranged for this guy and his partner to kill us?"

He did not wait for her response. "Whoever is killing lawyers also is out to get us and has the help of an insider—somebody *deep* inside. The best thing we can do right now is stay out of sight and continue the investigation on our own."

"What about Webster, Maxwell and Spade? Shouldn't we let them know?"

"If we contact them now they may inadvertently give us away. Maybe with us gone missing, it'll make them more aware of the danger they're in. Hopefully, they can make some progress on their end as to what's really going on." He didn't add that he had not ruled out any of them as suspects.

"Okay," she said, "what do we do in the meantime?"

"There's a group of old buildings on the hillside up there." He saw them when they drove past earlier and wondered if she had noticed.

"Old buildings?"

He felt some disappointment that she had not but he went on. "They looked like part of an abandoned mining operation. We'll lay low there until morning."

"Lay low in an old shed, all night. You know how cold it gets up here this time of year?"

"If our friend's pals track us down, we'll be a damn sight colder for a lot longer." He figured she got the point because she fell into silence as they rounded a bend and headed toward the hill.

After fifteen minutes of picking their way over rough, steep, stony terrain, they came to an old wooden shack that seemed sturdy. Moonlight found its way through the open door and allowed a dim look at the single room. The one window was paned though streaks of filth prevented a view.

"Must have been a storeroom at one time," Falk said. Constructed on a concrete slab, it contained a table, shelving along three walls and an old, wooden chair with three legs, for which someone had engineered a cure by propping a block of wood where the missing leg had been.

"Perfect hideout," Koski said sarcastically. "For sure, no one would expect two well-trained federal agents to hole up in here."

Ignoring her, he dragged a piece of cardboard from one of the shelves and pressed it against the grimy window. "Hold this cardboard until I find some kind of prop." He turned on the flashlight, finally located a couple of rusty nails and tapped them into the wooden frame with a piece of iron pipe. Then he placed the flashlight on the floor, partially covering the beam with an edge of the blanket, allowing a slither of light to illuminate the room.

Falk was removing the AK-47 from the blanket when suddenly he reached and switched off the light. "Listen!"

It was the throbbing sound of a car being driven very slowly that made Falk's body stiffen. Not a vehicle passing by on the highway, as others had. "I'm going to open the door a touch," he whispered. "Don't move, okay."

"Okay."

He leaned toward the door and inched it open a crack, the bottom dragging on the concrete floor. The engine sound was closer now. He saw headlights as the automobile crept slowly along the side road. Its high beams, wide and glaring, revealed the old Chevy in the ditch; the vehicle stopped.

Falk watched through the partially open door. Two men ran forward and checked the interior of the old car with their own headlights illuminating the eerie scene. Moving to the rear, they jammed an iron bar under the trunk hinge and levered up, forcing the lid open with a metallic groan, and lifted the wriggling body to the ground.

While one man ripped off the sign and read it, his companion removed the captive's gag and untied him. Wild gesticulations indicated a heated discussion, then one of them pointed up the hill in

Falk's direction. He pushed the door shut but his body reacted to a voice in his ear.

"They figure we're up here," Koski whispered. She had been looking over his shoulder.

"I told you not to move and you said..." He stopped. It was no use. She would do as she pleased.

"If we stay here, it'll only be a matter of time before they find us. Let's use the cell phone and call 911."

"Koski, we're in a deserted shack on an isolated hillside outside Virginia City. I couldn't even give an exact location."

"Those operators use global positioning, don't they? They can pinpoint general areas at least. It's worth a try."

Falk did not have time to argue. He felt around the floor for the phone, not daring to turn on the flashlight. "Where is the damn thing?"

"Here." She reached into his jacket pocket where he had put it after taking it from around his neck and produced the leather case.

The silence was shattered abruptly as the phone rang. Koski gasped, dropping the phone but its ringing continued.

Lunging forward, Falk scooped it up, ripped the door open and flung the thing as far as he could into the night. The ringing diminished as it arced out over the hill, thudded to the ground and then stopped.

Falk swore softly. "Our friend told them we took the phone and that it wasn't the type to chirp or vibrate so they dialed the number to zero in on our location by the ring."

The first arrow thudded into a wooden shack nearby and a bright flash ignited into flames.

"Quick!" He slammed the door shut and scooped up the blanket, keeping the AK-47 at his side. "They're burning the buildings...firing arrows with incendiary tips." While Koski gathered up the rest of their gear, he said, "When I open the door, move fast, stay low and hug the side of the building. Go around back, keeping the building between you and the fires." He slid the door open, seeing hot embers sparkle and singe the night air.

"Be careful. I'll cover you. If you hear shots, don't look back, just keep going to the top of the hill and you'll see the lights of Virginia City."

She burst out, her equipment slung across her back. Falk lunged through the opening into the darkness and the smell of ruined wood. He nearly reached the corner of the building when—*THWAK*—an arrow slammed into the door. He glanced back as it hissed into action, spewing blinding white phosphorus and splattering the building with fire. He bounded, crouching, following the sound of Koski's boots as they scraped over the rocks.

The fires would be visible from the city less than a quarter of a mile away and the alarm raised. He did not want to be discovered by fire or police units. Everyone was their enemy now, even innocents who might lead their pursuers to them.

He was breathing hard by the time he caught up with Koski just below the rim of the hill. Hugging the earth, she fought back a cough in the choking air, the veins in her neck pronounced. He dropped to the ground beside her.

"If we go over the top," she rasped, "we'll be backlit by the flames."

He patted her shoulder. "Good thinking. We'll stay just below the ridge. Keep moving to the right toward that large outcropping of rocks. Ready?"

She grunted and together they moved, hunched shadows, farther and farther away from the fires until they reached the outcropping. Calling a halt, Falk sank among the monumental, cave-like boulders, listening for the slightest sound of a chase. Koski landed beside him.

"Stay here," he said. "I'm going to the top of the ridge and take a look."

"Okay," he heard her say as he fell to his belly and elbowed his way to the ridge. Cautiously raising his head, he saw only the lights of Virginia City glowing in the distance.

"Why would they attract attention by torching the buildings?" Koski had wriggled up beside him, her normally husky voice even smokier. "They could have just come up the hill and shot us."

"They knew we had the AK-47 as soon as they spoke to scumbag. Playing it safe...burning the huts in an effort to smoke us out into their path. They'll either assume that we were caught in the fire or they'll come looking for us again in daylight when the emergency units are gone."

They returned to the boulders and he handed her the old blanket. "I think we'll be safe here for the rest of the night. I'll take first watch while you try to get some sleep." He cocked the weapon and thumbed the safety to off.

Who's Killing All the Lawyers?

Chapter 9

A radial engine seaplane banked over the Gulf of Mexico, early morning sunlight reflecting on the cockpit windows as the aircraft straightened direction for its approach. It swayed slightly in a light crosswind before touching down, its pontoons making a graceful feather of white on the blue-green lagoon. The engine throttled back, the sudden snarl startling a flock of flamingos from their wading and feeding to take flight, their outstretched necks resembling a squadron of supersonic transports.

The pilot made a wide, arcing turn, moving in close to a white, fine-grained beach. Big Pine Key was one of many in the chain stretching from Key Largo to Key West.

Palm trees crowded down to the sea, bright tropical flowers belied it was autumn in the Florida Keys. Before the propeller stopped, an inflatable Zodiac put out from the shore, its blunt nose curving upward, thrust forward by powerful twin outboards as it closed in on the seaplane.

A door in the plane's fuselage swung open and a powerfully built man with a strong face, a mass of red, unruly hair and dressed in a black jumpsuit waved toward the Zodiac that came alongside. The redhead, Rodney Eiker, a hard-boiled British soldier of fortune, sloshed gum from one side of his mouth to the other, chewing furiously, snapping and crackling it.

Ten minutes later, Eiker stood on the balcony of the hotel room that was reserved for him, overlooking the bay.

Rod Eiker was born in Manchester, England. At eighteen, he joined the British Army, served in the Middle East and Asia, then transferred to the Special Air Service at twenty-two. He relinquished his rank of sergeant, as do all non-commissioned or commissioned members of the British Army when they volunteer for SAS.

Time proved him an outstanding candidate in all phases of the elite service's strenuous training program. Posted to Belfast, Ireland, he re-earned the rank of sergeant in charge of a plainclothes detachment specializing in undercover and sabotage. Eighteen months later, he was commissioned first lieutenant and transferred to SAS headquarters, Hereford, UK.

Now, years later, Eiker had decided that this would be his last hire. Forty-three was old for the mercenary business.

He scanned the beach and surrounding area, remembering the day he was approached for the assignment. It was in the Green Man, a small pub on O'Connell Street in Dublin. Halfway through a pint of Guinness, Eiker felt a tap on his shoulder. He recognized the man as a mercenary recruiter he'd seen in other places around the world; a man who generally sought the best professional killers available. Eiker moved with him to a table in a dark corner of the pub. Two pints later, the deal was made. Two days later, Eiker flew to Miami, then here.

Now the phone rang and he went back into the room and plucked it from a side table.

"Yes?" he uttered in a voice lower and as unlike his own as he could manage.

A nondescript male voice softly asked, "Have I reached the party to whom I am to be connected?"

Eiker's quirky sense of humor made him wait to answer. It was the prearranged code question but it suddenly sounded so asinine that he was tempted to reply in the negative and hang up. Instead, he answered in the also prearranged counter code. "Yes, the green man."

"Right," the voice said, satisfied. "Get some rest. You'll need to be up early. You'll return to Miami tomorrow morning. Sorry about the circuitous route."

Eiker grunted, familiar with backtracking to avoid a tail, and the man continued, "There'll be a first class ticket to Las Vegas in the name of Taddington—an alias I understand you've used in the past and for which you have appropriate identification—at the Delta Airlines desk at Miami International for Flight 145. Someone will meet you upon arrival and take you to your meeting."

"Right," Eiker said and immediately hung up. He crossed the room again, glancing at his reflection in the wall mirror. Instinctively, his hand went to his left ear, which had an old scar and a mangled lobe —a constant reminder of a debt incurred in Nevada years ago and yet to be paid.

The next day, a black BMW and driver awaited him at McCarren International in Las Vegas. Eiker was familiar with the city and enjoyed the ride along Tropicana Avenue that paralleled The Strip, past the intersection of Paradise and Desert next to the Convention Center.

He looked forward to meeting with his new employer, who hired him for about the price of an American League baseball pitcher. His new boss also managed to stay at the top of the pyramid that was the Nevada Mafia.

Who's Killing All the Lawyers?

Chapter 10

The view from Tony Villachi's penthouse made the lights of Las Vegas appear to be twinkling jewels scattered across a black velvet display cloth. Villachi, however, was not a man to appreciate the aesthetic beauty of this display, only that it represented money and power painfully attained through ulcers, irritable bowel syndrome, diverticulitis and hypertension.

He pulled deeply on his Havana cigar, turned from the window and took his seat at the head of a long cherry-wood conference table, the gleaming surface of which reflected the faces of six men; the core of Nevada's gambling interests.

"Gentlemen," he mumbled as cigar smoke seeped from his nostrils, "I called you here to give you yet another example of why I sit at the head of this table while you are on the sidelines, so to speak." His pause gave the others a chance to redden, exchange glances or nervously sip from water glasses.

Attaining riches and power had not served to produce contentment, good health or a polished veneer to Tony Villachi's weathered appearance, frail body and rancorous personality. He was a short, small-boned man with thinning, stubborn gray hair and awning eyebrows. It was said that Villachi's wife also was from humble beginnings. She wallowed in her husband's wealth, a heart of gold type who gloried in the glamour with which the aging don surrounded her. Acquaintances secretly dubbed them "Happy and Grumpy."

The insiders at Villachi's table attributed the campaign of terror against lawyers to the don. In fact, it was hatched in the mind of The Fox; that was how The Fox wanted it. The Fox did not require a powerful, high profile presence. He preferred it to appear as if others were making the decisions when, in reality, it was the other way around.

"Hasn't it occurred to any of you," Villachi grumbled, "that there is money to be made in the fact that most of our local legal beagles are *against* the spread of Indian gaming because, like you, they want to keep as much money as possible in Nevada?"

He paused, his head steady while his eyes swept around the table but no one spoke, awaiting his point. "What would *you* do?" he growled. "How would *you* feel if you were a Nevada lawyer and your fellow attorneys were dropping like flies just because they opposed Indian casinos?"

This time he only paused for a nanosecond. He was getting to his bottom line and didn't want to take the chance one of his colleagues might guess what he was about to suggest and steal his thunder. He leaned forward. "You'd shit your shorts and scream for help, for Chrissake!"

Some of the men simply nodded. Others' eyes evidenced that they had begun to fathom the fortuitous circumstance to which Villachi alluded. The old don continued.

"Every lawyer in this state who's done anti-Indian gambling work is looking over their shoulder right now, wondering if they'll be next. They know better than to count on the local police." He stabbed his cigar into a large, smoked glass ashtray at his elbow, enlivened by his own words. "These people need *protection*..."

A heavyset man in an expensive suit to Villachi's left pounded the table, getting the message. "And *we're* going to provide it!"

Another middle-aged, overweight man frowned. "You're saying that we're going to ask *them* to pay *us* for protection against...what we're doing to them?"

Villachi eased back in his chair. "You bet your sweet ass we are."

The others began to get it and speculated aloud as to just how such extortion could be arranged.

Heavyset's deep baritone drowned out the other voices. "We'll need out-of-town, high-tech muscle to enforce payment...somebody who, if caught, can't be traced back to us...maybe somebody from the fuckin' Russian Mafia or—"

"Hold it, hold it, for Chrissake!" Villachi rankled. "As usual, I'm one step ahead of you." He looked into each face, appreciating the moment. "Tomorrow I'm meeting with a kick-ass British mercenary with a reputation for putting together the kind of small, efficient group we'll need to persuade our...esteemed..." Villachi lingered, "members of the bar that they need us on their side."

A tall, ascetic-looking man leaned forward and turned toward Villachi. "Harry's right, Tony." He nodded toward the middle-aged man who had questioned Villachi's logic. "It doesn't make sense that we're paying big bucks for somebody to do lawyers and, at the same time, we're going to hire a high-priced outsider to *protect* them."

Villachi's face reddened and his dark, cool eyes locked on the man. "Nobody's *really* going to protect them, Frank. We're just going to make them *pay* for it." He snorted and made eye contact with the others.

Satisfied they were all on the same page, he attempted to lighten the mood. "Jesus, Frank," he elbowed the man good-naturedly, "you one of those people who dimple your chads instead of punching 'em all the way through?"

A ripple of laughter went around the table and Villachi took the moment to get up and wave toward the full bar at one end of the room. "Stay, all of you…relax…have a drink. I wish I could join you but…" he patted the spot where his ulcers resided and let his words trail off.

Yes, Villachi thought as he left the room, the idea of extracting protection money from the lawyers was his inspiration; a serendipitous outgrowth of the terror campaign that even The Fox had failed to recognize.

Villachi was concentrated on that campaign. To date, his associate in Carson City had handled it pretty well; as yet no one had come up with any real suspects in the killings. The associate, however, only had one more job to do, then that aspect of the operation would phase out. It was time for the big guns.

The British soldier of fortune was perfect. He would operate in and out of state and could not be connected to Villachi in any way. He'd scare the shit out of the local lawyers until they paid through the nose and increase the pressure on the Indians, believing—as did those saps in the conference room—that Villachi's true objective was to stop the spread of Indian gambling.

Chapter 11

Maxwell sat in her Reno hotel room, nursing vodka over ice. The neon lights of the "Biggest Little City in the World" glowed outside her window. It had been two days since Falk and Koski disappeared. In the short time they were together during their briefing with Falk, she had quickly formed a fondness for the two.

Younger than Maxwell, Koski was what Maxwell called gritty, quick, capable but with a 'tude. Instinctively, Maxwell felt that the petite-size footprints at the scene in the woods were Koski's. She hoped to God that Falk and Koski were not in serious trouble.

Why hadn't they contacted the rest of the team? Webster could be reached at his office most of the time, fielding questions by increasingly irritated reporters. Why didn't Falk and Koski call? Had they, for some reason, determined that they couldn't trust the others? Certainly, they could trust *her*...and Spade and Webster...

She paced a few minutes before settling down again, awaiting a call from Webster as to their next move.

She decided to pass the time by reading a noir detective novel she purchased in the lobby gift shop. Her admiration for authors who wrote darkly about what they had lived in their professions was high. She wished she could do it, the prospect seen as scoring a double whammy in the marketability department. Not only was she a medical examiner, she also might be one of the few female African-American MEs writing in the genre.

Alas, she had long ago dismissed the idea as preposterous. She had never even taken a creative writing class. Beyond that, she firmly believed there already were too many writers and not enough readers.

She was reading the first chapter of the novel when the phone rang.

"Hi, Doc." It was Spade. "Got a minute?"

"Sure, Alex. What's up?"

"My wife and I were wondering if you'd like to have dinner with us here at the house. We're only ten minutes away. I could pick you up at the hotel."

She was both surprised and pleased at the offer. "Sure we wouldn't be breaking some federal rule?" she asked, mocking the many admonitions they'd received about secrecy.

Spade caught her meaning and laughed. "Don't think so. At least we haven't been forbidden to fraternize. Webster can reach you here. Will you come?"

"Certainly, give me a call from the lobby." She hung up and went to a mirror, running her fingers through her short, thick hair, wondering what to wear. She kicked off her terry mules and padded into the bathroom. Five minutes later she was ready. In a zip-front denim dress from J. Peterman and white NB 800 walking shoes, she slung an indigo boucle cardigan over one shoulder.

Now she looked for the right purse. She'd made up her mind as soon as the team was formed never to go anywhere without her Walther P38, which she both needed and reviled. Registered to carry the weapon in Nevada, she felt lost—even dining at a colleague's home—without the sense of security it offered.

She reached into a chest drawer beside her. She extracted her hand, as if stung. The gun's very presence stirred painful memories of her father. If she kept the gun available, would she, too, one day commit the unforgivable? Once this assignment was over she would officially dispose of it. Meanwhile, she'd tuck it down into the purse she chose for the evening and forget it existed.

Maxwell found she was at ease with Spade's wife, Flo, whose home-cooked meal was a pleasant break from hotel food. During the evening, Spade seemed careful to keep his part of the bargain with the government; there was no talk of the investigation or the missing agents. As far as Flo was concerned, Maxwell was in Reno doing routine work with the PD.

"When Alex told me you were stuck alone in a hotel room I said we must have you over."

They were seated in the living room; Maxwell on the sofa, Spade in what was obviously his chair, a well-used recliner. Flo dispensed coffee from her chair next to the coffee table. "I did wonder why you had to stay in town when you live in Carson City. I know so many people who commute every day."

Maxwell and Spade exchanged glances. "It's only for a few days," Maxwell lied, as she accepted a coffee cup from Flo. "Sort of a get-together…need to be on the spot, so to speak."

"That's the government for you. Alex will be retiring soon and it'll all be behind us. Right, hon?"

Spade smiled from behind his coffee cup. "Right," he said emphatically.

Maxwell excused herself to use the bathroom. While she washed her hands, she decided to peek out the window, idly curious to see the backyard. Switching off the light, she peered out. As her eyes grew accustomed to the darkness, she saw several small evergreens, a few bare deciduous trees, a patio and a medium-sized lawn featuring a Mexican fireplace with an Arizona flagstone surround.

Suddenly her peripheral vision picked up a quick movement where the fence and garage met. She pulled back automatically before easing forward. There it was again. Someone was out there. She had a moment of indecision.

Considering the events of the last few days with Falk and Koski gone missing, she shouldn't take any chances. She couldn't bring herself to reach into her purse. If she had, she would only fling the weapon from her, abhorring its hold on her instincts.

She saw the movement outside again. A darkened figure detached itself from the bushes and monkey-walked toward the house, hugging the garage wall to remain in shadow.

She envisioned the living room with French doors opening onto the patio…the drapes pulled back…light streaming out into the darkness, making perfect targets of those in the living room.

She opened the bathroom and quickly slipped out into the dark, narrow hallway. She had to think fast. If she went back into the room she, too, would be on the stage of light…Then she walked into Flo.

"Oh," Flo exclaimed, "there you are. I was wondering if you were having trouble with the flusher. Sometimes we have to jiggle the handle—"

Maxwell stopped her by grabbing her arm. "Do you have a phone in the bedroom?" Flo's face registered such surprise and fright at the sudden question that Maxwell had to repeat herself. *"Do you?"*

"Yes but—"

"Get on it right now. Call 9ll. Tell them someone's breaking into your house and they're armed. Hurry!"

She pushed past Flo and raced to the end of the hallway adjoining the living room. Standing back from the entrance, she could see Spade in the recliner and called softly, "Alex, come into the hallway, *quick*!" He looked up as if unsure he'd heard. "Now," she hollered. "Move it, Alex!"

The urgency in her voice removed his doubt. He flung himself out of the chair in the exact instant the sound of breaking glass split the air. He lunged into the hallway, stumbling and falling to his knees.

Righting himself, he wheezed, "What the hell..." He looked back into the living room and, after a moment of realization, gasped, "Where's Flo?"

"She's okay...on the phone in the bedroom, calling 911. I saw someone in the backyard moving toward the house." She peered into the vacated room. "Son of a bitch!" she said, hearing Spade inhale convulsively beside her. An arrow was buried in the upright portion of Spade's recliner, which backed up to the shattered French door. The ugly point of the arrow was jutting almost a foot through the back of his chair. Shards of glass were strewn across the carpet.

"Alex, are you all right?" It was Flo calling from the bedroom.

"Go talk to her," Maxwell said, "but keep her in the bedroom for now. Do you have another phone?"

"Only the car phone. Why?"

"I changed purses before I left the hotel and my cell is in there. I'm going to call Webster. He's in command in Falk's absence. He'll want to be here when the cops arrive."

Breathing heavily, Spade went to a sideboard and picked up the car keys. "Here, you'll have to switch on the ignition to make the phone work."

"Alex...can you hear me?" Flo wailed from the bedroom.

Maxwell grabbed the keys. Pausing to look around to be sure the assailant was not in the area, she bolted out the front door.

She reached Webster at FBI Reno and told him what happened.

"Can you remove the arrow from the chair?" he asked.

"I don't know. I can try."

"*Do it*. We don't want the local law enforcement officers messing with it."

"If I remove the arrow what do we tell the cops? The glass door is shattered…glass all over the floor…there'll be a hole through the back of Alex's chair that'll be difficult to explain."

"Think of something," he replied and the phone call turned to the buzz of a dial tone.

"Thanks a lot."

Maxwell returned to the house. She went to the living room and quickly extracted the arrow from the chair. The projectile was identical to the others. The seemingly indestructible weapon had suffered no discernible effects from the force of smashing through the tempered glass and the chair. It crossed her mind that whatever the arrow was made of should be used in automobile construction.

She raced out to the car and placed the arrow under the back seat. As she did, she noticed a blanket and scooped it up. Returning to the house, she told Spade about her call to Webster. She placed the blanket over the recliner, being careful to cover the front and back of the upright portion.

"Alex," she said, "quickly, tell Flo to sit in the chair. Ask her to not move, just sit and keep her mouth shut while the police are here. Can she do that?" Still visibly shaken, Spade nodded numbly. "Good," Maxwell continued, "I'll answer all questions when the cops arrive. I'll say you and Flo are too shaken up."

"You...you'll have that right," he mumbled and headed back to the bedroom and Flo.

Webster arrived, playing the visiting friend, just as the dumbfounded police officers were leaving after checking the grounds and writing the incident off as a bizarre attempted break-in.

When Flo went to put on a fresh pot of coffee, Webster turned to Maxwell. "That was inspired...putting the blanket over the chair... having Mrs. Spade sit there." Maxwell shrugged but there was some pride in her face.

"Webster," Spade asked, "what are we going to do?" His body language signaled fatigue and apprehension. "Obviously, whoever is killing lawyers is out to get us, too. They could come back and finish the job." He shook his head. "The last few days on the job and Flo and I are in danger of winding up dead."

Webster put a hand on his shoulder. "I'll put you up in a hotel and arrange for the house to be secured." He sank into an easy chair. "I have an update on Falk and Koski. An abandoned car was found in a ditch near Virginia City. The police have given us reason to believe that Falk and Koski were in the car, at least for a time."

"Any idea where they are now?" Maxwell asked.

Webster shook his head. "It's possible they might still be hiding somewhere in the area."

"Why haven't they contacted you?" Spade wondered.

"It's my hunch that Falk feels there's a leak in local law enforcement. He's taking no chances. If they did manage to escape from whoever was transporting them, they'll probably lay low for a while and then get in touch with us in person."

Flo entered, carrying the tray with cups and a coffee carafe. "A nice cup of hot coffee will make us feel better." She placed the tray on the coffee table.

Webster smiled disarmingly. "Mrs. Spade," he said, "Dr. Maxwell, Alex and I have an important assignment that may take us out of town for several days. Maybe it would be a good idea for you to get away, too…" He turned to Spade before Flo had a chance to reply. "Don't you agree, Alex?"

Spade opened and closed his mouth twice before finally muttering, "Yes, good idea." He turned to Flo. "I wouldn't want you here alone…if we have to be out of town. You can visit your sister in Little Rock since we were going to do that soon anyway."

Flo's eyebrows shot up. She was about to say something but Webster took quick command of the moment. "I'll arrange for you to fly. Alex can pick up your ticket tomorrow morning."

"Well…" Flo started.

"Good…great," Webster said and set his cup and saucer back on the table. "That's settled. I'll call and reserve the ticket tonight…round trip from Reno to Little Rock with the return date open." He stood and started for the door.

Maxwell gathered up her purse and jacket with renewed respect for Webster. His usually quiet, ingratiating manner could morph into a firm, take-charge approach when required and there was no competing authority.

Smiling at Flo, Maxwell said, "Thank you for a lovely dinner. I hope you have a nice trip."

Flo smiled, bewildered, and shrugged.

At the door, Webster turned to Spade. "I'll contact you shortly. I'll arrange for you both to stay at the Hilton tonight. See you at the office at ten a.m."

Maxwell shot a final look at Spade, who looked as if a tornado had swept through his life; no doubt he wondered when he would stop spinning.

Who's Killing All the Lawyers?

Chapter 12

Falk slumped against a boulder, his head propped against another, as he watched dawn streak pale light through weakening darkness, a rippling pink tint fringing the edges of low gray clouds. Winter soon would claim the mountains, bind them in white, freeze them solid and allow a frigid silence to settle until spring.

He had stayed awake for his last four hours of guard duty and was stiff, cold and hungry. His mind had been busy trying to make sense of the two *faux* deputies who tried to kill them. Who hired them? He must get some answers today.

He looked back, scanning the hillside in the distance where buildings had stood and only charred beams remained. The shed from which they escaped was only a pile of ash, wisps of smoke curling from its ruins. The odor of burnt wood hung in the early morning air.

He ducked quickly, seeing two firefighters on clean-up duty less than a hundred yards away, poking the ashes with long hooked poles. Koski, startled by his sudden movement, jerked awake. He pressed his hand on her shoulder.

"Stay still."

She rubbed her eyes, raked her slender fingers through her tousled hair and mumbled, "If I don't eat soon, I'll stay still, all right. I won't have the strength to get up."

She rolled over and squinted up at him. "How about *I* go into town, get something for us to eat, pick up a few groceries, while you steal a vehicle—"

"*Steal* a vehicle…?"

"*Commandeer* a vehicle, then. Isn't this a national emergency?"

He looked down at her. He wanted to kiss her. They had spent the night together, curled up among the rocks. They had faced death and survived. Perhaps it was because this complex female, with compelling green eyes with tawny specks, was capable of delivering a judo chop and being soft and vulnerable. She snapped open her hand, displaying an empty palm. "How much money do you have?"

A few minutes later, Falk watched her hike over the hill. She had picked up a stick and now swung it casually, looking like an early morning hiker headed toward the slumbering town. They agreed he would follow into town five minutes behind her and find a car to steal.

Once she was out of sight, he felt a strange sense of loneliness. There was a time, only hours ago, when he would have gladly left her and gone off on his own. Now it no longer was an option.

Once in town, Falk turned to the right down a side street, crossed the parking lot behind an old wooden church and noticed a large, black hearse parked under a carport across the street. The sign on the building read: TIDAL AND FLYNN UNDERTAKERS.

Hefting the blanket with the rifle rolled inside, he ambled closer to his objective. Seconds—and a few deft moves in the art of hot wiring—later, he was behind the wheel with the motor running. He checked his watch as he pulled onto the highway.

He was to meet Koski outside the store in three minutes. He heard the sound of a vehicle in the distance. It came up fast behind him. He shaded his eyes against the sun, higher now, a weak, late autumn sun, and glimpsed the automobile. It dipped over a rise shortly before dropping out of sight for a few seconds, cleared the second rise and came into full view.

A rush of adrenaline subsided when Falk saw it was an old pick-up truck, the object of past fender benders, one of dozens to be seen in and around the area. The relic roared past him, its muffler rattling, spewing a pale blue plume of smoke behind.

The clunker had just passed out of sight when Koski left the store, looked both ways and crossed the street. She took no notice of the hearse but scanned the highway for Falk and a fast car. He drove slowly up to her and stopped. She tensed, cautiously eyeing the highly polished vehicle. Recognition dawned as Falk swung open the passenger door. She jumped in fast and he took off.

"Well," she said sarcastically, "this is certainly a nice, low profile vehicle."

Her hair had captured the brisk morning air and when she settled in the seat beside him the hearse smelled fresher. "Figured it wouldn't be missed for a while," he offered in explanation. "You don't see too many funerals this early in the morning."

She held up a white paper sack. "Hot coffee and four bacon sandwiches."

He could have guessed bacon; the sweet, smoky aroma helped dispel the scent of formaldehyde that permeated the vehicle's interior. "Unwrap me one," he said then added, "please." She silently obliged and he stared ahead, chewing, his mind deep in thought. He finished the sandwich and gulped some coffee.

"Honestly," Koski said between bites, "do you really think we can get very far in a stolen hearse?"

Falk shrugged. "Someone said, 'There are those who dare and

89

those who don't, and those who don't sometimes get slaughtered anyway.'" He smiled, pleased that he remembered a quotation appropriate to the occasion. "We'll ditch it once we get to Carson City."

She eyeballed the ignition wires hanging from the steering column. "Marksmanship and grand theft auto were my two best subjects at Quantico, too."

He reached into the bag and started on a second sandwich as they crested a hill. He saw the Washoe Valley in the distance. He laid out his plan between mouthfuls. "Another fifteen minutes and we'll be in Carson. We'll park this monster in a church parking lot in town. Then —"

Suddenly, the two-way radio crackled to life. "Unit one, unit one, do you read?"

"I *knew* it!" Koski growled. "They've already discovered the hearse is missing."

Falk grunted. "Do they really expect us to answer?" He had an idea. "Koski, what else did you buy at the store?"

"Odds and ends in case we had to stay on the road; canned goods, bread, ham, fruit, a few power bars."

"Did you speak to the cashier…think she or he would remember your voice?"

"I was the only customer; they'd just opened. She'd probably remember my face but not my voice…I barely spoke."

"Good. Answer the radio."

"You want me to answer the radio," she repeated dryly.

"Yes but be vague. Say you had to get up to Tahoe in a hurry… some family emergency or some such."

"What! Why?"

"For God's sake, Koski, if they think you're on the way to Tahoe they'll head in that direction." He couldn't believe he had to spell it out for her. "Then we can make it to Carson without the Nevada Highway Patrol on our tail. We have less than ten miles to go." He reached for the microphone and handed it to her. "Wing it."

It was obvious that she still resented taking orders but when she chose to follow them she did it well.

A short time later Falk drove into the parking lot of a small, granite stone church in Carson City. He disconnected one of the wires hanging from the steering column and the engine shuddered to silence.

"Where to now?" Koski asked as she scooped up the groceries.

Falk carefully gathered up the blanket. "To a place where they don't ask questions as long as you pay the bill." She followed as he swung out of the hearse and strolled down a side street out onto Highway 395.

"What place?" she asked, taking two steps to his one in order to keep up.

He replied nonchalantly, as if there wasn't any reason for her to raise an eyebrow, "To a motel."

Who's Killing All the Lawyers?

Chapter 13

At nine in the morning pedestrian traffic on Highway 395—less than a block from the state building in Carson City—was double its normal volume. Civil servants rushed to their cubicles to contend with miles of red tape caused by the flurry of activity from yet another lawyer's demise.

Two FBI agents, in suits distinguished enough to be laid out in, hurried toward the silver-domed Capitol building. The tails of their jackets flapped with their stride. Increased aircraft activity in the area also was becoming the norm of late. The cacophony of a regulation chopper's rotors passed overhead going largely unnoticed.

A man in an empty shop doorway watched the two agents and surreptitiously maneuvered a small device until the red dot it controlled bobbed across the back of one of the agent's jacket.

"Yeah, well, I'm a lawyer, too," the unsuspecting, targeted agent was saying. "My wife doesn't even want me to leave the house in the morning…"

The dot moved in small concentric circles and stopped where a vital, vulnerable organ lay beneath the jacket's wool threads…"and my kids, they've seen enough about "killing arrows" on the six o'clock news to scare the shit out of them…before this, I thought I was too young to retire but right about now all of that Salsa Saturday and

Bingo Monday stuff is beginning to sound—" He never finished his sentence as the dancing dot determined its mark at the lower tip of his left shoulder blade.

The second agent might have heard the deep, thick *THUMP* that accompanied the arrow into his companion's heart. He might have seen the blood splatter out of the man's chest onto the beige coat of a woman walking six feet ahead but no one will ever know because he, too, was hit and fell.

"Relax, Don. Agents Falk and Koski going missing only serves to heighten the media's interest in them," claimed Nevada Senator Albert Reinecke. He had made one of his rare visits to Attorney General Lovesy's office and was forced to wade through a sea of reporters to get there. "After all, that was the initial intent."

"I don't like it, Albert," Lovesy said, his red, prickly face slick with sweat. "As ordered, I specifically formed this team to be highly visible at each of the crime scenes…to show the public that we have dedicated professionals on the job. Now, with the two best agents on the team missing, the heat's coming back to my department, defeating the purpose. The news hounds have worked themselves into a frenzy."

"Ah, relax," Reinecke repeated. "Publicity is what we want. All this helps to stoke the fires and put more suspicion on the Indians. He glanced toward the flat screen television set on the wall and leaned across Lovesy's desk, pressing a button on the remote.

A local anchor pictured over the "Breaking News" banner, which was above the crawl at the bottom of the screen, had reported the arrow killing of two FBI agents near the Capitol.

"We expect to have further comment from State Attorney General Donald Lovesy soon," the reporter said. "To date, however, Lovesy has said only that he has a top-level task force investigating these senseless killings. Meanwhile, local Native American leaders, encouraged by remarks from Democratic State Senator Albert Reinecke, are demanding a face-to-face meeting with the governor, claiming that hate and racism are being directed at local tribes—"

Reinecke hit the mute button and turned back to Lovesy with a slight grin. "We couldn't get more ink and air time if we'd hired a press agent."

It was three in the afternoon but Lovesy and Reinecke each held glasses of scotch in their hands. Lovesy set his down and twisted in his seat, his fat knees squeaking against the wood inside the kneehole of his desk.

"I repeat. I don't like what's happening, Albert. Washington has assigned this guy from the NSA, Samuel Ryland, to oversee this investigation. What if he finds out too much?"

Reinecke's voice was steady. "Then you'll have to take care of the situation."

Lovesy's squirming intensified. "When I agreed to be a part of this—and I *only* agreed because I was convinced that halting the spread of Indian gambling would keep Nevada financially strong—I was given to understand that there wouldn't be any killing."

Reinecke's eyebrows shot up. "None of your team has been killed, Don. At least as far as we know."

"Others have, including two of Tony Villachi's men, thanks to their own bungling. I guess agents Falk and Koski proved to be too much for them." He sipped his neat Johnny Walker Black and shook his head. "No, I don't like it, Albert. I don't like the whole thing."

Senator Reinecke was a tall, polished man in his sixties, widowed, with three grown children. He wore large gold rings on his fingers, expensive leather shoes and wool suits. Accustomed to political maneuvering, his face was capable of simultaneously registering self-importance and humility.

Through the years, it seemed that events conspired to bless him with what he most admired—power. In fact, it was his adroit manipulation of the state machine, coached by The Fox, that allowed him to rise in the political ranks until he emerged from nonentity to stellar social and political status.

No one knew about this manipulation. Ostensibly, Reinecke was a champion of Native American rights. The Washoe Indians owned nearly twenty million acres of Nevada. Reinecke, by exhibiting shrewd political prowess, controlled the Washoe tribe.

He was the natural choice to channel the political end of The Fox's campaign against lawyers. He appeared to be aiding the Indian gaming cause, while in fact he weakened it from within. In this way, Reinecke retained control over the tribes and The Fox retained control of Reinecke. Additional impetus for the senator to join forces with The Fox was the fact that Reinecke was dipping into the reservations' tills for years and The Fox knew it.

Reinecke stood up and slowly rubbed a manicured index finger across his sleek, silver mustache. "We don't have to *like* any of this, Don. We just have to do it."

Reinecke turned and left. One of Lovesy's aides immediately replaced him in the room.

"Sir, the reporters are waiting for a statement, sir," the young aide said nervously.

Lovesy stood and buttoned his jacket over his ample girth. "Kid," he said rhetorically, putting on a forced, philosophical air, "did you ever stop to think that ours is a planet of shit, a stinking outhouse dangling from a rightfully exploding universe?"

"Yes, sir." The aide apparently was accustomed to the AG's rambling, sardonic view of the world. "The reporters, sir…what do we do?"

Lovesy straightened his tie. "We give them a show. There always has to be a show, kid."

Reinecke got back to his office and called Villachi, using his scrambler line, as he always did when being publicly connected. The conversation was brief and one-sided.

"We'll have to do something about Lovesy. He's sweating heavily and the odor will ultimately attach itself to us." There was a grunt on the other end and the line went dead.

Who's Killing All the Lawyers?

Chapter 14

Maxwell was already in Webster's office at BLM Reno when Spade arrived, breathless as usual, and trimmed with camera equipment.

"You get Flo off to Arkansas all right?"

Spade nodded as he sank into a chair. "Yeah, she's excited about it, despite the fact that she's worried about me."

"Worried?" Webster asked. He poured Spade a mug of coffee from a carafe atop a filing cabinet.

"It's funny," Spade said, accepting the mug. "She never had reason to worry about me on the job before but now, after last night, she's afraid this assignment will be my last in more ways than one."

Webster showed obvious concern. "Alex, I'd hoped you would allay any fears she had before she left. Didn't you assure her that you weren't in any danger?"

"I may have not sounded too convincing. I've been married to Flo for thirty years." He paused and sipped his coffee. "She may be naive but she's not stupid."

"Married to you that long," Webster said with his personable smile. "I'm not too sure about her."

Maxwell was in her thirties and single by choice but a part of her silently longed to be in a relationship like what Flo and Alex shared.

She immediately corrected her thoughts: relationships were what you had with friends and family. Marriage was a partnership or else it didn't work.

"What's your take on long-term partnerships, Webster?" She had heard that he was thirty-seven, divorced, with no children. It was said that he led a quiet, self-indulgent life in which he sometimes partied hard but was dedicated and good at his job. This morning he looked a little bleary-eyed, as if he had worked late on this assignment last night or had too many beers with his friends.

He smiled with slight embarrassment, signaling his discomfort in discussing his feelings. After a moment he said slowly, "I think it takes a lot of work to make that tiny, inner magic—that can happen in the blink of an eye—last a lifetime."

The frankness and depth of his response impressed Maxwell. She also noted that he quickly changed the subject.

"I've already had two interesting phone calls this morning," he said. "Virginia City Police report that Koski was probably there yesterday morning. The owner of a small grocery store on the edge of town said a woman fitting Koski's description came in and bought coffee, sandwiches and some miscellaneous items. At the same time, a hearse was stolen from a nearby mortuary."

"A hearse!" Spade exclaimed.

Webster nodded. "It was found later in a church parking lot in Carson City."

"What about Falk?" Maxwell asked.

Webster downed the remains of his coffee. "The store owner said Koski bought two coffees, which leads me to conclude that Falk stole the hearse while she bought the provisions."

Maxwell sighed. "At least we know they're alive…or were…"

"So, we're going to Carson now?" Spade asked.

"Not *we*, Alex," Webster said, getting up and sitting on the edge of the desk, facing him. "Maxwell and I need you to stay here in the office." He gestured toward the well-worn couch and the adjoining restroom. "You'll be our base of communication as we try to find Falk and Koski," he paused for emphasis, "which means you cannot leave this office for the next few days."

Spade nodded, looking around. Maxwell thought he was somewhat relieved to have a desk job for the duration.

"Webster, you said you had two interesting phone calls. Who was the second?" Maxwell asked.

He glanced up at the white-faced clock on the wall, its black hands indicating 10:14. "We're having a visitor any minute. We get to meet the man from the National Security Agency Lovesy told us about…who is supposed to be overseeing—"

A light tap on the door interrupted him and all three looked up as the door opened.

"Excuse me," the man who leaned in said in a deep, soft voice. "Your secretary wasn't at her desk so I…"

"Come in, come in," Webster said, rising and extending his hand.

Maxwell took in the details of the NSA agent as introductions were made.

Samuel Ryland was of medium height, in his early forties and dressed in a dark, conservative suit. His hair was black; his face handsome, with a wide forehead, aquiline nose and dark gray eyes softened by a smile that Maxwell thought suggested gentleness and sensitivity.

With two quick strides, he closed the space between Maxwell and himself and took her hand. His palm was cool and smooth as he touched her. She thought his grip lingered a moment longer than necessary in its hold and was timed deliberately.

They took their seats. Ryland preferred to stand.

There was a sense of decisiveness about him, a firm set to his shoulders and a confident attitude that seemed to signify a career man at the NSA.

He said, "I know you're busy, as am I, so I'll keep this brief. Basically, I need some points clarified." He turned to Maxwell. "Doctor, tell me about the arrow that was turned over to you at the sheriff's office in Carson."

It was the embarrassing episode that she and her boss, Chief Bud Vigo, avoided discussing. "I placed it in the evidence locker myself after I examined it," she said, more defensively than intended, "but it subsequently disappeared."

"It was never recovered?"

"Not to my knowledge."

"It was the same as those found in the bodies of the dead lawyers?"

"Yes, employing an electronic guidance system."

They all turned then at a sudden interruption by Roz Newton, Webster's secretary, who had returned to her area and heard their voices.

"Oh," Roz said as she stepped inside the room, "we have a visitor." She turned intelligent blue eyes to Ryland. "Coffee?" she asked in the intimate way that came naturally to extremely physically attractive women.

Maxwell had wondered aloud to Webster earlier as to what secretarial attributes Roz possessed. He seemed indifferent to her striking looks, insisting that she was efficient and possessed extraordinary "people skills."

Now Maxwell scrutinized Roz with Webster's assessment in mind. She was a tall, leggy blonde, about thirty, a little over the age limit to be wearing the Jennifer Lopez outfit she had on: tight, powder-blue sweatshirt and super low-cut, leather-lace jeans. Maxwell thought her a curious mixture between soft-core dream date and, from what Webster said, a master's degree.

"No, thank you," Ryland answered and Roz retreated to her area. The J.Lo logo emblazoned in rhinestones on her butt pocket caught the light of syncopation as she moved.

Webster rose and closed the door. Ryland continued as if no interruption had occurred.

"I'm assuming the arrow embedded in the tree was just a miss of some kind...that some lawyer who was hiking in the area had a lucky day."

"I thought that, too," replied Maxwell.

Ryland nodded and included the two men in his next question. "We've been attempting to factor the range these arrows can cover. Does anyone have a guesstimate on that?"

"I'd say approximately five miles," Webster responded as he returned to his chair behind the desk. "The last few hundred feet could be under the control of a preset homing device. Whoever has control of these missiles has a pretty sophisticated piece of hardware."

"Yes," Ryland agreed, pacing the floor, "in fact, it may be worse than we thought...we've concluded that these so-called arrows probably have nuclear capability."

Spade, who had been silent until now, let his mouth fall open. "Nuclear!"

"Low-yield, of course," Ryland said, "but potent enough to be

103

termed a nuclear strike if used on almost any type of infrastructure. We can be thankful our enemy hasn't chosen to use the arrows that way."

Webster shook his head. "Does our military have anything like it?"

Ryland scoffed. "Dealing with Middle East terrorists, *Star Wars* systems and LGBs—laser-guided bombs—the Pentagon hasn't put much effort into developing laser-guided arrows." He stopped pacing. "Webster, any news on the rest of the team? I heard about the incident a couple of days ago with the man impersonating a deputy out near the lake."

Webster related the incident at Spade's home the night before. He also relayed what he heard from the Virginia City PD a short time ago and his belief that it was indeed Falk and Koski who "borrowed" the hearse and left it in Carson City. "Doc and I are about to head out to Carson now."

Ryland started toward the door. "Good. Hopefully, their trail won't be too cold."

"Mr. Ryland," Maxwell said, her words delaying his exit, "do you have any information about the man who was playing deputy sheriff... the man who apparently killed the real deputy out near Vista Point?"

"Not a clue." He shook his head. "Keep working on it." Then he was gone.

Webster accelerated to the maximum speed limit as he and Maxwell headed out Highway 50 toward Carson City. After a few minutes of Clint Black and some other C & W artist with whom Maxwell was unfamiliar but surprisingly enjoyed, Webster turned the radio off.

"Doc," he said, "I owe you an apology."

"Oh?"

"Yeah, when we talked for the first time, at the cattle chute where the vic in the tuxedo was found, I can honestly say I figured you for a wise-ass know-it-all. I suspected that either you and Falk or you and I might commit a major act of mayhem against the other before this assignment was over. I thought here is a woman I'll remember long after lunch."

Maxwell's warm brown eyes smiled but she remained silent.

"Well, anyway, I was wrong," he continued. "You're okay. You think like a cop, a good one, and have what I call mental agility and I admire that." He paused, nodding approval of his own words. "I just wanted to put that out there."

"Thanks, Webster." Something in what he said moved her to go to a place she generally avoided and never went voluntarily. "My father was a cop."

"Really? Where?"

"In a small Chicago suburb where I lived until I was seventeen." She had begun and, without any further word from Webster, simply started down the slippery slope of recollection. "God, I loved my father. I was an only child and as a kid, I was so proud of him. I listened to him tell about this or that which happened on his beat, about how he and his partner collared a perp, how they unearthed clues that led to solving cases. To hear him tell it, he was cop, detective, DA, judge and jury, all rolled into one."

"Ah," Webster interjected, "that's why you're into those detective novels."

"Maybe," she said, then went sullen, sucking on her bottom lip before she could go on. "When I was a senior in high school, my father, who had hardly ever unholstered his gun during his previous ten years on the force, shot and killed a brother...Mr. Peck, father of my best friend and classmate, Barbara."

"Oh, wow," Webster exclaimed, no doubt cognizant that he may be privy to thoughts that few, if any, had heard before.

"I *still* don't see why he had to *kill* him." Maxwell's voice quavered and she paused to bring it under control. "Everybody said it wasn't his fault. Apparently, Mr. Peck was a thief with ties to the mob du jour. An official Internal Affairs investigation exonerated my father of any wrongdoing. They found that Mr. Peck drew on my father while committing a robbery and my father fired in self-defense."

As he concentrated on the highway ahead, Webster tried to decide how he should weigh in on this subject. "That must have been tough on you," he ventured, "a teenager in high school…a very fragile time of life…and your best friend's dad…Yet, you couldn't blame your father if—"

"But I *do* blame him. Why *shouldn't* I? *He* did it. *He* killed Barbara's father…and ruined my life." Again she steadied her voice. "Oh, my friends at school didn't exactly persecute me but I believed they somehow blamed me. I felt that my mere presence among my classmates after that was a constant, bitter reminder of the tragedy that traumatized the whole school."

Webster handed her his handkerchief and drove silently, concluding that the situation Maxwell described had been a bum rap all around.

Maxwell dabbed at her eyes and slowly relaxed, pushing her thoughts back into perspective. "I managed to finish out the year and graduate…went off to college. I did go back now and then, mostly to see my mother, but she died five years ago and I haven't been back since the funeral." She handed back the limp, damp square of white cotton. "Nice hanky."

Chapter 15

Falk and Koski checked into a motel room next to the Greyhound bus stop on Highway 395 in Carson. A small parking lot and a liquor store anchored the rundown building. Falk sat on the edge of a sway-backed double bed and lowered the blanket roll to the floor. As he did, one side of the blanket opened and the Kalashnikov clattered to the floor with the sound only an ugly, lethal weapon can make. He picked up the rifle, along with the remaining items Koski had purchased in Virginia City—cans of corn and beans and several power bars.

Koski nodded to her video equipment. "For all the good this has been, I could have left it in the shack on the hillside instead of schlepping it all over Nevada."

"Just be sure to keep it in working order," Falk insisted. "I've a hunch we'll need it."

Koski wrinkled her nose and looked around the dismal room. "You get the blanket. I get the bed. How long are we going to be holed up here?"

"Just long enough to get some equipment together."

She shrugged. "What kind of equipment?"

"Snow gear. I want to check out an area near Bowman Lake where I came across an armed force of American Indians in training exercises a few weeks ago. They were on their own land and generally tolerated my nosing around. I'd like to rule out—or rule in—their involvement in these murders once and for all." He fished in his pocket for some change. "In any case, it's the last place anyone would think to look for us."

"*Us*? You've decided that I might be needed."

Needed? He certainly was not ready to admit that. "You might be *useful*," he corrected and handed her some quarters. "Look, I'll make my call for gear and wheels from the motel lobby. You go to the liquor store and call Webster. He knows the Sierra pretty well. Tell him to meet us three miles up the Bowman Lake road off Highway 20 before it joins the I-180. Tell him to come alone. I want Maxwell in her hotel in Reno in case we need the connection there."

He checked his watch. "It's almost five-thirty. Tell him to meet us at eight. He should look for a camper parked at the side of the road."

Koski nodded. "Who are you going to get the gear and camper from?"

"Someone I can always count on to deliver." He had one more order. "Tell Webster not to say anything on the phone and tell him to be on time or we go without him, no matter how well he knows the mountains."

At the liquor store, Koski got through to Webster's cell phone. "Don't say anything, Webster. Just listen."

When she finished relaying Falk's orders, Webster responded, "But Maxwell and I are on our way to Carson now—"

"Webster!" Koski snapped, stopping him. "I just said Falk doesn't want you to talk on this line." She sighed. "Look, you have plenty of time. Take Maxwell back—she'll understand—and meet us as Falk instructed."

"Right," he said without further protest and the dial tone hummed on the line.

Webster made a quick U-turn and headed back to Reno. Maxwell looked surprised and asked where they were going. Webster brought her up to date and she was naturally disappointed, being out of the loop, but she respected that Falk had his reasons.

"Where are you, Falk and Koski going?" she asked.

"Into the mountains," was all he said, although he probably saw no reason to withhold the exact location from her.

Through the smudged window of the motel room, Falk saw a dented, dusty camper truck drive into the parking lot and stop. A young man got out, looked around and walked into the liquor store.

"Stay here," Falk said.

Koski went to the window. The store had two entrances, one to the parking lot and the other to the street where a Greyhound bus was picking up passengers. She watched Falk go to the driver's side of the truck, remove the keys and lock the door. He opened the camper's rear door and climbed in, only to reappear in minutes, carrying a large, bulky canvas bag. The bus turned onto Highway 395 and the camper driver nodded in Falk's direction from inside the bus as it gained speed and headed south.

"Like I said, my man always delivers," Falk said, re-entering the room.

"That young guy is your man?"

Falk ignored the question as he swung the heavy bag onto the bed then tugged open the heavy-duty zipper. "The camper is equipped with food, five-pound, goose-down sleeping bags, ordnance...everything."

Koski took another glance out the window at the ratty vehicle. "Doesn't look as if it will make it to Bowman Lake."

"Looks can be deceiving. It'll make it." He quickly checked out

109

the sack's contents, which included an alcohol compass, a small Primus stove, enough dehydrated, individually wrapped meals for three people for six days—supplementing the canned goods already in the camper—three personal packs containing first aid supplies and toiletries, including non-freezing liquid soap.

"In the camper I saw three, one-piece, white coveralls, a couple changes of nylon mesh underwear, lightweight silk gloves to be worn under padded mittens with trigger slips and vacuum insulated boots."

"Sounds like your man *did* think of everything."

Falk reached back into the pack. Wrapped in an oilskin pouch near the bottom of the bag was a thoughtful addition: a Glock 17 9mm automatic with a loaded 17 round magazine.

"In the right hands," he said, "this is capable of placing five-shot groups inside a 2.5-inch circle at a range of 25 yards."

"Right," she said, disappointed, "but there's only one of them." When he nodded, she shrugged. "Oh, well, those can openers are always jamming anyway."

Falk went into the bathroom. He had extracted a small manila envelope from the bottom of the canvas sack. Falk's name was written on it in a scribble he recognized as Tom Stewart's of Cerberus. He had asked Stewart a question when he called for the camper. He hoped the note contained the answer. The message read: IT IS RUMORED THAT UNDERWORLD UNSUBS TO MEET ON LEVEL 15 OF MINE NEAR BOWMAN. PURPOSE UNKNOWN. BOLO. IN ANSWER TO QUESTION RE MINE, DEED TRACED (WITH DIFFICULTY) TO INDIAN NAME "MUKUAMP." T.

"Mukuamp?" Falk whispered to himself. He had hoped for something more specific. That name, however, sounded familiar… something Falk heard or read in the past. He sighed. He had no idea what the cryptic rumor of a meeting at the mine meant or who the unknown underworld subjects were. Moreover, why were they meeting at the mine? Did they have some connection to the Indian militia members Falk himself was planning to investigate?

On an abstract level of understanding, this information tied into his unformed thoughts. Yes, he would BOLO—be on the lookout—for anyone and anything that posed a threat. He tore up the note, flushed it down the toilet, then returned to the room where Koski had finished repacking the bag.

"Now what do we do?" she asked. "We've got some time before we meet Webster."

He decided to do something he seldom did—share his thoughts. "A couple of things bother me about this operation," he said. Koski sank to the bed and he sat in the only chair in the room. "According to Lovesy, we were supposed to be visible but silent, right?"

"Right."

"What does that suggest to you?" Koski shrugged, not sure where he was going. "Ever go duck hunting?"

"No."

"When you hunt ducks, you put a brightly colored wooden duck in plain sight to attract other *real* ducks. The wooden version is called a decoy."

Koski rolled her eyes. "Fascinating."

"That's *us*, Koski. You and I and the whole team. I'm convinced we were meant to be decoys from the start."

Her expression turned serious as she realized what he was saying. "But why?"

"To give the public evidence that something is being done about the lawyers' deaths—while something *else* is being done in another place."

"What? Where?"

"If I knew the answers, I wouldn't have to sound out the situation. I might even go so far as to say that we're expendable."

"Are you saying that people in our state government are using us…maybe even trying to kill us?" Koski's forehead furrowed beneath her silken bangs.

"I'm saying that their plan was to put us out there, cut us loose and if we got killed in the process…so be it. By disappearing and going off on our own, we must be, to put it mildly, frustrating them royally."

"You think that Lovesy…?"

"I don't know anything for sure yet—but he certainly has a stake in this. To halt the spread of Indian gambling in California would keep the state that pays Lovesy's salary fiscally strong." He shook his head. "If you try to mentally round up all the usual suspects, everybody's questionable."

He leaned back in the chair. "I have a friend in the Bureau of Indian Affairs with strong ties to the Indian nations. A Native American chief in Arizona mentioned a name that rang a bell with me: Senator Albert Reinecke of Nevada, chairman of the powerful Ways and Means Committee and outspoken champion of Native American welfare.

"The senator has been the driving force behind increased funding for all Indian tribes in the state for the last ten years. The report indicated, however, that there hasn't been any significant improvement in the tribes' way of life. In fact, in many instances, conditions have worsened. Millions in aid targeted by the Interior Department for them is going…where?"

Koski was propped against the headboard with her arms folded across her chest. "That would suggest that Reinecke is getting rich off Native Americans. He wouldn't want them weakened...blamed for the killings."

Falk's vision was abstract. "At least not publicly," he mumbled, "or at least not *voluntarily*." His eyes narrowed slightly and he looked at her. "Another thing: why would the tribes need to resort to murder to get more casinos in California? Governor Gray Davis endorsed, and the voters passed, Proposition 1A in March 2000, which initially envisioned small casinos in remote rural areas but in fact resulted in mega hotel casinos.

"Then in January 2001, President Clinton signed legislation that allowed the building of the San Pablo Casino on Interstate 80 between Oakland and Vallejo. It was the first Indian casino to operate in a major urban area in Northern California. As I recall, Davis even signed an agreement with sixty tribal leaders to legalize gambling on nearly all large reservation lands in California."

"That's true," Koski said. "I remember when California's Miwok Indians announced their intention to build a $100 million casino hotel along U.S. 50."

Falk nodded. "There's even an Indian gambling operation adjacent to the entrance to Yosemite National Park, for God's sake. Indian gambling is not only increasing in California but all over the country."

Koski leaned forward. "So, if your last statement is a defense against the Indians having motivation to kill the anti-gambling lawyers, it's an indictment against the people those lawyers represent, which means a large portion of the public that's against gambling. On the other hand, Nevada's organized crime, which opposes any gambling pie they don't have a piece of...top echelon officials in Nevada state government who want to protect the status quo—like, possibly, Reinecke and Lovesy here in Nevada—and God knows who else."

She sighed and let her back return to the headboard. "Which of these scenarios are we buying into and if we're decoys, for what?"

Falk's vision rested somewhere in the space between his eyes and the wall. "I'm not sure yet." He paused. "I'm pondering the motivations of those *who else* people you mentioned. Casinos are popping up everywhere—creating traffic problems, environmental concerns, etc. —but they're changing the very character of rural communities..."

"Environmental concerns?"

"In some California communities, local authorities have warned there isn't enough water in the areas to meet the needs of local homeowners and the casinos...that wells are running dry."

"What's the Indians' response to that?"

"Pretty scary. They flatly state that under their agreement with Governor Davis they are not obligated to obey California environmental laws."

Koski was surprised. "Do the non-Native American Californians know that?"

"Even if they do, there's nothing they can do about it."

"Doesn't California have a gambling commission to regulate all of this?"

"Yes but I haven't heard of any substantial regulation or oversight on their part. Some tribes even refuse to disclose how many slot machines they intend to operate in any given casino."

"So, you're saying that *lots* of disgruntled citizens have what you might call motivation to want to make the country afraid of Indians?"

"I'm not sure what I'm saying. For now, remember that we trust no one." He silently hoped to figure out the answers before it was too late. He bent forward in his chair and checked his watch. "Time to meet Webster."

Her green eyes narrowed and her head tilted to one side. "Who, by the way, we can't even be sure is someone we should trust." She got up from the bed. "Are we being paranoid?"

Falk got up and slung the canvas bag over his shoulder. "I only know that this situation is more complicated than it first seemed. There's more at stake here than the spread of Indian casinos. Native Americans suddenly represent something a lot more threatening than a few more slot machines."

Who's Killing All the Lawyers?

Chapter 16

Koski sat silently in the passenger seat of the old camper listening to the *clack-clack-clack* of the turn indicator as Falk switched to the right lane and exited Highway 20 onto the lonely Bowman Lake road and their prearranged rendezvous with Webster.

The farther they moved into the backcountry, the more remote the rest of the world became. On Highway 20, despite little traffic and miles between exits, there were homes in the distance. Their lighted windows were beacons in the darkness. Now, trees and bushes were their only companions and the exterior isolation heightened a sense of camaraderie in the warm truck.

In the glow from the dashboard, Falk's strong features softened as he glanced her way. A spontaneous, friendly, disarming smile turned up the corners of his mouth. A tenderness long denied welled up inside Koski and dismayed her. She immediately pushed away her emotions, trying to deny a girl-like shyness that remained.

The voice inside that had dogged her since David's arrest and imprisonment whispered in its darkly feathered way. *You can't trust your instincts, Susan. You're in danger of reading something into a situation that isn't there.* She thought of David doing time at the Ely State Pen in the high desert for stealing and selling eight pounds of coke.

"A penny for your thoughts," Falk said softly.

She shook her head dismissively. He didn't really want to know despite their protracted conversation in the motel room; that was business, not personal.

A muscle quivered at his jaw. "Okay, a nickel then."

She decided that conversation might be a good thing right now. "To be perfectly honest, I was thinking of my ex-significant other doing time up at Ely because he and a bunch of other rogue cops were caught dealing."

He nodded. "I read something about it. Was it a bum rap or was he really involved?"

"Oh, he was involved all right. Up to his nostrils."

"Ah, a user; signed his own arrest warrant."

Koski made the conscious decision to relax and spoke comfortably, as if she were talking to herself. "It's not that he didn't respect the law initially—he did. He revered it, as if it was a god and he was its prophet. I imagine that once you place yourself in that role nothing can stand in your way. Eventually, a warped sense of survival —his own—grew out of that philosophy. He lost the sense of shame that most people naturally feel if they think exclusively of themselves. Ultimately, all but the most superficial feelings became subordinate to the sense of power David derived from his work in Las Vegas Vice. It was so intoxicating that it was difficult to turn off when he came home at night."

She paused but Falk's interested silence encouraged her to go on. "I should have questioned the paradox; he could be gentle and kind— not boyish; he was never that—yet polished, slick, duplicitous."

She shook her head. "Damn! I never saw it coming. Until that day, I was sure I could read people, had passed Psychology 101 with flying colors, yadda, yadda, yadda…What a fool I—" She stopped abruptly, thinking she already said too much.

Falk's voice was low and soft. "Do you still love him?" When she didn't answer immediately, he added, "I think it only fair to tell you that in my last life I was a lie detector."

She sighed. "I don't think I ever did." Then she turned to the window. "If we can be mistaken about so elemental an emotion as love what feelings can we trust?"

Falk noticed she reached into the breast pocket of her jacket, as if to extract something. The hand lingered for a second but came out empty. He'd seen her do this before, reminiscent of a person who fingered a charm for luck, touched base with a treasured trinket or brushed a Buddha's belly.

He had a sudden, overwhelming desire to take her in his arms. In response to her question about trusting one's feelings, he wanted to reply that such were not so elemental but that he trusted his and they seemed to involve her more and more.

Webster came up behind them, the lights of his jeep blinking, and Falk pulled to the side of the road. Further conversation with Koski on the subject of feelings was fatefully interrupted. Perhaps that was a good thing.

Who's Killing All the Lawyers?

Chapter 17

Because his pale hand trembled, Donald Lovesy slowly raised a glass of scotch to his lips. He sat at his desk and stared at the flat screen on the facing wall. The impact of his part in the horror hit home as he caught the breaking news on television.

"Attorney John Hamlington and the three-member staff of his law firm were found dead in Sacramento today. The firm represents more than a dozen Northern California card clubs and various Bay Area charity organizations whose card rooms are struggling to stay open amidst new, flourishing Indian gambling facilities." The co-anchor managed an appropriate pause before continuing. "Police will only say that all four individuals, each in a separate office in a high-rise suite Hamlington leased, were killed by arrows."

Lovesy continued to hold the glass, unable to drink. Disgust at himself and his fear increased the tremor. When his private line rang, the glass jumped in his hand, blotching amber liquid across his desk and its contents. Even the phone was his enemy now.

"Lovesy," he grumbled. There were the usual gulps and gurgles from scrambler equipment and then Tony Villachi's deep growl came on the line.

"Morning, Don. In your office bright and early, I see."

Lovesy thought that the bastard, whose tone was usually grumpy, sounded as if nothing happened; as if four more innocent people hadn't just lost their lives. "It's all a show, Tony," Lovesy said honestly. "I'm here in body but not in spirit."

"Chrissake!" Villachi seemed surprised at his associate's bad humor. "I take back the bright and early remark. Why so glum?"

"I just turned on the TV and learned about that attorney, Hamlington, and his staff in Sacramento. I imagine your people are behind this?"

Villachi sounded indignant but controlled. "What a thing to say, Don. My people wouldn't do—"

"Oh, no, not your people. You're right. You wouldn't use anybody who can be traced to you. I'm sure you *imported* the talent for these atrocities." He paused and tried to drink, again unsuccessfully. "When is the slaughter going to end, Tony?"

Villachi's voice turned to ice. "I'm gonna chalk this conversation up to angst and pretend you never said that, my friend. I'm calling because you'll need to meet with Reinecke and me this morning. There are a few things we need to touch base on…make sure we're on the same page."

Lovesy knew not to refuse. One word from Villachi or Reinecke and he'd be revealed as a co-conspirator. He sighed heavily. "I suppose I can clear my calendar—"

"Good. Reinecke will send a car for you."

The phone went dead in the same instant that his intercom buzzed. "A car is here from Senator Reinecke's office, sir," his private secretary said.

"Thank you." Why hadn't Albert called himself? Lovesy seldom dealt directly with Villachi, which was as he liked it. Consorting with the Las Vegas don—even on a secure line—was not something the state attorney general was—or should be—comfortable doing. Beads of perspiration formed on his forehead. He wanted to go to this meeting about as much as he wanted to undergo the bypass of his blocked left carotid artery scheduled for next week. He had no choice; a situation he found himself in a lot lately, a situation he hated.

He put on and buttoned his jacket. When he started through his secretary's office on his way out, he said, "Push back my meetings for about an hour."

"Yes, sir," the middle-aged woman said. "You'll probably want to take the private exit, sir. The outer office is full of reporters...you can imagine...four more deaths and no word on the missing members of your investigative team..."

"Buzzards," Lovesy muttered. "Everybody's thirsting to be first with the worst." He turned and went back into his office and was passing his desk when his private line to the governor rang.

"Donald." The governor's voice was high-pitched and crisp. "You've talked to local law enforcement officials. This vendetta against lawyers continues to spread. Should it become out-and-out terrorism against the citizens of California and Nevada, are you satisfied that sufficient high alert security is in place at the Capitol and every major state and federal facility in Nevada?"

Lovesy gripped the glass of scotch and managed to down the liquid. The sensation was exhilarating, spreading from a fiery explosion in his mouth and throat to every part of his body. His mind cleared. "Yes, governor, I am." He took a deep breath, poured another couple of fingers and added an ice cube from the leather bucket. The cube cracked and crackled and he quickly moved it away from the phone, hoping the governor hadn't heard.

"What about the dam?" the governor asked. "If whoever these

terrorists are—and I'm beginning to doubt they are Native American weekend militia warriors—should decide to play havoc with Hoover Dam and that 726-foot-high concrete wall holding back twenty-seven million acre feet of the Colorado River was damaged..."

"Not a chance, governor. The dam is totally secure; has been since September 2001...the National Guard is there and—"

"Speaking of warriors, Donald, it wouldn't be a bad idea to..."

Lovesy nodded at his directives as the governor continued, "Yes, governor, I'll call General Stone of the National Guard...a squad of men will be deployed...yes, sir, immediately."

Concluding the conversation with more assurances to the governor, Lovesy finished the remainder of his drink and made a brief call to an old friend, General Rocky Stone of the Nevada National Guard. Then he walked to the back of his office. Touching a panel on the wall, he waited while a pocket door disguised as wood paneling slid open. He walked through the opening, which returned itself to the appearance of a seamless wall behind him.

Soon Lovesy sat slumped in the back seat of Reinecke's limo, staring out at the city. Traffic was light but Lovesy was aware of an air of expectancy surrounding the moment. The car felt uncomfortably warm...maybe the scotch...It was more than that. He reached for the intercom and asked the driver to cut back on the heat.

He cursed silently and pressed the button to lower the window beside him to allow a cold draft to sweep into the vehicle. He removed a handkerchief from his pocket, wiped away a film of perspiration that had collected on his upper lip and leaned back in the seat. Reinecke and Villachi should know the governor wanted a National Guard unit deployed to monitor the militia camp where Bowman Lake bordered Nevada and California. Lovesy should have called them immediately.

No matter, he would see them in a few minutes; he'd tell them then.

The limo slowed and stopped for a traffic light near the Nugget Casino a few blocks from the Capitol.

The target was perfectly placed. The window of the limo was partly open, giving a powerfully built, redheaded man and his partner, poised behind the tinted windows of a parked car at the corner, a clear view of the attorney general and the red dot moving down the side of his face. It settled just above his collar. At this range it was a cinch. The arrow flew fast and true, thudding into Lovesy's neck and pinning him to the seat. He was dead before the light changed.

Who's Killing All the Lawyers?

Chapter 18

During his meeting yesterday with Tony Villachi in a secret place behind the counting room in one of Villachi's Vegas casino hotels, Rod Eiker, British mercenary par excellence, was given a goal and a nearly bottomless budget. He also was informed that how he accomplished that goal was pretty much his business, within reason. It was the way Eiker preferred to carry out an assignment; unencumbered by moral or fiscal considerations.

Villachi's unnamed associate in Carson City had completed phase one of the campaign with the killing of the two FBI lawyers outside their offices at the state building in Carson. Eiker had picked up the torch, solved what Villachi called "the Lovesy problem," contracted out an assignment in Sacramento and had an important personal date in Reno at noon today. Now he would begin the campaign to collect extortion money from frightened Nevada attorneys.

Eiker first chose the prominent Nevada law firm of O'Connor, Cox and Brace that occupied three floors of opulent office suites at the top of a twenty-five-story steel and glass tower in Las Vegas. Here, amid muffled legality, associates and soft-spoken executive secretaries generally ministered to the absolute power of Ralph O'Connor. He leaned toward rejecting the mob's offer of security against death by an arrow through the heart.

Eiker had secured a blueprint of the high-rise and a schedule of the members' appointments.

He planned his visit for nine a.m. on the day all the firm's attorneys met in the twenty-fifth floor conference room. Eiker and two of his men entered the building in predawn darkness, bypassing the security system with ease. Earlier, he had carefully handpicked these men, flying them to a rendezvous point in the desert midway between Vegas and Carson City.

With only a few hours to prepare them for this assignment, Eiker was forced to push the envelope but he was satisfied they were the best local talent available. Now, the three were dressed in state-of-the-art anti-terrorist attire, clad entirely in black clothing and body armor, black Kevlar helmets and shatterproof goggles. Flame-resistant Nomex balaclavas protected their heads and faces. Their assault vests and leg pouches held an assortment of grenades and other gear, a terrifying sight to the uninitiated.

Eiker's dramatic plan was to be hidden in the drop ceiling of the conference room when the meeting began. One of his men carried a portable laser beam guidance system. In addition to his regular weaponry, Eiker toted a bow and two arrows. Having had only a short time to practice with the unusual weapon, Eiker and his archer had nevertheless mastered the skill needed to work as a team. Their third man was assigned to toss a low-powered Flash bang concussion grenade into the room when Eiker gave the order to plunge from their hiding place behind the ceiling panels.

Eiker had fitted a length of flexible fiber optic tubing through a small hole in the ceiling tile and attached it to a palm-sized TV. Then he plugged the whole assembly into a battery pack attached to his vest and he and his men, balanced on beams, waited silently.

Soon a sharp, clear picture of a bevy of male and female barristers appeared on Eiker's tiny TV screen as they entered the room and took their seats, sipping coffee and awaiting the main man. The sound of a grandfather clock striking nine floated up through the ceiling.

"Good morning," O'Connor's voice boomed as he entered the room. Eiker adjusted the tube and held on the large Orson Welles look-alike as he seated himself at the head of the table. "Before we consider regular business, let's take a moment to discuss our in-house security. As you know, we have spared no expense to ensure that we have the best available. Nonetheless, some of you have suggested that in light of the recent killings, it might be prudent to consider the, shall we say, *particular* type of security offered by a local gaming and resorts organization."

One of the partners gulped a handful of pills, downed some water and mumbled, "Nothing but the old protection racket. They want to take advantage of us. Gangsters, all of them."

O'Connor nodded. "My sentiments exactly."

Another partner leaned forward and said in a solicitous, negotiating tone, "These people you call gangsters happen to be, for the most part, our bread and butter. It's possible they're only thinking of our welfare."

"Our welfare, my foot!" It was obvious the discussion was over. O'Connor reddened and banged a fist on the table intermittently as he spoke. "It's nothing short of extortion (thump) and I for one am appalled that you'd even consider going along with this strong-arm tactic. I will not (thump) be—"

Eiker tapped his closest companion's shoulder and whispered, "It's show time."

The man kicked at a ceiling panel and tossed his Flash grenade down onto the center of the conference table. An ear-splitting roar and a flash of blinding light accompanied Eiker and his men as they landed on the large, long slab of glossy mahogany, terrifying everyone in the room. Women screamed. White-faced men sat, unmoving, with their mouths agape, fingers gripping the arms of their chairs. The third member of Eiker's team jumped lightly to the floor and stood in front of the door, his Uzi submachine gun covering the room. Eiker nodded and his archery partner took an exaggerated stance with the laser transmitter, snapped on the switch and with a flourish placed a red dot on the panelled wall.

"A preview, counselors," Eiker said, his voice ringing through the room, "of what can happen if certain people ignore sound security advice. The lawyers whose demise you've read about in the newspapers," he continued, "were dispatched in the following fashion." He held the arrows aloft. "Laser-guided shafts. The victims were marked with a laser dot aimed by an accomplice while a second person fired the arrow."

The smoke from the Flash bang had cleared and the red dot on the wall was visible to all. "The shooter," Eiker continued, "could be, and in most instances was, out of sight of the target. The arrow was released and by the wonders of modern electronics, homed in on the little red dot." He paused and smiled perversely. "Just like the laser-guided bombs the Yanks use in Afghanistan and Iraq."

Eiker's man moved the dot from the wall and centered it on the forehead of a terrified attorney sitting at the far end of the table. The dot slowly went from one lawyer to another, bouncing around the table until it stopped and held on O'Connor's chest.

"No one is safe," Eiker said menacingly, "once the bead is drawn on the victim." He nodded across the room to a large oil painting of O'Connor's great-grandfather twenty feet away. His partner moved the laser dot onto the subject's forehead and held it motionless. Eiker notched an arrow into the bow, aimed in a direction deliberately to the left of the target and released the arrow. The twang of the bowstring was still in the air as the projectile was corrected in flight then veered to its goal, thudding into the forehead of the likeness of the law firm's illustrious founder.

"I think you get the point," Eiker said in O'Connor's direction. He and his companion jumped from the table and backed toward the door. "Don't attempt to exit this room for one hour after we leave; it will be booby trapped." He flicked his eyes to the oil painting. "You may keep the arrow as a symbol of our determination." His crooked, boyish grin slowly transformed his face. "Someone will be in touch regarding the premiums due on your new insurance policies."

Outside the room, Eiker led the way to a freight elevator he had wired earlier with a hidden bypass switch to override its normal operation. Closing the lift's gate, he activated the override and spoke an order into his wrist microphone as they continued non-stop to the basement.

Like clockwork, a van pulled up to the back door as the three men exited the building and climbed aboard. Within minutes they were on The Strip and headed back to their desert location, where Eiker would reveal the details of their next and infinitely more dangerous assignment.

Who's Killing All the Lawyers?

Chapter 19

Sitting in her hotel room in Reno, Maxwell put down the book she was reading and switched on the television to a local news channel. A co-anchor announced the lead story: the murder of Nevada's Attorney General Donald Lovesy. His two closest aides and private secretary were being interviewed, extracting their fifteen minutes of fame by tearfully proclaiming that the AG was a kind, honest, optimistic straight-shooter who didn't have an enemy in the world.

A meeting that the governor convened at his mansion less than an hour earlier resulted in his announcing that martial law was in effect in Nevada until further notice. The governor also expressed his sorrow at the loss of the attorney general, promising his killer would be brought to justice.

"Enough!" Maxwell said as she depressed a button on the remote and the television screen went black. She was angry, sad, uneasy, frustrated and curious. Why Lovesy? Yes, he was the state's chief law enforcement officer but there was someone ready to step in and take his place. What would Native Americans—or anyone—gain by killing him? At that moment, she sorely longed to talk to her teammates.

The phone rang and she grabbed it eagerly.

"Dr. Maxwell?"

She thought she recognized the deep, powerful voice. "Mr. Ryland?"

"Yes, but call me Samuel, please. How are you?"

She felt relieved at the sound of a familiar voice and decided to be honest. "A little antsy, a little angry…I just heard about Attorney General Lovesy."

"Yes, it seems so senseless."

Maxwell sighed. "I also think I've got cabin fever."

"Cabin fever, why?"

"My part in the investigation at the present time is to stay here at the hotel in the event I'm needed but so much is happening out there…"

"Where is Falk? Have you talked to him?"

"I haven't the faintest, except that he, Koski and Webster are headed into the mountains somewhere."

"Well, look, I just flew in from HQ at Fort Meade and I'm about to have an early lunch with Lester Carter. He's not only an old friend but Falk's bureau chief here in Reno. Would you care to join us? I'm not far from your hotel. I can pick you up before I collect Lester."

Maxwell's inclination was to jump at the invitation but she had her orders. "Thanks but Falk—"

"He has my numbers. If he doesn't get you there he'll probably check with me, in which case I'll say I insisted that you get out of the "cabin.""

His reassuring words were all Maxwell needed. She concluded the conversation and was ready before Ryland arrived.

Fifteen minutes later they were seated at the Steak House in Harrah's on North Center Street.

Lester Carter was a short, thin man who looked like he was in the habit of skipping meals. He was pale, with fine features and curly light hair that tended to frizz around the edges like Gene Wilder's. Maxwell soon realized that the man's lean body was probably due more to an overactive metabolism than Weight Watchers' meals.

Carter had devoured a deep-fried Monte Cristo sandwich, fries and coleslaw and was working on a large wedge of apple pie.

"Nice place," Carter said, glancing around. "When it comes to steak houses, you can't beat Binion's Horseshoe on Fremont Street in Las Vegas. If you haven't tried it for dinner, you should."

"I remember it, Lester," Ryland interjected. "You and I ate there years ago."

"Oh, yes, that's right." Carter turned to Maxwell. "I forget how far back this guy and I go. Anyway, Binion's Steak House has the best prime rib this side of Texas." He put down his fork and gestured with his thumb and index finger. "I swear, it's at least two inches thick... rare...tender..." He shook his head. "It'll cost you but worth every penny. The restaurant's on the twenty-fourth floor and the view—"

"Lester," Ryland interrupted softly, "you should know that I got word a few hours ago that FBI Reno is under investigation."

Maxwell silently watched Carter as he discontinued scraping the last vestiges of pie crust from his plate and studied Ryland's face. Despite his responsible position at the Bureau, Maxwell got the impression that Carter was a man whose biggest challenge in life to date was how to avoid a second mortgage on his home.

"You're serious?" Carter asked Ryland.

"Dead serious, I'm sorry to say."

Maxwell leaned forward and whispered, "The NSA is investigating the FBI?"

Ryland smiled slightly, enough for Maxwell to see his strong, sparkling white teeth. "Actually," he said, "the FBI will be doing an internal investigation of its own field offices."

Maxwell looked around. "Should you be telling us this?"

Ryland's dark, solemn eyes softened. "Probably not." He looked at Carter. "A heads-up among friends."

Carter nodded, then wiped his mouth and put his napkin down. "I hate it when that happens," he complained. "Internals always disrupt routine…morale drops to zero…everyone's pores are dissected under a microscope."

"Including yours?" Maxwell asked.

"Especially mine, Doctor. They start at the top and work their way down."

"Sorry, Lester," Ryland said. "I know you have enough to deal with right now without contending with a witch hunt." He signaled for the check and turned back to Maxwell. "Bad news for you, too, I'm afraid. If the scuttlebutt is correct they'll also be digging into the sheriff's offices in Carson and Virginia City."

It was Maxwell's turn to be surprised. "If there's someone connected to the murders working in the Carson City office, I'll be more than shocked." She shook her head. "I guess I can't blame them for checking out everyone—whoever's behind the killings might have internal access—but my boss, Chief Vigo, and his deputies…the other personnel…they're all honest as the day is long."

Mention of her boss made her wonder how Vigo was doing without her. She resolved to call him when she got back to the hotel. Surly bastard that he could be, she missed him.

"If you ask me," Carter was saying, "it's an import that's doing the lawyers. If I was heavily involved I'd check out an ex-agent from the Mossad's Saudi Arabian desk, Tamar Aderet. She has the brains to mastermind something like this." He paused and finished the last drop of coffee in his cup. "Of course, there's the British mercenary with whom I have a history..."

"British mercenary?" Ryland asked.

"He uses several aliases but his name's Eiker, Rodney Eiker."

"I've heard that name," Ryland said. "What kind of history are you talking about?"

Carter said, "Several years ago my partner and I caught him and a couple of his men red-handed near Hoover Dam. They had nearly three hundred pounds of stolen plastic explosives and several hundred detonators. We spotted them and called for backup but decided not to wait.

"When we broke cover, our perps opened fire and in the ensuing gunfight, Eiker's men were killed. He got away but not before I got off a round that caught his left ear." Carter paused and grinned slightly. "I didn't get the son of a bitch but I can guarantee that his ability to wear a diamond stud in that lobe was seriously impaired."

Maxwell silently took back her earlier assessment of Carter as untried.

"Think he's here in this country?" Ryland asked.

Carter shrugged. "You might want to check that out."

As the three walked back to Ryland's car, Maxwell felt grateful for the advance warning Ryland had provided about her office being under investigation. She felt no compunction to act upon that information. She was guilty of no wrongdoing and was certain Vigo was equally unstained.

Maxwell would remember the next few minutes the rest of her life, in flashes collaged upon the background of her mind.

The three approached the car. Ryland took out his remote and pressed a button and the alarm chirped. He opened the door behind the driver's seat for Maxwell while Carter walked around the vehicle to the front passenger door.

Maxwell did not see the red dot of light that moved across Carter's shoulders, lowered slightly and remained fixed, burning to penetrate its chosen spot. Before ducking to sink into the back seat, Maxwell heard a sound like the rushing wind captured by a large bird as it fluttered to earth. Something made her glance toward Carter. His eyes were like a deer's impertinent question as it stares out of the darkness.

Maxwell later envisioned the arrow's passage as it pierced the illuminated dot on Carter's back, tore through his left lung and sliced through his aorta, stopping only after it passed through the front of his chest and pinned him to the car.

"*Jesus*!" Ryland breathed and Maxwell felt his hand shove her into the car. His head whipped around, desperately scanning nearby vehicles. Several rows away, one surged from its spot and screeched toward the other end of the parking lot. Ryland sprang behind the wheel and started the engine. Backing out, he stomped on the gas and careened across the lot, burning rubber in a cloud of stinking smoke, so intent on pursuit as to be oblivious to Carter's body.

Maxwell was unable to move, speak or breathe. She saw Carter, still pinned to the passenger door, face pressed against the side window, blood pumping from his lips, his eyes retaining the eternal question.

Ryland had to swerve in an attempt to avoid another automobile but Maxwell heard the sickening crunch of metal and bones as Carter's body hit the car, snapping him free from the shaft.

Ryland shouted, "*God damn son of a bitch*!" as he braked the car and pounded the steering wheel. The suspect car had disappeared, merging into the flow of traffic. For a second he was undecided whether to go back for the bloody pulp that was his friend lying in the parking lot. Making a decision in the next instant, he pressed the accelerator to the floor.

Maxwell groaned and passed out.

Who's Killing All the Lawyers?

Chapter 20

Falk, Koski and Webster spent the night in the camper on the deserted trail off Highway 20, splitting the hours into shifts so that one was on watch while the others slept. They were on the road by dawn. Webster followed in his jeep as they neared their destination. Falk steered out of a long S-curve and checked the rear view mirror again, expecting to see the jeep but it didn't appear.

"Webster," he said to Koski, "he's not there."

She looked back. "He was right behind us…"

Falk slowed the truck, not highly concerned. Their companion might have had to stop for one of the many deer in the area that crossed to get to water…might have had to take a leak…

He drove to the right shoulder and waited and then turned off the engine. It was silent except for the ticking from the hot engine manifold. Thirty seconds passed and then Falk reached into the glove compartment and grabbed the Glock.

"Something's wrong. Wait here. I'll be right back."

Koski watched Falk in the side mirror as he jogged back along the side of the road. She pulled the collar of her jacket around her ears and squirmed deeper into the seat. With the heater off, a chill was already seeping into the vehicle.

Suddenly she jerked to attention. A gunshot cracked the freezing air, echoing across the mountains. She immediately reached for the AK-47 she had stowed behind the driver's seat, opened the door and slid out, cocking the weapon. The metallic sound was particularly harsh in the still, cold air as it slid to the killing position. Crouching with her back to the camper, she eased toward the rear, allowing herself a clear view of the road. She could not see Falk. She would wait sixty seconds…Then she heard a sound in the direction Falk had taken. The crunch of footsteps…but no voices…no sounds of conversation…

She took a deep breath, then crawled beneath the vehicle, gripping the automatic weapon in front of her, never taking her eyes off the empty road. If there had been an ambush she did not intend to walk into it. She wriggled closer to the right back wheel and pressed the butt of the cold weapon against her cheek. Then she saw them.

Webster and Falk rounded the bend, walking toward the truck, hands on their heads.

Several feet to one side and to the rear, a stranger had the drop on them.

Koski fingered the fire selector switch and it softly clicked to automatic. *Son of a bitch.* She watched as the three came closer. The stranger was silent but directed Falk and Webster with his weapon to continue toward the camper. Soon they were so close that Koski could have reached out and tapped the toes of their boots.

"Open the door," the man commanded. "Tell her to get out, hands on her head."

Falk opened the driver's door, letting it swing wide, surprised himself to see there was no one inside the vehicle. The man moved a few steps closer. Koski could see his weapon, a SPAS, Special Purpose Shotgun, Model 12. The swine could blow the damn camper apart with that kind of ordnance. He spoke again.

"I know there were three of you. Where is she?"

Falk sounded calm. "There's no one else here, I tell you. Take a look."

The man gripped the shotgun and moved slowly, until he was only inches from Koski. She zeroed in on his boots, legs and belt buckle.

"Unless you tell me where the woman is," he snarled, "I'll shoot one of you, now. My orders are to bring you in. It's no problem for me if I have to kill one of you."

Falk asked, "Whose orders?" not expecting a response.

The man grinned with sadistic wickedness as if, having the upper hand, he could afford to divulge a titillating portion of a secret. "Some Limey with a fat wallet." His face closed then and he demanded, "Where's the woman?"

"I don't know," Falk said honestly.

Koski saw the man's boots shuffle impatiently in Webster's direction.

"If I shoot your friend here, maybe that'll help you recall. Get over here," he commanded Webster, "away from the truck. I'll count to three. One..."

Oh, God! Not daring to breathe, Koski positioned the AK-47 and took aim at a spot a few inches below the man's belt buckle and waited, praying he would change his mind.

"Two..."

She saw Falk's feet shuffle slightly, too. Was he preparing to dive at their captor? The man stepped back, however, and she heard the chilling, metallic rattle of the shotgun being cocked; her own finger tightened on the trigger...

"Three—"

The automatic weapon roared and kicked against her cheek, the sound deafening in the close confines of the truck's underbelly. The raw, acrid pungency of cordite filled her lungs. The man's shotgun was flung across the clearing and dropped unfired into a mound of boulders more than twenty feet away. His body fell to the ground, ripped from groin to sternum.

Webster and Falk stared at her in disbelief as she wormed from beneath the truck and staggered to her feet. Gravity collected in her legs and for a moment she couldn't move. Then she ran headlong into Falk's arms, burying her head in his chest, stifling a gag as bile rose in her throat. She killed a man. "He was going to kill Webster," she stammered, "I…I had to…to…"

Falk held her close. "It's okay," he whispered. "It's okay." She remained in his arms, shaking and drenched in sweat.

She couldn't know his thoughts; that he marveled at her toughness, as tough as they come, yet she was like the soul of a sparrow, fluttering in his arms.

Finally she pulled away. "Why would he…"

"I don't know." Reluctantly, he released her.

She realized she had reached into her inside jacket pocket for the postcard she always carried. As if the inked writing beneath the laminated surface was Braille of love, she gently smoothed her fingers over it. It was the last communiqué from her parents before they perished in a train wreck five winters ago—a touchstone of her courage representing the fiercest test of her life to date. It was a test that had taken all her mettle to survive.

Touching this material memory of a moment of loss had become more than a habitual reaction to distress. Suddenly aware that Falk and

Webster had noted the card and the pressing of her fingertips across it, she quickly tucked it back into the folds of her jacket.

"He got the drop on me," Webster said, continuing their discussion as if Koski's action had not intervened. "He just seemed to materialize from the side of the road back there..." He paused and offered his hand to her, saying, "Thanks, Koski, although thanks doesn't begin to cover it."

She smiled weakly. "It's covered."

Falk walked over to the body splayed in the dirt. Sinking to one knee, he went through the man's pockets. Keys, wallet. "Nice," he said as he turned him over before removing a Bowie knife from a leather sheath attached to the man's belt and positioned out of sight in the center of his back. "This guy routinely expected trouble." He picked up the wallet and quickly flipped through it. "About sixty dollars cash...no ID."

"No ID," Webster repeated.

Falk grunted. "Yeah, a pro, a hit man." He replaced the wallet in the man's pocket and headed for the camper.

"Ride with you or take my jeep?" Webster asked.

Koski watched Falk tuck the AK-47 behind the seat in the cab. "May as well leave the jeep," he said. Then he added something Koski thought she'd never hear him say. "It's best if we all stay together."

As he eased the camper onto the highway, Falk asked, "Webster, being in BLM you must know a little about the Native American population. How many of them are there in the United States?"

Webster was surprised by the question but had a ready answer, "Close to three million."

Falk whistled. "Three million?"

"Yes and I recently read a report that the Census Bureau expects that number to triple by 2050."

"Do you know how many total acres of land they own in the West?"

"Well, let's see…The Navajo reservation is the largest in the country, with 16 million acres in Arizona, New Mexico and Utah…"

"Sixteen million acres," Falk interjected in Webster's pause. "That's a lot of land to control."

"Pyramid Lake became a 475,000-acre Paiute Indian reservation way back in 1874," Webster went on. "The Washoe tribe owns almost 20,000 acres in Nevada."

"Twenty thou…" Falk grimaced. "Thanks, Webster. That gives me some idea of what we're looking at here." He paused and added, "Right, Koski?"

"Right," she said weakly. He took his eyes off the road long enough to watch her brow wrinkle as she tried to establish a nexus between Webster's answers and Falk's remark.

"One more question, Webster. Are there any Algonquin Indian tribes living in the western part of the United States?"

"They're mostly concentrated in the New England states."

"Yeah, I know about those in New England. Well, thanks again." He reached into the pocket of his heavy jacket and produced a folded road map. "If you promise to refold this correctly later," he said lightly as he handed it to Webster, "I'll let you be our guide. I basically know the area I want but it'll help if you pinpoint it exactly for me."

Webster silently flipped open the folds as Falk continued. "The camp I visited near Bowman Lake, where some militants of the local tribes go to train, is on the premises of an old, inactive gold mine. I crudely marked it on that map." Falk's concentration on the winding road did not preclude his wondering aloud. "How did that guy know

146

there were three of us?"

Koski shrugged and Webster replied, "Beats me. I didn't even tell Roz I was going to be with you."

"Roz?"

"My secretary." He was silent for a moment, then added, "At least I don't *think* I told Roz…"

Who's Killing All the Lawyers?

Chapter 21

Tony Villachi and Senator Reinecke arrived at the mine at eleven on the morning following Lovesy's death, summoned to a meeting with The Fox. As they walked from the parking lot toward the high, steel mesh fence surrounding the premises, Reinecke looked down at his runty companion. He adjusted his steps to accommodate the frail man's minced stride and asked, "Been here before, Tony?"

Villachi took a long draw on his cigar. "Never."

The guard at the entrance recognized the senator and pulled open the tall gate, nodding a silent greeting.

Glancing around at the rows of run-down, mostly single-story wooden cabins, Villachi mumbled, "Can't say I'm impressed. Seems deserted. I thought you said some of the local Indians pow-wowed here."

Reinecke grinned at Villachi's politically incorrect phrasing but didn't mention it, not wanting to let the mobster know that Reinecke considered him gauche.

"The Native American militia members only train here on weekends." He pointed toward a two-story structure at the back of the facility.

"It's all supposed to be quite harmless. When I was here on a Saturday I was allowed to observe maneuvers taking place in that building. It actually was quite frightening: Indians armed with weapons made in Israel that were a cross between Russian-built AK-47 assault rifles and American M-16s. Don't ask me how they happened to have those weapons. I was told they were practicing what they called "shooting and ducking."

"First one man then another would run up and down the stairs, covering himself by firing live bullets while being shot at by a machine that fired rubber bullets…bullets that can do a lot of damage if they connect at close range. I suppose it was good exercise as well as good practice."

"Chrissake," Villachi said, "sounds like they're preparing for war."

Reinecke shrugged and ran a manicured index finger across his silver moustache. "In any case, the training camp is just a cover."

They had reached the main entrance to the mine; a large, stone building, the earthen path to which was edged with uniformly sized, white painted rocks. Faded letters on a weathered sign above the door read "Colonial Mine." The guard stationed just outside the door waved them through.

Reinecke leaned toward the gangster at his side and said, sotto voce, "It's rare for The Fox to call a meeting at his headquarters."

Villachi shivered and tugged at the collar of his calf length, black wool coat. "Some kind of emergency, I suppose. Just what we need." He paused and looked up at the senator. "What do you mean the camp is just a cover?"

Reinecke's slight, condescending smile betrayed the pleasure he derived from always being on top of events. "Even the Native Americans who train here don't know of the secret sanctuary beneath the camp. They only know there once was an operational gold mine beneath the surface.

"Now a skeleton crew maintains the main shaft and fourteen lower levels at the eccentric, unknown owner's request, despite the fact that veins of the precious ore were depleted sometime back in 1956. Federal authorities concentrate on militant Indians, who are allowed by the landowner—even encouraged—to train here above ground."

Villachi grunted. "I know that even though mining operations ceased, BLM agents, state safety inspectors and other bureaucrats inspect it periodically. You telling me there's something they're missing?"

While they continued into a long hall, Reinecke went on as if he was a tour guide. "The Colonial Mine ownership passed to several different companies until 1966. The present owner is listed as a legitimate corporation. That owner, however, created a level fifteen and turned it into what he refers to as "Control"—the exclusive headquarters from which he manipulates events that he imagines will one day allow him to...to..."

Villachi was getting impatient with talk. "To what, for Chrissake?"

"I don't know exactly...some sort of grand plan. I wish I did know The Fox's ultimate goal."

Villachi was pleased there was something Reinecke didn't know. Villachi, however, also wasn't able to fathom The Fox's motivations. Villachi did know that the senator's ambitions were to continue to build his own power base and save his own skin. He went along with the scheme to discredit the Indians because The Fox had him in an awkward position. He led Reinecke to believe that in the end there would be increased money in Indian aid, much of which would find its way into the senator's pockets.

Villachi also was aware of the single-minded motivation of his friends in the Nevada organization: to create enough fear in the public's mind to halt the spread of Indian gambling and keep Las Vegas' coffers full.

Nevertheless, Villachi's associates, like Reinecke, didn't get it. There *was* no way to stop Native American tribes from overrunning the United States with casinos.

Like his associates, Villachi had fought that battle initially; until he recognized the odds. His Sicilian mother didn't raise foolish sons. There was only one thing to do. "If you can't beat 'em…" If there was finally to be a substantial Indian pie, Villachi would get a piece of it.

Quietly, singly, he began injecting millions of his own money and money from the organization into the pro-Indian gambling referendums in California and other states. For now, he would be the Indians' silent partner.

One day, his vision of the entire country being one big Las Vegas would come true. Despite whatever plan The Fox may have in mind, Villachi would let his associates in on his coup. This would further ensure his place at the head of the table in his Las Vegas penthouse for years to come.

Meanwhile, he would back the campaign *against* his Indian friends, convinced that the more pressure they felt, the more readily they would feel obliged to share a wedge of the ultimate dessert when the time came.

"This place is spooky," Villachi grumbled, his unlit cigar moving from one side of his mouth to the other. He began to breathe laboriously, taking two steps to Reinecke's one in the dimly lit hall. The walls were lined with old sepia aerial and ground photographs of the mine in its earlier days, pictures of bearded, moustached men with picks and shovels, dressed in dingy clothes, boots and round domed hard hats. At the end of the hall, a guard ushered them into a steel cage elevator that dropped at a stomach-churning velocity in total blackness through a shaft drilled through solid rock. The lift jolted to a halt in a lighted horizontal tunnel fourteen hundred feet below the earth's surface. A heavyset man in clean street clothes opened the iron-trellised door and waited for them to step out.

"Each of you take one," the man said, indicating a row of numbered laminates hanging from wall hooks. "Wear them around your necks at all times. This enables security to know how many persons are below the surface in case of an emergency. You'll be reminded to replace them when you leave." He opened a wall-mounted cabinet and issued each man a hard hat with a battery-operated lamp attached.

"As you see, we have lights along this gallery." He indicated the low wattage bulbs hanging from the rocky, cave-like ceiling every fifty feet. "This lighting system is used throughout the mine's galleries. The lamps on the hard hats are for the tributary areas in drifts and stoops where there is little or no overhead illumination. You probably won't need them but in case of emergency..."

"Stop saying *emergency*," Villachi grumbled. "What are drifts and stoops?" he muttered. Crude mining terms were beyond the realm of his comprehension.

"In mining terms, a drift, sir," the man explained patiently, "refers to any horizontal passage. It's also known as a gallery or level of the mine that follows, or once followed, a lode or vein of ore. A stoop is an area where the miner has to kneel or stoop due to the lack of height in the tunnel."

Villachi then asked, "How far is it to this control center?"

"About a mile, sir."

"You mean we're expected to walk a mile through this tunnel?"

"No, sir." He gestured toward the ground where narrow gauge rails ran through the center of the gallery. "There'll be a tram along in a few minutes. Here it is now." The man turned to Villachi, "And don't light up that cigar, sir."

The old don grumbled. "Hey, you think I'm stupid." A steady hum filled the air followed by the rhythmic clatter of iron wheels on the track.

"No, sir. Stay close to the wall until the tram comes to a full stop."

The tram consisted of an electric engine and three high-sided ore carts with wooden seats and entry doors cut into the iron sides that had been converted for passenger use.

"Keep your hands inside the cart at all times," the driver grunted as they climbed aboard.

"I feel like I'm on a kiddie ride at Disneyland, for Chrissake," Villachi rankled in Reinecke's direction. His companion was silent, apparently thinking it uncouth to complain.

When they reached what looked like a solid wall of rock, the track U-turned and the tram stopped. The driver slid out, signaled the others to follow and walked to the wall. He waved a hand before an unseen sensor and a door in the breakaway rock wall opened, exposing a brightly lit stairway.

"Chrissake," Villachi said, "what next?"

"Only six steps, a landing, then six more steps," their guide explained as he led them down the stairs to another door. A keypad on the left wall glowed beneath a soft red light. "Protection against unwarranted approach," the guide explained and then punched in a sequence of numbers and symbols. The red light flashed to green and the door opened to Control—a connected series of rooms—the hub of a multi-million dollar operation governed by The Fox.

Two male technicians sat at a security console against one wall of the cavernous main room and concentrated on a bank of screens fed by cameras positioned throughout the facility. The feeds were crisp and in color. All critical interior areas were covered and exterior robot camera eyes panned desolate areas of the mountainside. Except for the movements of security guards, there was no activity.

"From that console," Reinecke advised, recalling his previous visit, "the operators monitor all levels of the mine 24/7." He removed his hard hat and set it on a large round table in the center of the room, then sank into one of the twelve ample swivel armchairs surrounding the table. "No one gets near this mine without a technician at the monitors knowing it. I'm told the security systems are so sensitive they can detect two flies copulating a hundred yards away."

"Copulating?" Villachi repeated quizzically.

It seemed distasteful to Reinecke that he should have to resort to such common terms. He said softly, "It means *fucking*."

The man who had been their guide gestured to a tray of glasses and a water pitcher on the table's mahogany-finished surface. "The Fox has asked that you make yourselves comfortable. He'll be arriving shortly." He turned and left by the door through which they had entered.

Following Reinecke's lead, Villachi discarded his hat and sat at the table. "Albert," he said in his frail baritone, "I'll take some of that water."

Reinecke, accustomed to being waited on, nevertheless reached and poured a glass of ice water for the older man.

"Who else is supposed to be here?" Villachi asked.

Reinecke shook his head. "The message I got only mentioned an urgent, top-level meeting."

Villachi sipped his water and wiped away a little dribble that ran down one side of his chin. He glanced around the room. "Some setup." The floor was marble. Three of the windowless walls were concrete, designed to accommodate the technology the room contained. The third wall, however, was glass, behind which could be seen an interior garden, replete with tropical plants, a small pool and a waterfall.

"Nice touch," Villachi added.

Reinecke nodded toward a phone on the table with one red and several unlit white buttons. "I understand the phone system has a bypass setup whereby a call can be made from here to anywhere in the world. For anyone attempting to trace the call, however, it will be recorded as having originated from another state or country."

Villachi raised his gray awning eyebrows and nodded. He was impressed. Pointing to a bank of computer terminals against the wall to their right, he said, "I'll bet people in every federal agency in the country would give their right arms to hack into that intelligence control system." He glanced at the ceiling. "This place seems to have everything but a cone of silence."

The two sat quietly for a moment, then Villachi glanced at his Rolex and in his grumpy way said, "Well, where is our esteemed boss, for Chrissake."

Reinecke, ordinarily very much at ease in any given situation, was antsy, unaccustomed to being kept waiting and thus determined to make the time pass in conversation.

He leaned toward his companion and whispered, "I don't know if there's any truth to it but I heard that years ago a demolition expert worked on the construction of this control center and other parts of the mine. He planted explosives in the infrastructure's concrete. They can easily be detonated in the event Control is in danger of being overtaken by an enemy force."

He took an empty glass from the tray and eased back slightly. "A sort of scorched earth policy, you might say."

Leaving his listener with an assessing expression, he rose and went to a wall at the back of the room. He opened a cabinet containing a three-tiered Lazy Susan liquor assortment and swiveled one section until a bottle of Johnny Walker Black came into view. He poured some into his glass and glanced at the clock on the wall. He had no idea as to why The Fox had summoned them here. Suddenly it bothered him that he, like Villachi, had never seen The Fox, never actually heard his voice.

Here he was, a so-called top-level player in this scheme, yet his dealings went through an intermediary—an unrecognizable voice on the phone. On his previous visit to Control, like now, he had waited for The Fox but the meeting was cancelled. The Fox was unavoidably involved in an emergency and could not join him.

He returned to the table and Villachi. "So, you have *no* idea why we've been summoned here, Tony?"

Villachi chewed on his cigar before deciding to answer. "My guess is that it has something to do with our British import."

"Eik—" Reinecke started to say but caught himself, glancing at the technicians across the room who were engrossed in their work. "What *about* our British import?"

Villachi shrugged. "Like I said, it's just my guess but I'll wager that the boss thinks it's time to call our friend off, that the point has been made and that people are starting to turn against the...the..." he searched for the right word…"proliferation of Indian gambling—"

Villachi stopped in mid-sentence. He and Reinecke turned at the sound of someone entering the room, walking confidently, seemingly familiar with Control, heading toward them. It would seem reasonable that both men at the table might make parallel observations.

Police Chief Bud Vigo, whom they knew as a loud, surly man given to overt gestures, was unattractive, of medium height, fifty pounds overweight and oval, with a bowl haircut and bangs. His light blue eyes were so pale that from where Reinecke and Villachi sat, it appeared they had no pupils, held no clue to his soul.

Villachi thought Vigo had never appeared to be overly ambitious or overly bright, yet…Could it be?

Villachi whispered, "Bud Vigo—The Fox?"

Chapter 22

Earlier, heavy dark clouds had swollen the sky. Now cold rain turned to sleet as first the temperature fell, then snow. Falk switched on the wipers, clearing two paths on the windshield but beyond their sweeping jurisdiction, whiteness gathered.

"Should I call Spade?" Webster asked, reaching for his cell phone.

"Call Spade?" Falk demanded, surprised. "Why?"

Webster shrugged and pulled his empty hand from his jacket. "It's just that when I talked to him earlier, he asked me to keep him...he and Maxwell are naturally..."

If it had not been necessary to concentrate on the slick highway, Falk thought he might have reached over and choked Webster. "What do you *mean*, 'When you talked to him earlier?'"

Webster raised his eyebrows and leaned back, keeping Koski's head between himself and Falk, staring straight ahead. "He called this morning," Webster said, "when you and Koski were still asleep and I was on watch...just to see how we were doing and to bring us up to speed about Maxwell."

"Goddamnit, Webster! *Nobody* is supposed to know where we are or what we're doing."

Koski started to say something but Webster, trying to justify his

actions, stammered, "Don't tell me you suspect Alex Spade of being
—"

"Whether I suspect Alex Spade or you or anyone else of anything
is not the point. That cell phone of yours and Spade's could be tapped
into by now. Damn! *Never* use it again unless I specifically tell you
to." He sighed and brought his frustration under control.

Koski turned to Webster and whispered, "Webster, you are sooo
off this island." Immediately seeing that her attempt at flippancy did
not ease his humiliation, she asked seriously, "Since Alex has talked to
Maxwell, how did he say she's doing?"

At first reluctant, Webster finally relaxed and briefly told about
the incident at Spade's home and how he narrowly escaped death when
an arrow was shot into his recliner. Then Webster related Spade's
account of Maxwell's luncheon with Ryland and Carter, following
which Carter was killed and Maxwell taken to a safe place to
recuperate.

Falk could not believe it. Carter was dead. He had known his
bureau chief for many years—a small man with a big heart and keen
dedication to his work. "Why?" Falk demanded aloud. "If all this is
about killing those who are against the Indians why kill Carter?"
Certainly, he thought, Carter had made enemies in his profession. It
was a given at that level of Bureau stratification.

Falk and Carter had held private conversations, some—
unfortunately not enough—in which they exchanged their own
personal "most wanted" lists. Now Falk tried to remember those on
Carter's list who might want to kill him but it was no use. It took too
much time and acute concentration to recall.

"And you heard about Lovesy?" Webster asked after a long
silence.

"We've been a little too busy staying alive to catch the eleven o'clock news, Webster," Falk snapped. "What about Lovesy?"

"He was killed by an arrow, too...in a limo on his way to a meeting with Senator Albert Reinecke."

Falk cursed. Not that he believed Lovesy's death was of a particular loss to the world as compared to Carter but any man's death, as someone once said, diminished us all. Now there was another puzzle. If, as Falk and Koski had speculated earlier in the motel, there was a connection to Lovesy and the arrow killings, why did his co-conspirators kill him?

Koski turned to Falk. "Maybe we were wrong about Lovesy."

"Or maybe he simply outlived his usefulness," Falk replied.

All three fell silent. There still were so many questions and so few answers.

Webster, occupied intermittently with the map during the past hour, took one last look at it. They had climbed to twelve thousand feet. The snow-covered highway snaked into woods heavily furred with age. "According to your map markings," he said, "we're close to the mine now...little less than a mile." He deftly refolded the topographical map and returned it to Falk.

"Okay," Falk said. He let the vehicle crawl a short distance farther, dropping into deep ruts, climbing over small rocks that had rumbled down the steep cliffs at the side of the roadway. Finally, he pulled to the dextral side of the one-lane gravel road and killed the engine.

Without the rumble of the snow tires, hum of the motor and blow of the heater and defroster, the sudden muteness seemed big and palpable. The temperature dropped immediately.

"Time for a little reconnaissance," Falk said, opening the door. A furious flurry of snow flew and eddied into the truck as he slid out, the Glock in his hand.

With a curtness meant to discourage debate, he quickly added, "You two stay together until I get back." He pulled the jacket collar up around his neck.

Koski slithered from the seat and jumped out beside him. "We're joining you," she said with her usual determination, her cheeks pink with eagerness and cold.

Webster watched them, unmoving.

It was Falk's habit, his nature, his job to reconnoiter on his own, damn it. He certainly didn't need a nursemaid on this little side trip. He pointed an index finger directly into her face. "You'll join me when I'm *ready* for you to join me."

With an exaggerated pout, she scrambled back into the truck beside Webster, extracted the AK-47 from behind the seat, laid it across her knees and folded her arms.

Even with Webster there, she suddenly looked vulnerable. The automatic only served to punctuate that danger might be all around them.

"Okay," he growled and led the way into the woods.

"Hey! I've been to this mine before, months ago," Koski whispered, as she and Falk huddled by the steel mesh fence. "I didn't recall until we got close to it."

"Do you know who owns it?" Falk asked.

"Some veiled corporations, DBA some other corporation's statutory client trust account…in other words, who knows."

"Why were you here?"

"BLM got a request to check out a complaint from some small independent miners in the area. They were concerned about water usage, the possibility that streams were being diverted."

"What happened when you checked it out?"

"Not much, we made recommendations, they complied and we left."

"Were they diverting streams?"

Webster, who had been scouting the area behind them, emerged from the trees and crouched next to Koski. Having heard Falk's question, he added, "I remember reading the report. We couldn't prove anything."

"Oddly enough, though," Koski said, "we suspected some diversion near an old mine entrance that went unused for years."

"You mean near an old mine shaft?"

"No…it was a horizontal entrance, an adit. The miners dug into the side of the mountain, their path slanting downward until they reached what they called the "working face," the actual wall of rock that contained the vein they were mining. Later the practice was discarded in favor of sinking a shaft." She smiled slightly, as if pleased that her work at BLM gave her opportunity to enlighten Falk.

"I knew that," he said. "So, what did you do?"

She shrugged. "As Webster said, we couldn't prove anything. The old entrance looked unsafe to me. We went several hundred feet into it and then got the hell out. We ordered them to re-timber the roof and shore up the walls."

"And did they?"

She shrugged. "I assume so. We never re-inspected. We were told to take their word…orders from someone above our lowly station." She paused. "Come to think of it, I could find that entrance now…take us right into the mine."

Yes, Falk wanted that. Suddenly he felt a presence behind him.

He pivoted and saw two National Guardsmen approaching—rifles at the ready.

"Drop your weapons," one soldier commanded quietly, not wanting to be seen or heard by the guard at the mine's main gate several hundred feet away. He gestured impatiently, his dark eyes threatening from beneath the rim of his white camouflaged steel helmet.

Falk let the Glock slip to the ground and Koski's AK-47 followed suit.

"Damn!" Falk mumbled as they turned and raised their hands. They were led back into the woods.

Five minutes later, seated in an old cabin, the trio faced a bored-looking officer whom Falk recognized as Colonel Staudinger of the Nevada National Guard.

Once identifications were established and Staudinger notified Command of the three interlopers, the officer seated himself behind an old table he used as a desk. "What are you three doing in this dismal place, Agent Falk?"

"My team was assigned by Attorney General Lovesy to investigate the recent deaths of lawyers in the state. We're up here to talk to the Indian militia who train in the area."

Staudinger nodded. "Weekend warriors; they only train on weekends."

"The actual exercises, yes but we thought some of them might be around."

"You say Lovesy requested your investigation?"

"Yes."

"Mine, too," Staudinger said. "Before he died, he called General Stone, who ordered me and two platoons up here." He shrugged. "It

164

seems that our mission is moot. We haven't found any increased activity in the vicinity and, as you see, the mine's nearly deserted."

"You went into the mine itself?"

"No, not yet." He paused and added, "The powers that be are concerned about the kind of press we get. Everything must be low-key here. Should an incident occur, we don't want the media to get wind of it and come up here. They'd shoot video, decrying the tragedy of poor, misunderstood American Indians, who were doing nothing more than bonding in this bucolic setting and being attacked without provocation, blah, blah, blah. It's obvious that all's quiet right now. We thought it best to observe for the time being...see what develops."

Falk studied Staudinger, a tired old soldier who would most definitely fade away when the time came—and that time was not too far away.

The sound of helicopters thwacking low overhead drowned out any further conversation and the communications officer burst into the cabin.

"Received nothing on the radio, sir," the breathless man reported. "No warning of approaching helicopters. Unidentified, sir...they came out of nowhere."

Falk followed the colonel and his lieutenant as they raced outside, staring up as an unmarked chopper passed over the wooded area and continued to the east.

"The first one already has dipped out of sight," Staudinger snarled just as the second vanished below the tree line. "Raise Command and ask them what the hell's going on. Tell them we received no notification of impending aircraft."

He stormed back into the cabin and went to his desk. "Take a patrol and scout the area where those birds landed," he commanded his lieutenant. "Find out who the hell they are and what they're doing here." He gestured toward Webster and Koski, who had been sitting silently the past few minutes. "Stay put," he ordered, as if they had made some threatening gesture.

Falk had a premonition that the colonel's luck was about to change, and Falk and his two companions' with it.

Following the violent death of Lester Carter, Ryland decided Maxwell should be housed in a secure location until the case was over. He chose a little-used military hospital at the U.S. Navy "Top Gun" Fighter Weapons School near the city of Fallow east of Reno.

Maxwell raised her eyebrows.

Ryland gently touched her arm. "I want to be sure you're safe."

She stood at the window in her room on the second floor and stared out at the rain. Already she was bored out of her mind. The weather channel predicted that rain would turn to snow before the end of the day. It also reported that snow was falling in the higher elevations.

More than ever, she was frustrated. She decided to tell Ryland that she must either get back into the investigation or return to her job in Carson City. Instead, she called Alex, who also confessed to being bored at his assigned location, Webster's office. At least Alex was contributing. He was being helpful by keeping her apprised of the others' activities. Thanks to Alex, at least Maxwell knew that Falk, Koski and Webster were alive…or *were,* early this morning.

Chapter 23

"What!" Bud Vigo said harshly to Reinecke and Villachi when he walked into Control and saw the look of inquisition in the men's faces. "I'm only ten fucking minutes late," he exclaimed, thinking his tardiness was the reason for their silent inquiry. He flailed his arms in the air. "Do you have any idea what kind of precautions I have to take to be sure I'm not tailed when I come here?" He sat down.

"It's a good thing the boss doesn't call us here often." When Villachi and the senator were still silent, no doubt reassessing their hasty assumption that Vigo was The Fox, he went on. "Where's the boss?" He glanced around the room. "Ya know, I was here once before. Had to pick up some instructions that he didn't want to have delivered...never did see him...the guy's a fucking phantom." He looked at his watch. "He'd better show pretty soon. I got a life, ya know."

Reinecke looked at Villachi. The older man broke into a grin while Reinecke laughed out loud, turning to Vigo. "We thought that *you...*" Reinecke started to say but decided that it was too absurd a premise to bother mentioning.

Vigo turned toward the technicians seated at the monitors thirty feet away. "Any activity topside we should know about, fellas?"

Realizing they were being addressed, the older of the two replied,

"Activity normal at all levels, sir."

His attention remained riveted on images of the main gate, the interior and exterior of the entrance building.

"Maybe so," Vigo fretted, "but something doesn't feel right to me."

It was two years ago when The Fox incorporated Bud Vigo into his grand scheme. Vigo knew he was a perfect candidate for the job for several reasons. He was police chief of Carson City with clout and access to local law enforcement resources. He was a stubborn, determined man who didn't covet the limelight like Reinecke. Once persuaded, Vigo could be relied on because he was a man whose past could be used against him.

Vigo, in his late fifties, was married for twenty years to a woman he loved and who gave him six children. On one occasion, however, he succumbed to a weakness in his groin for a teenage girl and The Fox had learned of the liaison. When The Fox required an associate in Carson City to begin implementing phase one of the campaign against anti-American Indian lawyers, he only needed to meet secretly with Vigo and remind him of the tabloid-type details of his single, unfortunate amour.

The subsequent association with The Fox had altered Vigo into sycophantic submission, and chain-smoking, dramatic passive-aggression. He and his well-bribed helicopter pilot had done exactly as instructed from the start. Their only misstep was the arrow that missed a hiking lawyer and ended up in the tree near Wally's Hot Springs.

Vigo had retrieved and destroyed the arrow from the evidence cage where Maxwell had placed it. Since then, any attempt to keep the murder weapons a secret was forgotten in favor of getting his job done.

"What feels wrong, Bud?" Reinecke asked.

Vigo rubbed his chin. "My contact—that high, singsong voice that gives me all orders from The Fox and, for all I know, could be The Fox himself—ordered me to pull back right after the demise of the two FBI agents in Carson. Then there were the murders in California, then the FBI man, Carter and Lovesy—"

"Carter!" Villachi made the exclamation but it might have been Reinecke; he, too, was that surprised. "I *know* Carter," the don said. "He's been around awhile. What happened?"

If Vigo wondered why the two men were surprised at the news that foul play had befallen Carter but exhibited none regarding Lovesy's fate, he did not stop to ponder it. "Poor son of a bitch was killed in Reno on his way home from lunch with the Carson City ME and a NSA man."

"Chrissake," Villachi mumbled.

"Yeah," Vigo agreed, "that's what I mean. Things are out of control…maybe even out of The Fox's control."

Villachi slumped solemnly in his chair, chewed on his cigar and wondered if he had created a monster by hiring Rod Eiker.

"Trouble!" one of the technicians at the security monitors barked. He and his companion tensed in their chairs as a klaxon alarm pulsed in the air.

Vigo, Reinecke and Villachi, in that order, rose from their chairs at the round table and immediately rushed to the console.

The monitors that had slumbered earlier with benign images of routine, seemingly unneeded, security, now flashed with activity as the alarm sounded throughout the facility.

"Shit!" the younger technician spat as his vision zeroed in on two unmarked helicopters landing in a clearing the size of a football field away from the mine's outer fence. Seven men, obscured by falling snow and indistinguishable in their snowsuits, jumped from the aircraft. Loaded down with weaponry, they dispersed to a staging area at the tree line.

"What's happening?" Reinecke insisted, echoing the concerns of his companions.

If the technician he addressed knew, he didn't have time to answer. A red phone on the wall by his ear shrilled and flashed with stroboscopic intensity. He lashed out his left hand and grabbed it.

"Yes, sir," he said crisply. Listening silently for a minute, he repeated, "Yes, sir." Holding the phone away from his ear, he relieved his partner's apprehension by nodding toward the screen that displayed the helicopters and saying, "Friendly…they're okay." Then he handed the phone to Reinecke. "The boss wants to speak to you."

"Albert," the soprano-like voice on the line said without preliminaries, "I've just learned that minutes before his demise, Lovesy ordered National Guard troops to the mine at the governor's request. Not because they had any idea we were to meet there—your ass is covered—but as a precaution against any possible militant Indian gathering.

"I've instructed our British friend—because he's the only one who can do it—to get you and our associates out before the troops start nosing around." The voice paused and said pointedly, "That's *all* that son of a bitch is authorized to do. I'll be in touch once you're back in your office." The Fox hung up before Reinecke could respond.

As instructed, Eiker had earlier arranged for himself and his six-man team to be combat-equipped at their desert location, picked up and flown to a clearing near the mine. Now he instructed the men to remove the mortar tubes from the aircraft and ready them for use.

Although Villachi initially hired him, Eiker soon learned that his orders came from a singsong voice that reached him on his cellular phone from various public phones. The last call reamed him a new asshole for killing Carter, which was a personal score Eiker needed to settle.

It was now imperative that Reinecke, Villachi and Vigo be safely spirited away to prevent any possibility of their being found and questioned. How Eiker accomplished this was up to him. In his flamboyant fashion, he decided not only to rescue the three men but also to eliminate the National Guard troops.

The Fox's last words to Eiker were, "If you fail to get the three men out safely, the last installment of your fee will be forfeited."

While his men prepared the mortars, he pulled slightly on his maimed left ear lobe, savoring the satisfaction that the man who was responsible for that affliction had paid the ultimate price for branding Eiker with a constant, visual reminder of the failed Hoover Dam episode years ago. He turned his eyes to the cool flakes that melted on his warm cheeks. "Let it snow, let it snow, let it snow," he sang softly. No adverse element Mother Nature thrust at him could smother the inner fire that the anticipation of battle inflamed in him.

The sound no soldier experienced in combat ever forgets assailed Falk's ears. "Get down!" he shouted, grabbing Koski's arm and yanking her to the floor. Webster, Colonel Staudinger and two of his men reacted, too. They hit the deck in the same instant a thunderous explosion ripped one side of the cabin apart. A gusher of bright orange flame leapt out of the ground a few feet from the office, throwing rocks and debris through the air.

"Mortar attack!" Falk hollered, pulling Koski up by her jacket. Both jumped through the gaping hole where the wall was seconds earlier. He was vaguely aware of Webster vaulting through the air beside them.

As his two companions dove for cover behind a tree, Falk looked back at what was left of the cabin. He saw Staudinger sprawled face down on the floor. He whirled and lurched back inside but he knew the colonel was dead as soon as he rolled him onto his back. A piece of window glass had severed his throat as if sliced with a knife. Falk whispered an Amen to the man's life and removed the 9mm from his holster.

"Mayday…mayday…"

Falk turned in the direction of the distress call. The radio man lay on the floor ten feet from him, one side of his body a bloody, amorphous mass. "Mayday—," the shell-shocked man repeated into the transmitter as his intestines spilled onto the floor before his mouth gaped and he lapsed into final silence.

Falk heard the sound of another incoming round and burst from the cabin as it hit the remains of the roof and exploded. What was left of the cabin went up in a searing sheet of flame along with several more of Staudinger's men nearby.

Falk dove behind the pine tree that sheltered Koski. "You okay?" She nodded but her hands, pressed to her ears, trembled. "Webster," Falk called to the figure lying on his stomach, his face buried in the snow. "Webster!" Falk started to go to him but Webster slowly raised his head.

"I'm…I'm okay," he rasped. A burning slab of wood from the demolished building lay beside his head. Groggily, as if just awakening from sleep, he slowly pushed it away.

The staccato repetition of automatic gunfire sounding in the distance led Falk to speculate that whoever mounted the mortar attack

172

also was attempting to wipe out Staudinger's lieutenant and the small unit sent out earlier to investigate the choppers. Falk said a silent prayer that the dead radio operator's "Mayday" got through to someone.

A third round whistled in, landing a few yards from the remains of the cabin. When the debris from the explosion settled, Falk slowly raised his head. The mortar fire came from the direction where the helicopters had landed near the mine. Damn! He sorely wanted to get into that mine but the crackle of automatic gunfire was closer now.

"What'll we do?" Koski asked. "Whoever mounted the mortar attack will move in…"

Falk looked up into a flurry of falling flakes. The sky, a deep dove gray and pregnant with more snow, seemed to reach down and touch the earth. Unless they found a place to hide and keep warm, they would freeze to death before the day was over. The Sierra Nevada gave no quarter to the unprepared.

"We'll get back to the camper then decide our next move."

Fifteen minutes later they were inside the camper. Falk got the motor running and kept the revs high until he was sure the motor wouldn't stall. He eased forward slowly.

Koski shivered. "Where will we go?"

"I noticed a trail running into the woods a couple of miles back that's wide enough for us to squeeze this old beater into until the storm lets up." He switched on the wipers, squinting through the fan-shaped clearings at clumps of snow that stuck to the blades and then slid down the glass like fat, white slugs. He switched the blades to high as the flakes thickened.

"What the hell happened?" Webster asked, his voice vibrating as the truck's right front wheel dropped in and out of a rut.

Falk was pleased to hear Webster asking questions. He had been concerned about his dazed demeanor immediately following the attack. "I'm not sure who they are yet," Falk replied. "In the meantime, we don't want them to find us."

Webster put a hand to his head. "We don't want them to find us," he repeated.

When they reached the small trail, Falk headed the vehicle into it and stopped. "Koski," he said, "you take the wheel. I'll guide you into the trees and bushes as far as you can go." He turned to Webster. "There's a shovel behind your seat. Use it to break away some good-sized branches we can use to cover the camper."

Following Falk's directions, Koski drove the truck deep into the forest and stopped. She opened the door against protruding tree limbs and squeezed out.

"Good," Falk said, "now we'll camouflage it some more. The snow will do the rest." Snowflakes that had melted and run off the warm hood of the vehicle now found acceptance as it cooled.

Webster walked through the brush to collect branches and scrub, his gait slow and hesitant.

As Koski sighed and leaned back against the camper, Falk silently moved closer to her. She turned a tired face up toward him and, squinting against the barrage of disintegrating whiteness, she asked, "What are our chances of getting out of here?"

He moved nearer, his boots crunching in the snow. He stopped inches from her. "Not bad."

Emotion ordained physicality. She was acutely conscious of his stance now, which emphasized the force of his thighs. Something stirred in her, a blazing locomotion of awakened embers that compelled her to move…

She twisted away. "I'd better see what I can do to secure the gear," she said, her hood falling to her shoulders as she raked a hand through her hair and climbed into the camper.

Falk nodded slightly to himself. He had better help Webster, whose camouflaging efforts seemed to be flagging.

Ten minutes later the camper had melded into the white foliage. Falk backtracked through the trees to where they had turned off, assuring himself that their tracks were already nearly covered by snowfall. In less than an hour no one would know they had driven through the area.

Returning to the camper, he found Webster bent double beside the rear wheels, one arm to his forehead.

"Webster?"

"Headache..." the lanky younger man stammered. "Dizzy..." Falk grabbed him just as he passed out.

Who's Killing All the Lawyers?

Chapter 24

The interior of the camper was crowded, in disarray and smelled of wet clothing and canned food they had devoured. Their jackets hung from wall hooks, boots scattered in various places and three sleeping bags snuggled together on the floor. After gaining consciousness two hours earlier, Webster was asleep in his bag and Falk and Koski seated on theirs.

Koski shot a twinkle of sympathy in Webster's direction. "I'm worried about him."

Falk nodded. "He was conscious after the attack…able to carry brush and tree limbs."

"He didn't want to be a burden to us…" She turned to Falk. "Even when consciousness is *not* lost, symptoms of a concussion can show up hours later." She sighed. "I hope he's going to be all right." She eased down to her back on her sleeping bag.

"He will be," Falk said, trying to sound optimistic as he twisted and lay on his stomach beside her. Gently, slowly, he ran an index finger over the back of her hand. He repeated it and she silently allowed his touch to continue.

"Are you familiar with the term "bundling?"" he asked.

"Isn't that something people did back in New England in Colonial times?"

"Right, when two young people were ready to start courting, their parents let them bundle. That is, lie side by side but in separate bundling bags. That way they couldn't get into too much trouble, unless, of course, they were ingenious and determined."

She smiled but her expression turned serious. "May I ask you a question that may be too personal, in which case, just say so?"

"Anything." He continued to trace concentric circles on the back of her hand.

"Who is Meg?"

The question surprised him, although he had known since the night they spent together near the burning buildings on a rocky hill outside Virginia City that one day he would tell her about Meg. "Where did you hear that name?"

She sighed, "When I was on watch last night in the camper, before we started up the mountain. You called her name in your sleep."

He nodded. "Can talking about the past change it?"

"Of course not, but sometimes it can give one perspective, maybe even perception."

He cleared his throat and turned over to his back, hands under his head. "Meg was my wife. She's dead now. It happened two years ago…"

Speaking in low tones so not to wake Webster, and pausing intermittently to assure himself there were no exterior sounds, he related the events surrounding Meg's accidental death that day in the woods; events he often relived in sweaty nightmares and in the accusing light of day.

When he finished, she slowly lowered her head to his chest. "You've been blaming yourself," she whispered, her green eyes gleaming, "yet you know it wasn't your fault."

That's just *it*. It *was* my fault." He felt the old agitation rising. "I *left* her. I left her there in the woods—alone." He rose up on one elbow and Koski pulled away. "I...I never expected..." he went on, "I hurried...I ran all the way back...she'd be afraid of darkness...of a bear maybe but never..." He stopped.

"Guilt is such a destructive force. Joe, we're not responsible for everything that happens in life. We can't be. None of us is that powerful. Did it ever occur to you that you might have returned earlier, got into the car and been sitting there with her when it happened? Would you still blame yourself?"

His head rolled from side to side. "I know. I know...bad things happen to good people."

"You can apply all of the clichés but the bottom line is that it was an accident."

Falk glanced away from her. "If I believe that there's no one to blame...and the hurt goes on."

"It goes on anyway. Maybe you have to learn to manage it." She touched his chin, forcing his face back to hers and her voice was soft. "Freud said that guilt is the way our super ego punishes us for violating its standards."

"Meaning?"

There was amused tenderness and understanding in her eyes. "Meaning you should stop punishing yourself."

Webster stirred and groaned and the two sat up and turned to him. "Oow..." he moaned, opening his eyes and raising both hands to his head.

"How bad is it?" Koski gently inquired. "We have morphine in the survival kit."

"No," Webster mumbled, "I'll be okay."

Koski lifted his head and put a cup of water to his lips. After a sip, he turned over and closed his eyes again. "Just need a little rest…" He was asleep in less than a minute.

Koski turned to Falk and whispered, "He has to have expert medical attention, Joe."

Falk shrugged into his heavy, hooded jacket and turned up the collar, explaining as he did, "I have to get help. It's possible the Guard's "Mayday" got through and that area is swarming with troopers."

"It's also possible there are no reinforcements or they're all dead." Koski was not in an optimistic mood.

"A chance I'll have to take." He glanced from her to Webster and back. Damn! He didn't want to do this. He hated to leave them. In the beginning, he resented having to take them along. That was so long ago…eons, it seemed. They were an important part of his life now, like family; they were his.

"You'll be safer here than with me," he said, as if she had protested his leaving. He gently ran a hand up and down her arm. *Oh, God, it hurt his heart to leave her.* He reached into his pocket and handed her the 9mm he had taken from Staudinger's dead body. "Here."

She pushed it away. "You'll need it."

"If I'm lucky, I'll only need stealth for this assignment." He held her gaze pointedly. "Don't leave this camper for any reason, understand?"

"Okay."

His eyebrows pulled together in a frown. "You have a way of saying 'okay' to an order and then doing as you damn please."

"Okay," she repeated in a way that said she meant it. She quickly stuffed some power bars into a small backpack. "You'll need all the energy you can get."

Struggling into the backpack, he said, "Take care of yourself and Webster until I return." He paused and then added, "I *will* return."

She put her hands on his shoulders and lightly turned him away from her. "I know you will, Joe."

Who's Killing All the Lawyers?

Chapter 25

As Falk vanished into the pines amid lightly falling snow, Koski closed the camper door. She had to keep busy as her mind tried to assimilate the emotions of the last few minutes. She began sorting through the survival kit, finally finding what she was looking for: a plastic tackle box full of miscellaneous items. She located glue and a roll of twine and set about making a crude trip wire mechanism using odd pieces of metal, which, carefully connected, would touch each other and sound an alarm if disturbed.

Holding a section of the twine, she stretched her arms apart and surveyed her handiwork—three tin plates, two aluminum mugs, an assortment of metal fishing lures and five metal tent pegs. She had placed a dollop of glue on each of the knots to assure they remained in place.

Gently shaking the twine, she created a jangle of sounds reminiscent of a wandering group of Hindu musicians. None of the sounds awakened Webster, yet she quickly lowered the noisemakers to the floor to quiet them.

She exited the camper and returned in minutes, removing her gloves and breathing on her numb fingers to warm them. Her alarm was set, concealed beneath brush but with enough clearance to allow the noisemakers plenty of room to do their job.

Webster still slept, breathing quietly, his face pale. Koski settled down beside the window, the 9mm in one hand. Her empty hand slid into her inside pocket and she fingered the laminated postcard that was suddenly in it.

It was five years ago when her mother and father took their last and fatal train trip through the Northwest. As the train began its descent from thirteen hundred feet to the Christmas card beauty of Klamath Falls, Oregon, the tracks suffered an inexplicable defect. Two sleeper cars derailed, tumbling into a deep, diamond-ice ravine, killing twelve people, Koski's parents among them.

As was their habit, they had sent their only child a postcard from Eureka, California. That fateful mailing arrived in Koski's mailbox two days after their funeral. She had laminated the card, which depicted a photograph of Eureka's historic Old Town on its obverse, and always carried it near her breast.

She glanced out the camper window just as a small sliver of sunshine briefly sliced through the falling snow and clouds, igniting the icy tips of a stand of spruce. She tucked the memento gently back into her pocket and decided to concentrate on the silent clearing outside, praying for Falk's quick return.

Falk was sweating, notwithstanding the cold. It began to snow more heavily, bringing the eerie silence that had a tendency to dull the senses. He bent and scooped up a handful of freshly fallen snow and took it into his mouth, bit by bit. He knew that eating snow wasn't wise but the continual gasping for breath as he plodded through the gathering drifts exposed the membranes of his mouth to the air and quickly extracted their moisture. Exertion, coupled with high altitude, became a race against fatigue and dehydration.

Because clots of glassy old ice hid beneath the new layer of snow, he slowly and cautiously made his way to the site where Staudinger's cabin had been.

As he rounded a large noble fir, two men seemed to rise out of the ground, their weapons aimed at his head. These were not National Guardsmen. They were U.S. Army Special Ops soldiers and the one hauling out a pair of Flexcuffs before Falk could explain himself had cold blue eyes and an attitude.

Who's Killing All the Lawyers?

Chapter 26

"What do you mean, we have to leave by a secret exit a mile away," Reinecke demanded of the big redhead in hard hat and Kilimanjaro coat. He suddenly had entered into Control with two of his men, AR-18s slung across their shoulders. "We're aware that The Fox sent you to get us out," the senator went on, "but our cars are in the parking lot. Why can't we simply drive away?"

"Because my orders are to get you out *safely and secretly*," Eiker snapped, "and there are still a couple of National Guardsmen out there somewhere. My understanding is that you don't want them to see you. I'm also assuming you don't want them to *kill* you."

"Kill—Why, they have no reason to kill *me*...to think that I—"

"You don't know what they're thinking," Eiker barked.

"Chrissake," Villachi grumbled, pushing his cigar to one side of his mouth and pulling up his collar. "Let's just go!"

Vigo, anxious to get out by any means, started for the large double doors through which they had entered.

"This way, sir," one of the technicians said and Vigo stopped and turned. The young man pointed to a five-foot vertical cabinet against the wall to his right. Turning back to the console, he reached down and depressed a button recessed beneath the working surface. The cabinet opened like a door, revealing a five-foot rectangle of darkness.

"You'll need your hard hats," the technician who seemed to be the senior of the two said. "The lamps atop the hats will be your only illumination."

Vigo and Reinecke scrambled to retrieve their hats but Villachi, his fragile neck and shoulders bobbing in protest, said, "I'll walk behind you all and follow your lights."

"So, where does this black hole go?" Eiker demanded of the men at the console. He retained his hard hat but checked his gear for the added insurance of the flashlight he found there.

"This unlit passage connects to an old entrance that hasn't been used for years," the older man said. "The pipes that provide our pirated water supply run beneath it. Here in Control we're just below the area once considered to be the working face of the mine, where the original vein of gold was worked.

"The passage you'll follow will gradually slope uphill until you reach a wooden ladder running vertically through a natural, chimney-like cleft that rambles up through the mountain to the surface on a ridge east of the mine. It's a long climb but you'll be well outside the fence that surrounds the mine proper. After that you're on your own."

As he was about to turn away, he added, "By the way, three months ago there was an earthquake, a strong one, up in the Mammoth Lake area. I was told that the old slant entrance to the mine—the one on that ridge you're headed for—lost some of its ceiling timbers. Repairs were made but it could be dangerous should anything…Well, good luck."

There was a moment in which all six who were about to depart stood still and looked at each other, their faces darkened with doubt.

Then the other technician shouted, "Helios!"

"Say again," Eiker commanded.

"*Helios!* Helicopters! One...two..." As he counted, the others raced to the console. "Three...four. Four U.S. Army Blackhawk's approaching the perimeter are circling at three hundred...two hundred feet above the main gate..."

The senior technician hit a large red button on the console, activating loud alarm klaxons attached to the walls throughout the mine. Then he began answering phones as each security station reported in.

"Shit!" Eiker raged, "One of those National Guard assholes got a Mayday through. The Army's sent in the fucking A-team."

"Oh, my God, the United States Army," Reinecke said, his face waxen. "They mustn't find me here—" He grabbed the front of Eiker's jacket. "Get me out of here!"

Eiker threw off the senator's sweaty hands and studied the monitors, two of which captured the threatening rotorized aircraft descending through the falling snow. A reconnaissance team was already rappelling down from the first, dispersing to the shelter of the mine's outbuildings. "Shit!" Eiker repeated.

Reinecke's face turned white. "For God's sake, Eiker, don't you have a contingency plan? Didn't you *expect* the possibility of—"

"I had no reason to expect the fucking United States Army," Eiker said, cutting him off.

"One more thing," the senior technician said loudly but calmly, "If our situation here gets critical, which is unlikely, but...my orders are to destroy the mine." He paused to be sure they understood the import of his words. "If you hear a steady, shrill red alert whistle, you'll only have twenty minutes to clear the perimeter."

"Oh, my God," Reinecke moaned.

Eiker signaled his two men toward the passage and then turned to

Reinecke, Villachi and Vigo. "Come on, let's get your sorry asses out of here."

Once the six men had vanished into the darkness, the senior technician closed the door and refocused on the console. For a moment the two were silent, their vision caught on the screens before them, which now displayed dozens of arctic-suited soldiers rappelling down ropes that dangled from still hovering helicopters.

"What happens if the soldiers find level fifteen…Control…us?" the junior man asked.

"They won't." The man's eyes darted from monitors two through five that offered underground level views and revealed more Special Forces with ready rifles racing through the galleries, rounding up security guards, exchanging small arms fire with those who resisted.

"They're through on levels six and eight," the younger man shouted, panic rising in his voice.

"Chill," his companion commanded firmly. "We've always known this day might come. We're well prepared for it."

"But *look*. They're already in the main elevator shaft." Sweat moistened his upper lip. "The commander probably has maps of the mine and can trace the galleries, entrances and exits…"

"Control's not on any map, you idiot. They don't know about level fifteen." As he made deft adjustments, snapping switches and viewing the intense activity at each descending level, the older man also began to lose conviction. Then he saw two security men on level fourteen draw their pistols and fall to the automatic gunfire of the invading troops. A third guard surrendered and stood trembling and gesturing wildly, no doubt offering whatever he knew of the secrets of the complex.

"Holy shit!" the younger man shrieked. "We're gonna get fucking killed."

"Hold it," one of Eiker's men shouted, his voice resounding above the cacophony of pounding feet as the six men raced through the dark tunnel. "Man down."

Eiker led the column now. He stopped, turned and rushed back past Reinecke, Vigo and the second guard. The latter was helping the Mafia don to his feet.

"You've got to keep up, you son of a bitch," Eiker shouted. The old man already was breathing heavily and it hadn't been five minutes since they left Control. He concentrated the beam of his flashlight on Villachi's face. "We've got almost a mile to go to that exit."

Villachi shoved the light away and swiped at the mud on his overcoat and pants. "The ground's slippery, for Chrissake," he grumbled, steadying himself against the rock wall. "I slipped."

"Well, don't slip again." Eiker turned to his man. "Take his arm. Keep him upright and moving." He ran back to the front of the line, muttering, "I don't have time for this shit."

That Falk was FBI didn't seem to impress the Special Ops soldiers who found him plodding through the snow. His disclosure that a female BLM agent and her wounded companion were stranded in a camper less than a mile away, however, piqued their sense of responsibility. One had switched on the squad intercom attached to his right chest and requested and received permission to check out Falk's story.

Falk stood next to Koski in an abandoned lodge a quarter mile west of the mine, facing a flint-eyed, fortyish officer. He was U.S. Army Colonel Alvin Cromwell, Commander of a Special Operations Force. Cromwell's unit, consisting of four six-man teams, had deployed here after Staudinger's troops were wiped out by mortar fire.

They had flown Webster to a Reno hospital. Falk could only hope that his concussion was not as severe as Falk and Koski initially feared.

"Look, Colonel," Falk said, "we've told you everything we can." Throughout the informal interrogation he and Koski had just undergone, they were helpful but provided only general information. "Like I said, and as our credentials attest," Falk continued, "we're federal agents on a high-level assignment, the details of which we've been sworn not to divulge." He displayed his most innocuous smile. "We're here because we have reason to believe that at least one suspect in our investigation may be at the mine."

Koski's eyes widened slightly, hardly betraying her surprise at this disclosure.

Falk turned to her. "Right, Agent Koski?"

She sucked in her bottom lip and said without conviction, "Right, Agent Falk."

Colonel Cromwell swiped a finger under his long, narrow nose and spoke crisply but with amusement. "It isn't irritating enough that my deployment is in the Sierra Nevada in near-winter but I also have to suffer with wannabe G-men…" He looked from Falk to Koski…"G-Persons."

He sighed. "Yes, well, you should know enough to take orders, I imagine. And, to reiterate mine, you both are to be airlifted out of here as soon as I'm sure I don't need the chopper." He kicked at a chunk of dirty, encrusted snow-ice that had been tracked into his command post. "I can't take the chance of non-military personnel jeopardizing my operation."

"Colonel," Falk protested, elbowing Koski's arm, "Agent Koski, being with the Bureau of Land Management, is familiar with this mine. She has intimate knowledge of areas that can be helpful in this regard." Less gently, he nudged her again. "Right, Agent Koski?"

"Yes…right." Koski cleared her throat, this time prepared to step up to the plate. "You said you have troops in the mine, correct, sir?"

"Yes, they're engaged and encountering extreme resistance, I might add."

She continued, "Well, sir, your troops no doubt have general knowledge of the mine but are they aware of a particular, old, forgotten surface entrance? The entrance that would provide an ideal escape route for anyone—like whoever launched the mortar attack on Staudinger's unit—who may be inside and trying to get away even as we speak."

She paused long enough to be sure she had his attention. "No doubt, you'd want to have such an entrance covered, sir. I know where it is. I've been there."

Falk was silent, watching Cromwell deliberate, running a finger across his upper lip. He would be skating on thin ice, allowing a civilian female to be involved in a dangerous operation. It was tempting. Seeing Cromwell's indecision, Falk decided that it was time to feed the commander enough insight into Falk's conclusions to gain trust or at least gain an advantage that might make Koski and him more valuable.

"Colonel," he said, assuming a more solicitous tone, "Agent Koski, a videographer, has something on video that might be extremely interesting to you." He pointed to Koski's video equipment that he had insisted she bring when she and Webster were taken from the camper. He turned to her. Koski's surprise was less subtle than earlier, her recovery slow. "Ah…yes." She nodded. "Right."

Colonel Cromwell waved his assent and two crisp young uniforms helped Falk and Koski sort out cables and hook them up to a portable battery-operated color monitor. Koski tentatively switched on the camcorder, glancing at Falk for a clue as to what exactly they were about to demonstrate but got none.

The video shot on attorney Mark Sharpe's balcony at his home at Lake Tahoe came up on the screen as Falk set the scene for Cromwell. He fast-forwarded to the outdoor shot he had requested at the time in which Koski panned and held for a full minute on a red tile roof opposite Sharpe's home. Hitting the pause button, he leaned forward and tapped the screen.

"There." He ran the tip of his finger across the tile roof. "See them?"

Cromwell squinted at the screen, his steely eyes searching for what he was supposed to see.

"Nice work, Agent Koski," Falk said, looking at her. He couldn't help himself. He had discovered that he enjoyed putting her on the spot. He knew that she, like Cromwell, couldn't possibly make out the feature he indicated. Without knowing precisely what he or she was looking for, no one could. Yet, he calculated that she could take the teasing.

"There they are," he repeated, gesturing toward the screen. "See them? Clear as day." Koski's eyes never moved from the screen.

"Of course," Falk continued, "when enhanced they will be more readily revealed. Nevertheless, those, Colonel, are marks made by a helicopter's landing skids when it hovered above the red tile roof for a few seconds and accidentally touched down on the tiles. The helicopter was equipped with a sophisticated firing mechanism used to project the arrow that killed the lawyer living in the home next to this one."

Cromwell turned from the image. "But a helicopter?"

Falk snapped off the video. "No doubt Sharpe came out onto the

A. G. Hayes

balcony, wondering why a helicopter would be hovering so low, when the arrow was fired from the aircraft into his chest."

"What about the neighbors? Wouldn't they have seen and heard the copter?"

"Not necessarily. Many of the homes in that area are only used on weekends and only for a portion of the year."

Cromwell stood and started to pace. "Who is in possession of this phantom helicopter?"

"We have an idea," Falk said, his head nodding to include Koski, "but I doubt—"

""*We*" don't have a clue, Colonel," Koski interrupted honestly. "My partner here might have an idea but *I* don't."

Falk let his eyes half flicker to her but went on casually. "In any case, I doubt we'd find it. By now it's probably hidden or the mechanism dismantled and the chopper no doubt easily converted back to standard."

Cromwell shrugged. "Where does that leave us?"

Falk's reply was hard edged, "In the middle of a conspiracy of national magnitude."

The Colonel stopped pacing. "What do you mean, mister?"

Falk did not intend to disclose all of his suspicions but if he was to get into the mine, he needed to throw out enough breadcrumbs for Cromwell to want to follow the trail.

"Colonel," he said, "I suspect that from the start, my task force and I were decoys, meant to be seen investigating—and thereby giving credence to—the supposition that Native Americans are killing lawyers. It seems there also are others who oppose those Native Americans' gambling rights."

He paused and raised a forewarning finger in the air. "While my

195

team and I were supposed to deflect attention, someone was busy setting the stage for something a lot more sinister than the growth of gambling casinos."

Cromwell returned to his chair, aware he was being made privy to intrigue on a grand scale. He put his elbows on his desk and made a steeple of his fingers. "And that is…?"

"If I knew that, this investigation would be over."

The Colonel's mobile phone interrupted and he took the call. "Roger, Major," he said with quizzical satisfaction and hung up.

"I only know," Falk continued, "that I was given a tip that some important people were meeting at the mine. I suspect at least one of them is connected to the killing helicopter we just talked about."

Cromwell snorted, "Important people, here?" He nodded toward the phone. "That call was reporting that all fourteen levels of the mine are secure at this time. To date, my troops found only maintenance and security personnel. There is no evidence that anyone who might be considered important in a military or political sense has been there."

"As you no doubt know, Colonel," Falk said, "there's a saying in the intelligence community that goes: 'The absence of evidence is not evidence of absence'."

Cromwell nodded. "Yes, well, they're still searching for those responsible for the mortar attack and expect to have them in custody soon." He paused and ran the finger across his upper lip, a gesture that Falk had ascertained was a sign of uncertainty. "I must say," Cromwell continued, "that the degree of resistance by mine personnel is puzzling. In any case, that bird is available now to evacuate you two."

Falk contemplated divulging the seed of suspicion that had sprouted in his mind earlier, when Koski mentioned the mystery of water diversion in connection with the old entrance. Now that seed was nurtured by the Colonel's mention of "all fourteen levels." Tom Stewart's note to Falk, delivered to him at the motel along with the gear and camper, had indicated a meeting on level *fifteen*. Stewart seldom made mistakes.

"Colonel," Falk said, bringing the conversation full circle, "what about the mine entrance...the one Agent Koski mentioned as a possible escape route?"

Cromwell sighed heavily and stared at him. "Can you guide some of my men to this secret entrance?"

"We can do—"

"*I* can," Koski interrupted, jumping to her feet— "Most definitely, right now."

Falk saw the Colonel's mouth momentarily twist into something resembling a grin. Cromwell turned to one of his officers. "Get these two equipped with snowsuits and vests right away. Take three men with you. Notify me when you find the entrance—but nobody goes into the mine. You got that?" The officer nodded and Cromwell turned back to Falk. "As soon as we have secured that entrance, you two are out of here, mister."

In the control room, the senior technician's mind burned with shock and indecision. How could this be? His had always been a quiet, mundane job in which he put in his hours watching monitors that, day after day, displayed a series of tranquil scenes that merely prepared him for more of the same.

He was trained how to react in an emergency. Indeed, he had sworn to die willingly here at these controls if necessary to keep the computers and files generated by The Fox's crusade from falling into the wrong hands. He fully understood that should invaders threaten Control, his responsibility was to implement the plan.

The demolition packs were in position at every level of the complex and would have to be activated. The time-destruct mechanism then would count down the minutes until those strategically placed explosives destroyed Control and the rest of the mine with it. Nothing must remain that could lead authorities to The Fox or other players in his campaign. Even now—when it seemed possible that the government's elite fighting force might actually discover level fifteen —the man could not believe that he must set that final plan in motion.

He glanced at a particular monitor and saw soldiers standing at the false breakaway wall that separated level fourteen from the stairs leading to the lowest level. It was a matter of time before they drew the critical conclusions; ten or fifteen minutes to get through the outer door. He already had delayed too long.

He sighed and turned to his companion, who was screeching and imploring by turns. "It's time," he said calmly. "I'm setting delay destruct for…" he concentrated on the Seiko on his wrist…"two p.m." He glanced at his companion, who fidgeted silently now, his mouth agape.

"Synchronize your watch," the senior man commanded. "It's one-forty…now." He snapped open two red-capped metal covers flush with the console surface and simultaneously pressed the two recessed buttons. A high-pitched whistle shrilled through the facility. He jerked his head in the direction of the concealed door and pressed its release button. "Go!" he commanded. "You've only got twenty minutes."

Jumping up, the terrified man grabbed his coat from a hook on the wall. "What…what about you?" he asked before he stepped into the black aperture.

"I'll be along. It's my job to be the last to leave."

Chapter 27

"Oh, no," Reinecke screamed. All six men in the gallery stopped running. Their ears filled and burned with the sound of the shrill red alert whistle of which the technician had warned.

"We've got less than twenty minutes to find and get up that ladder," Eiker shouted, reacting quickly. "Move it!" He dashed forward. His flashlight and the lamp on his hard hat cast bobbing, erratic streamers of light into the dark passage ahead.

He ran full tilt; Reinecke, Vigo, Villachi and the two guards at his heels, their footfalls, wheezing and fear echoing with the sound of the whistle off the damp, dark walls. For a time, they made swift progress, despite the steady uphill slant of the rock and earthen floor. Then Eiker heard the guard at the rear shout something indistinguishable. Waving Reinecke and the others past him, he waited for the guard, who halted his labor of dragging the frail Villachi along with him.

"Somebody's coming behind us," the guard said, catching his breath.

Eiker listened long enough to distinguish two footsteps. "It's just one man."

He turned and shouted to the other guard, who stopped abruptly and came back. "You take up the rear position," Eiker ordered. He nodded to the darkness behind them. "If he's Special Forces, kill him."

Eiker raced to return to the head of the column of desperate men. In minutes he heard voices from the rear and turned to see the junior technician from Control flying past the rear guard. His eyes wide with terror, the young man now shoved past Villachi and the guard who upheld him, nearly knocking Vigo and Reinecke down, too, in his race to be first out of the tunnel. Eiker merely watched as the terrified youth flew past him, his forward pitch so impatient as to be in danger of becoming a stumble.

Eiker and the others raced on. Finally, without slackening his gait, Eiker dared to glance at his watch again. "Two minutes," he wheezed, hope sinking. Maybe his watch was not exactly coordinated with that of the man in Control…maybe his was fast…maybe—

His light caught horizontal shapes on the right wall beyond the runner, little more than a hundred feet away. They were wooden rungs…built into the side of the wall…*the ladder*! Then the shrill alert whistle died. Eiker and the others halted and froze. There was a moment of silence; indeed, breathing itself halted.

Three simultaneous surface explosions blew open the earth beneath the mine's main gate building and surrounding areas, spewing large chunks of wood, cement, metal, snow, dirt and shards of rock and boulders into the air.

Black smoke plumed upward with fragments of timber and other debris that returned to earth with the damp, lightly falling snow. The earth jolted and trembled, as similar explosions rocked all underground levels of the old mine, coughing more torn and twisted matter into the atmosphere.

Cromwell's soldiers stationed outside the perimeter of the fence watched the instantaneous destruction of the mine in horror, knowing that many of their fellows bled in final agony inside.

The explosions came in the instant Eiker's vision had fixed on the ladder that represented the exit and freedom. He looked up as an old, neglected ceiling timber several feet ahead jolted and split instantly. It was followed by others that cracked and splintered and, in a roar, fell with rock and earth, collapsing the tunnel before his eyes. Only his exceptionally responsive reflexes, burying his chin in his chest and letting the hard hat take the brunt of the falling debris, saved him.

The force of the explosion behind them as Control erupted sent a rush of air like a wall into the frenzied group of men, plunging them, screaming, through the air and headlong into each other.

Minutes earlier, Koski's unerring sense of direction had led Falk and four attendant soldiers to a spot on a hillside less than a mile due east of the mine where they halted. Only the sound of sporadic gunfire in the distance had attested to the fact that the Delta unit had moved farther into the mine complex.

"There it is," Koski said, pointing to what appeared to be no more than a concentrated overgrowth of shrubs. "It probably hasn't been disturbed for months."

"Let me," Falk said and started forward but Cromwell's serious lieutenant stopped him.

"Let *us*," the officer insisted, as much protectively as representing an order. The four men pushed through the dense, snow-covered vegetation. It was no more than a five-foot-square opening on the side of a hill, reinforced with timber and covered with a fine mesh screen.

The lieutenant pulled a flashlight from his utility pack. He had led Koski, Falk and his men twenty feet into the entrance. Now he trained his flashlight beam into the black abyss. "There are wooden ladder rungs built into—"

He never finished his sentence. He was knocked to the ground by the percussion of smoke, dust and dirt that erupted like molten lava from the black hole as explosions rocked the earth for miles around.

In the instant of the explosions, Falk turned and lunged through the air to Koski, carrying them both as far as possible from the belching hole.

Eiker, forced to his knees by the power of the blast, was pummeled with fragments of wood, rock and other debris, as dust and smoke continued to whirl through the passage, burning and scratching his eyes, nose and throat. Then he heard Vigo cough.

"What the fuck happened?" Vigo's voice was thick from the dust he had inhaled. "I thought if we got this far—" Then another paroxysm of coughing overtook him.

Eiker shook his head. His flashlight was gone, blown from his hand, and his shoulders ached from being hit by a piece of falling timber. His hard hat was still on and he sensed that he was generally unharmed.

"Don't move, Vigo," he said. Hearing no other voices, he moved his head to illuminate the area but only swirling dust beams were revealed. "Reinecke…Villachi…" he called but got no response.

Squinting through the dust and smoke, he spat out a mouthful of dirt and moved ahead slowly. Then the beam reflected on the head and shoulders of the guard who had been assisting Villachi. The already expanding pool of blood flowed from a massive and life-ending slice to the guard's jugular, the offending knife of splintered wood still embedded in his neck. His lower body was buried beneath a jumble of rocks that had dislodged from the ceiling.

Now there was movement around Eiker as dazed figures groped haphazardly in the chaos, trying to focus. He saw Ray, the other guard, who sustained cuts and bruises but was not seriously injured.

"Eiker..." It was Reinecke's voice. Eiker trained the miner's lamp on his hard hat in the direction of the sound.

"It's Villachi..." Reinecke rasped between coughing spasms.

Eiker turned his head to light the area Reinecke indicated. The settling dust allowed him to see the frail body crumpled against the jagged wall. It was the old don, all right, although he was hardly recognizable. His head, not sheltered by a hard hat, lay open. Blood mixed with pieces of bone and brain splattered the dusty ground.

"Debris from the blast killed him," Eiker said without emotion, "sucking away the soul of a gambler to join his ancestors. Bad luck."

A quick survey of the tunnel confirmed what Eiker already had surmised. The explosion had deposited ruined sections of the gallery in front and behind them. Eiker, Ray, Reinecke and Vigo were marooned in a pocket of thick, musty air between that portion of the passage leading to the now destroyed Control and the ladder, the condition of which Eiker couldn't know.

He was thankful for one thing. The water pipes the senior technician had mentioned buried beneath this tunnel apparently had not broken, at least not in this section. The men would have drowned. Eiker thought of that technician, who must have been the last to leave Control and never had a chance of making it out alive.

"Okay," Eiker said, "we've got to work fast." Any minute, he figured, residual cave-ins could occur. He gestured toward the wall-high heap of rubble that separated them from the ladder. "Ray and I'll start clearing this passage. Senator, you and Vigo find a place to sit that's out of our way. You'll need your strength once we're out of here."

He grabbed a slab of wood and, using it as a fulcrum, threw all of his strength into rolling a stubborn boulder that had been part of the ceiling from his path. Beside him, Ray's body twitched at a sudden rumble overhead that caused a small landslide of dirt and stones to rattle into the narrow confine. Ten minutes later, they had scraped and clawed their way to the top of the heap and achieved an opening between it and the ceiling large enough to wriggle through and escape.

"Thank God," Reinecke breathed.

Eiker scoffed, "Reinecke, you're always invoking the deity. Whatever gives you the impression that God would ever intercede on *your* bloody behalf?"

On the other side of the wall of rubble, they discovered what must have been the body of the technician who earlier shoved past them on his way to be the first one out. He was literally flattened by an I-beam and only his broken, twisted extremities and the litter that followed its violent descent were visible beneath it.

Eiker stepped over him and rushed to the ladder, testing its strength, finding only several of the lowest rungs unusable. He looked up into the shaft. From what was visible through the smoke, he determined that it had sustained little damage and that it contained about a hundred rungs.

"Good luck," he said to Reinecke and gestured for him to ascend first, followed by Vigo, Ray and Eiker himself. Being last to leave the deadly passage in this instance was no heroic courtesy. Eiker knew that The Fox wanted Reinecke and Vigo alive, if possible. He would get out somehow but these milquetoasts needed special consideration.

Chapter 28

Following the explosions, Falk and Koski wanted to descend the ladder the lieutenant saw in the mine opening but the officer reached Colonel Cromwell on the squad intercom. In turn, Cromwell ordered massive reinforcements in the wake of the explosions and commanded his men and their two charges to stand clear of the entrance until those reinforcements arrived.

As they waited, the soldiers rested on boulders that had resembled large marshmallows before the men swept the snow from their surfaces. Like Falk and Koski, they were in white snowsuits that, when they were still, nearly masked their presence in the silent scene in which snow had ceased to fall.

Falk and Koski paced slowly but impatiently. Looking down the hillside toward the smoldering mine, she asked, "What do you suppose happened?"

He shook his head. "From the locations and totality of the explosions it appeared that they were deliberately triggered from within the mine...no accident."

"So, you think whoever was in charge rigged the place to self-destruct in the event of any hostile intrusion. Who do you think that was?"

"I don't know yet."

In an effort to avoid being surprised later, she replied, "But you do know *something*. I can tell. What have you figured out so far?"

"That we're getting closer to The Fox." He had told her what he knew about The Fox and that Stewart suspected that person may be involved in the lawyers' deaths.

Suddenly Falk turned, having caught movement at the nearby mine entrance. Koski and the others followed him in the direction of the hole. His instinct was to draw his weapon but Cromwell had confiscated it. A weapon didn't seem necessary, however, when Falk saw the weary, unarmed man who emerged.

"Senator Reinecke," he said, not entirely surprised.

Reinecke wheezed and coughed as he staggered into the cold air, puffs of dust and dirt attending his emergence. "Now," Falk whispered to Koski, "what do you suppose Reinecke is doing here?"

Koski caught sight of the next man to surface. "Bud Vigo!" she exclaimed, recognizing Maxwell's boss, the Carson City police chief. Vigo lumbered from the hole like a bear coming out of hibernation but he was panting, doubled over in a fit of coughing.

On later reflection, Falk would have to admit that their recognition and tacit acceptance of these two men were greatly responsible for what happened next.

It wasn't until the final two men jumped from the hole with their ready AR-18s aimed at them that the military men became aware of their critical misreading of the situation.

Nothing that followed could be misinterpreted, however. The appearance here of Reinecke and Vigo served to confirm the hunch Falk had nursed for days. It was as if the lens through which he viewed the puzzling investigation suddenly cleared and all but a few remaining pieces fit together. Obviously, Reinecke and Vigo were two of the unknown subjects Stewart referred to in his note. Who were the others?

The militia's mistake allowed Reinecke, who might not have been a physically fit or courageous man, to exhibit a skill he possessed in abundance—quick-wittedness. "We..." he began, trying to read the group's faces, "we were taken prisoner by this..." he nodded toward the big redhead, "this terrorist and brought here to this godforsaken place to...to..."

Apparently, Falk mused, the senator's quick thinking had its limits.

Vigo jumped in to assist, as well as to salvage himself, no doubt. "Exactly," he said, "we were taken hostage at gun point and forced to divulge official police and state secrets to aid this man in his scheme to murder all the lawyers in the state. You have no idea—"

"Save it," the redhead commanded, not commenting on his companions' allegations. Something in his inflection gave Falk the impression that he was English.

After patting down Falk and Koski and finding no weapons, the big man with one mangled ear lobe walked over to the soldiers, whose faces burned with the acrimonious fire of those who have been outmaneuvered. Their rifles hung at their sides.

"My name is Eiker," the Brit said.

A bell rang in Falk's head. Yes, he had heard of the man...not on the Bureau's Most Wanted list but somewhere in one of their databases...maybe on the ITL, the International Terrorists List.

"We'll take your weapons now," Eiker said. "Ray," he summoned and the bald, bearded, thick-necked menacing man came forward to carry out his leader's order.

The first two troopers immediately opened their hands and let their rifles thud to the soft snow. The third hesitated only slightly then followed suit. The lieutenant seemed to be measuring something.

"I said *now*," Eiker repeated.

Without taking his eyes from Eiker's face, the soldier let his rifle fall to earth. Then, as Ray bent to gather up the weapons and Eiker let his eyes flicker momentarily to the others, the officer's right hand foolishly whipped to his hip and pulled a 92F Berretta automatic.

He got off one round—a hurried, ineffectual shot—before Eiker's automatic blazed. Hit, the soldier nevertheless brought his gun down from recoil to squeeze off another round. Eiker's storm of bullets punched into his body and he lurched back, taking several more rounds in the head.

The soldier standing beside him, a youngster with visages of the acne of puberty still evident on his face, turned toward the lieutenant, as if to keep him from going down—a ridiculous, spontaneous reflex. Eiker chose to read it as an attempt to grab the handgun and fired, killing him along with the veteran.

Eiker calmly looked at the dry clip in his AR-18, thumbed the clip release, then reached into his belt and drove a fresh clip home.

Falk was aware of a profound silence there on the hillside among the pristine sparkle of trees iced in white. Koski had involuntarily screamed during the exchange of gunfire. Now she, too, was silent, malevolence in her eyes trained on the redheaded killer.

Reinecke and Vigo were obviously shaken, too, as if questioning whether they had chosen the right side in this fight. If what Falk suspected was true, it was too late for the duo to question their choice. They committed to the wrong side long ago.

His rifle always at the ready, Eiker herded them into a tight group and addressed Falk and Koski. "Just exactly who the hell are you?"

"Bureau of Land Management," Falk quickly offered, trying to make their presence here as benign as possible, at least for the time being. "Sent to do an inspection in the area of the mine when suddenly there were these explosions."

"What's Land Management doing here? I thought you Yanks had something called the Bureau of Mines."

"We do. However, there appears to be a water dispute...our jurisdiction."

Eiker seemed to buy it but Falk figured that he did so either because he didn't have enough time to probe further or because it didn't matter. He was not the type of man to accept anything at face value if it were pertinent to him. Falk thought something else about this Limey. He obviously had the opposable qualities of detached calm and exploding urgency; often juxtaposed in a hired killer.

"Okay," Eiker said and turned to Koski. "I need to rendezvous at Bowman Lake in exactly two hours. You and your friend here, being BLM, should know your way around the area enough to lead me there."

Eiker chewed his gum slowly. Its sound snapped crisply in the cold air. "You have the right to remain silent," he said, "in which case, I have the right to kill you."

"You expect *me* to help *you*?" Koski said slowly and levelly. "I would regard that on a par with feeding an alligator in hopes that he would eat me *last*."

Falk stepped forward. "Look, Eiker, I'll—"

Bud Vigo, not sure what Falk's response would be, was already in the act of bursting between them. "I know the area well, Eiker...I have a cabin near the lake...I'll show you how to get there."

In that moment Falk thought that Vigo probably did the only

decent thing he had done in years. Maybe because Eiker was his ticket out of here. Maybe because his stomach couldn't take the prospect of more dead bodies in the snow.

Eiker shrugged. "How long will it take us on foot?" he asked Vigo.

"A couple of hours if we hurry and don't get more storms."

"Then let's move out."

Koski's green eyes blazed anew. "You're just going to leave them here? There are wolves and coyotes in these woods. They'll—"

Eiker dismissed her with a wave of his gloved hand. "Don't worry your pretty head. More troops will be along to collect them soon—too soon." He turned to his partner. "Ray, Vigo will lead." He gestured with his rifle to Falk, Koski, Reinecke and the two remaining soldiers. "You follow Vigo and Ray will follow you. I'll be…everywhere."

Before they stepped into the encompassing forest, Falk looked back down the hillside at what remained of the mine.

Regular Army troops, several fire trucks and other first response units converged on the scene of blazing rubble. Special Forces units were probably on their way to the hillside entrance Falk and the others had just left.

Once more, Falk glanced back toward the entrance and the two brave, fallen soldiers. Before this day ended he would avenge their deaths.

Chapter 29

Maxwell jumped when the phone rang. This room in the military hospital in Fallon had been her home for the past twenty-four hours and she'd had no calls.

"Webster!" She was jubilant to hear his voice.

"Didn't Alex tell you I was transferred here from the hospital in Reno?"

"No, Alex hasn't called me in two days. I assumed he either had no news or was told to discontinue broadcasting our whereabouts...if he even knows our whereabouts." She paused. "How are you?"

"I'm fine now."

Maxwell detected a great tiredness in his usual, congenial tone. "'Now?'"

"I had a moderate concussion that kept me hovering in no man's land for a while but I'm...it's a long story. Look, I just discovered that only a couple of rooms separate us. Want some company?"

"Of course."

By the time Webster arrived and gave her an account of the mortar attack near the mine and his, Falk and Koski's detention by the U.S. Army, he was thoroughly exhausted. He looked around the militarily sparse room; a hospital bed, a portable tilt-top table and two comfortable arm chairs. A scarlet duvet woven with gold thread lent an ambiance of personality to the room. "I don't have a pretty bedspread like that on my bed," he said, as if deprived.

She smiled. "Are there patients in any other rooms on this floor?"

"No and the nurses' station is unattended, too. This place is more like a hotel than a hospital."

"Well, at least we're safe here," she said sympathetically.

"Yes, but our being safe doesn't help Falk and Koski."

He slumped in one of the easy chairs and Maxwell thought of the strong, take-charge man he was the night at Alex Spade's home when an arrow was nearly buried in Alex's back. "I understand your frustration," she said, "but what can we do?"

He stood up suddenly, reached into the pocket of his western style shirt and extracted a small piece of folded paper. "I'm going to call Ryland…tell him that we need to get back into action, that…" His words trailed off and he weaved slightly, repositioning his feet to steady himself.

"Whoa!" Maxwell said and was at his elbow, urging him gently back into the chair. "I think you need another day of rest."

A quick, light tapping on the door made them both turn toward the sound.

"Ryland told me that nobody knew I was here," Maxwell whispered. The tapping repeated, louder.

"Maybe we should see who it is," he said.

She got up and stood by the door. "Who is it?"

"It's Roz Newton, Wes Webster's secretary. Do you have a moment, Dr. Maxwell?"

Webster roused with recognition, started to get up but Maxwell waved him to stay in his chair. She couldn't explain it. It was as if somewhere some hidden evil had stuck its head out of a hole and she shivered. Looking back at Webster, she mouthed, "How did *she* know I was here?"

Webster shrugged naively. "I might have mentioned..."

Maxwell rolled her eyes. "Why do you want to see me, Roz?" she called out.

"I have some information you'd be interested in. It's about Agents Falk and Koski."

Maxwell envisioned Roz as she had seen her in Webster's office several days ago—Roz and the J.Lo jeans with rhinestone pockets. She had seemed harmless and Maxwell had no reason to mistrust her. Nevertheless, events of this investigation had heightened Maxwell's vigilance. She decided to ask one more question. "How did you know I was here?"

"Wes told me, of course. In fact, he sent me."

Maxwell was chilled that her seemingly unfounded suspicion was confirmed. She turned and walked back to where Webster had silently risen from his chair, his mouth hanging open.

"You *sure* you didn't tell her to come here for any reason?" she whispered.

He nodded blankly, unable to comprehend Roz's motives. "I'm sure."

"She doesn't know you're here. She must think you're in your own room." She walked back to the door. "Look, Roz," she called, "I was just about to jump into the shower. Why don't you come back say, in half an hour?"

They both stared at the door. Maxwell could almost feel the woman's anger. Then there was the rattle of the doorknob and Maxwell was grateful she'd had the foresight to lock it after Webster arrived. Finally, hearing Roz's heels clicking along the corridor, she sighed and walked away from the door.

"She's gone." Would she be back? That depended on what she had in mind. If she did come back, what would Maxwell do?

Inexplicably, she thought of her father's words when she was young. He was speaking of preparedness. "Don't assume everybody wants to hurt you but expect it."

"We should call security," Webster said.

Maxwell started pacing. "I'm not sure…I don't even know if we can trust *them*. We could call Ryland but I doubt he's close enough to do us any good." Every ounce of her being resisted her next thought but finally inbred preparedness prevailed.

"I'll be right back," she said and went to the bathroom, pulled off her skirt, jacket and panty hose and slipped into a robe and slippers. Carefully, fighting disgust, she removed the Walther from her purse on the countertop, checked that it was loaded and cocked and then thumbed the safety to off.

Draping a thick bath towel over her right arm, she arranged the folds to conceal the weapon. When she returned to the room, Webster was standing by the door and pronounced what she had expected.

"She's coming back and it's been less than ten minutes…" Moving away from the door, he glanced up at the overhead light Maxwell had turned on earlier to expel the gloom of the dark afternoon. He instinctively hit the wall switch, which extinguished all but one low wattage lamp. He crossed to Maxwell and protectively placed an arm around her shoulders. "Don't worry," he whispered. "I'll protect you."

Maxwell knew he meant it but she was aware of the slight sway of his body against her own. The footsteps paused at the door and she heard the jangle of a key in the lock. Maxwell could think of only one purpose that would make the woman this determined. She curled her finger around the trigger of the automatic and waited, unsure if she could pressure that trigger if the need arose.

Who's Killing All the Lawyers?

Chapter 30

It was late afternoon and a white sift fell on the Sierra again. Falk felt apart from the other seven people in the straggling column, his mind constantly assessing the chances of his and Koski's escape before they reached Bowman Lake. The Brit was a tough opponent in a battle of wits and strength yet, like any man, he had weaknesses. Falk watched for one to show itself. Only moments ago, Falk remembered where he heard the name Rodney Eiker.

The ITL listed him as a freelancer, for sale to the highest bidder. Now he'd been hired to extricate Vigo and Reinecke from the mine before the Army found them. "Hurry it up." The Englishman's voice cut through the cold air from his present position at the end of the column. "I won't look kindly on anyone who makes me late for my rendezvous at the Lake."

Falk figured that Eiker, like any good warrior, never underestimated the enemy. One of Cromwell's units could be in the surrounding hills. That reflection might be reassuring to Koski, Falk thought, and he whispered, "Once the Delta troops discover the two dead soldiers and our tracks, they'll locate us." Koski, preceding him in line, nodded silently. Snowflakes tumbled around them as the wind, up to fifteen miles per hour a short time ago, dropped to zero and the still air grew deathly cold.

Falk thought of how he reassured Meg in her time of need before he left her in the vehicle in which she died. He quickly barred the haunting memory. He had not failed Meg and he would not fail Koski.

Then he realized Koski was not waiting for anyone to fail her.

She had dropped back slightly, putting some space between herself and Vigo. "Psst," she whispered, turning her head so that her voice travelled back to Falk.

"Yes?"

"The direction we're travelling will put us in open country soon." Falk nodded silently. "We want to get to Bowman in one piece," she said. "That Delta team could wipe us *all* out."

"The Brit will kill us anyway when we get to the lake." Falk was sure of this. Earlier, Ray had covered the column while Eiker and the two captive soldiers went into the woods. Two shots rang out and Eiker returned alone.

"We can lose Eiker when the time is right," she said.

"We can?"

"Of course." She paused. "Right, Agent Falk?"

"Right," he answered, noting that he had not seen her reach for her postcard in hours.

She turned and called to Vigo. "Tell our fearless leader that I can show him a better way to Bowman so we don't get picked off like rabbits out on the open slopes."

Eiker heard and walked ahead to Koski.

Falk positioned himself at Koski's side and, for the first time, took a close look at the man. Late forties, he guessed and younger shape. His left ear was deeply scarred and there weren't any laugh lines around his eyes, which were deep blue, flashing like Novas.

"I had a hunch taking you along would eventually pay off," Eiker said to Koski. "What's on your mind?"

"If we're being tracked by the Army, and I've no doubt we are, they'll sight us easily if we tramp across an open slope."

Eiker considered her comment. "So?"

"So, if we walk straight down the mountain we'll reach the tree line, which will afford cover. Scrub pines overlap ridges that by heading northeast, will take us within yards of the lake where dense tree cover is available."

"You can find your way through the woods?"

"Definitely."

"You lead then. I'll be right behind you but remember, any false moves and—"

She waved him away. "I know. I know. I saw the movie."

Soon the weary column plodded through scattered underbrush, evergreens and interspersed deciduous alders. All was silent except for the occasional slap of snow falling from an overloaded branch and the soft squeak of powder underfoot. They travelled this way for thirty minutes before Falk heard Reinecke complain of muscle fatigue and their leader called for another brief rest stop.

Falk huddled with Koski next to a giant pine, seeking to give, and get, warmth. "We must be almost there," he said.

She pulled the collar of her jacket tightly around her throat. "We'll be over the ridge in less than twenty minutes and then we're basically at Bowman."

As a sudden spurt of wind whirled icy streams of snow from the powdered surface around them, Falk thought the Englishman would eliminate the excess baggage.

The column started moving again, making slow but steady progress. Falk saw two Delta men on skis cross in front of a stand of aspens, visible only for a split second, less than a hundred yards away. Eiker saw them, too. Falk watched him scoop up a handful of snow and lob a snowball at Ray, who was behind Koski at the head of the column. Ray spun around and saw Eiker tap the top of his head and point in the direction of the skiers.

Falk lurched behind a giant pine, whipping his arms around Koski and taking her with him. The others also dispersed and hit the ground among the dense trees.

"Soldiers," Falk whispered, his breath creating a cloud between them. "White suited and on skis."

"How many?"

"I only saw two…probably part of a split six-man team."

"We're only ten minutes from the lake," she said softly.

"Isn't there a Ranger Station somewhere near Bowman? We could call Ryland from there."

"Yes but we'll have to go around—"

Suddenly he clapped a hand over her mouth and pulled her deeper into the drift beneath snow-laden branches as an Army captain and a two-man team passed within five feet of them moving eastward.

When they had gone, Falk whispered, "Obviously, that team is not equipped with heat sensors."

"I'm thinking that maybe it's not such a good idea, hiding from Special Forces. After all, they're the good guys."

"I know, but we have work to do and we can't do it if we're detained in another session with Cromwell."

She nodded. "Or if we're dead."

He pointed to the edge of the woods. "They came from that direction so we'll head out that way." Moving from tree to tree and using all possible cover, they reached the border of the thickest tree growth. Falk peered across the white expanse of mountainside and saw the troopers' discarded skis sticking upright in the snow.

"We're out of here," he whispered. "Those skis are fitted with military bindings and designed to adjust to nearly any boot size and type." Within minutes, the two were ready to push off.

"Look!" Koski said, pointing to the tree line. Bud Vigo was running and stumbling toward them.

"Chief," Koski said, "are you all right?"

Falk was silent. Apparently, Koski had bought the story of how Vigo and Reinecke were hostages of Eiker. For the time being, Falk let it seem that he did, too.

"I saw you two leave and took a chance," Vigo said, sucking air and looking back over his shoulder.

"Where's Senator Reinecke?" Koski asked.

"Still hiding...with Ray and Eiker," he wheezed, "among the trees."

"What was he doing at the mine, anyway? And—"

"Koski!" Falk glared at her. "Later." He turned to Vigo. "You ski?" Vigo nodded. "Then grab a pair—hurry."

Falk pulled the remaining skis out of the snow. "No sense leaving these for anyone pursuing us." He tucked them under his arm.

Silently they hissed over the snow like low-flying gulls, leaving the woods behind. Soon Falk let the excess skis go and watched them race like stoats down the mountainside and vanish from sight. He heard the rattle of automatic weapons in the direction from which they had come but he stabbed the snow with his poles and never looked back.

Eiker took down two of the soldiers at nearly point blank range, having watched them approach from the hiding place he chose because it afforded an ideal crossfire condition for Ray. The remaining trooper of the first half of the team was fast and took cover, returning fire with amazing speed and accuracy.

Bark chips flew from a tree inches above Eiker's head. He rolled away to his next cover, a downed evergreen half hidden by fallen branches, as snow was whipped up by the fire of two Special Forces troopers. They had popped into view with astonishing speed, reminding Eiker of spring-loaded targets on a firing range. He snaked behind the log, one bullet tearing the heel from his boot.

Ray waited until he was sure he had the sharp-shooting trooper lined up. Then his finger froze on the trigger. There was a sound near him—something barely heard...but felt...He pivoted. "Wha—" and saw Reinecke. The senator had been crouching behind a nearby tree, afraid to move, afraid not to move. Either unaware of the trooper in Ray's crosshairs or oblivious to all but his need for the safety of an armed companion, he suddenly stood and took two steps in Ray's direction, alerting the sharpshooter to Ray's position.

The soldier fired, strafing a six-foot path in the bark of the trees around him. Pain, like the whack of a sledgehammer, seared Ray's left upper arm but he knew instantly that the bullet that found him had not tunnelled deeply into his flesh. He shot a malignant glance at Reinecke, who had taken cover beside him.

Eiker, having pinpointed the shooter when he fired at Ray, reacted swiftly, turning his AR-18 on the soldier in time to trigger twice, silencing the man forever. Then he took another blast of bullets from the two who had pinned down his position, but the domino effect continued. Ray let loose a barrage of bullets in their direction, firing until no fire returned.

Eiker took off, bent double, sprinting between trees for two hundred meters. He stopped, fell into firing position and waited. He assumed that Ray would leave the shivering Reinecke behind, bolt in the opposite direction and wait.

The Delta captain of the final three-man unit was the next in Eiker's sights. He squeezed the trigger, his AR-18 roared and the captain, hit in the throat, spun in a spray of blood, his life wrenched from him. Before disappearing into the trees, the two remaining troopers opened fire, raking the branches inches above Eiker's head.

Ray saw one of the remaining soldiers finger the squad communicator attached to the right side of his suit. If he got through to Command, he would give away their location. Inching forward, Ray closed in on the man who was moving out of the trees.

This would have to be a wet job. Sliding a bone-handled knife from its sheath, Ray stealthily crept through the soft snow. To kill the man without a sound would prevent the remaining trooper from gauging their location. Ray lunged. Before the soldier had time to react to danger, the razor-sharp knife had found its way to his jugular.

The snap of a twig behind him caused Ray to spin around. The remaining trooper was there, his body levelled into a combat stance, rifle angled in Ray's direction. Ray lurched sideways and blood spouted from the side of his left shoulder, yet some part of his mind registered amazement that he was still alive.

The sight of his fallen companion had diverted the soldier's aim. In the next instant, in the soldier's pause to assess what obviously was an advantage, Ray bolted to his feet and lunged savagely at the man, slamming him to the ground and knocking his weapon from his grip.

The soldier recovered quickly; a Bowie knife was suddenly in his hand. Grasping the wrist of his attacker, Ray brought his knee up into his groin. The soldier grunted and groaned but never lost the grip on

223

his knife. Before he could duck and avoid it, the blade swept across Ray's face, laying it open from below the right eye to the top lip.

Blood gushed into Ray's eyes as he spun sideways to avert a second slash but it sliced through his snow jacket and cut a gash in his side. The trooper was built like a door. Ray would have to rely on speed and agility in this battle of blades but his wounds were slowing him down.

Clutching his knife in the classic position, he jabbed upward with all his strength, hoping to plunge the blade into the attacker's groin but the thrust was deflected. Again, Ray stabbed upward but the big man pitched to the side and the knife only caught the threads of his snowsuit.

Ray's hands were slippery with blood; the same vital fluid poured from his face and shoulder. He was losing strength, the knife now alien in his weakening grip. Turning his head, he saw the trooper leap, too, and his knife sliced down through Ray's collarbone on its way to his heart.

Eiker broke through the trees in time to see Ray receive the mortal wound. The soldier turned, his knife dripping with blood and in that instant Eiker fired from the hip. The trooper took the shots full in the face and his head disintegrated.

Slowly crossing the clearing, Eiker stopped and looked down at his dead companion. Then he fell to one knee and removed the knife from Ray's bloody grip. "I'll keep this in memory of a warrior," he said softly.

Tucking the weapon into the inside of his jacket, he turned and walked back into the trees. Where in hell was that pitiful excuse for a man, Reinecke, and Vigo and the two BLM agents? This battle was not over.

Chapter 31

Roz Newton was suddenly in the room and in her hand was a silenced Sig Sauer automatic.

True to her J.Lo image, Roz wore a tight tee and a denim miniskirt under her long tan leather coat, exaggerating her leggy appearance. Her blond hair was long, straight and wispy. She nodded at Webster.

"I was *afraid* I'd made a mistake when I answered Dr. Maxwell's last question. I knew by her response that I'd given myself away and that you were probably here." She kicked the door shut with her heel. "It's convenient, actually, you both in the same room."

Gesturing for them to move to the bed, she saw a *noir* paperback novel on Maxwell's nightstand and referenced its title. "You two are about to take the big sleep."

"But *why*, Roz?" Webster asked gently, adopting the tone of a negotiator. "Why do you want to kill us? How are you mixed up in all of this—?"

"I'm not *mixed up*!" she interjected defensively, mistaking Webster's remark.

Her response, however, was telling. Maxwell guessed that here was a young woman whose defense mechanism was a hair trigger; she hoped that her firing finger was not.

Maxwell's own finger was steady on the trigger of the Walther beneath the towel draped over her right arm.

Roz smiled then laughed, a full-throated laugh delivered through very white teeth and cherry red lips. It crossed Maxwell's mind that perhaps Roz was mad.

"I'm in this for the thrills, Wes," Roz said, "and the money and the experience." Her eyes flickered to the automatic in her hand. "This is something I've always wanted to do.

"My mother shot my father when I was six…" It was as if she was talking to herself. "I've played it over and over in my mind." She paused and seemed to reach to the bottom drawer of her madness. "It's time for an empirical experience."

"Look, Roz," Webster said, "if it's a question of money—I know BLM doesn't pay you much—I'll see what I can..."

Her shrill, crazed laugh stopped him. "I'm getting more money for these few minutes than BLM could pay me in a lifetime." She levelled the gun and her finger began to pressure the trigger.

Maxwell seemed to watch rather than experience what happened next, as if viewing an out-of-body experience. The Walther discharged twice. Maxwell was less than three feet from her would-be killer when the shots sounded.

Jolted back, Roz staggered and fell—a stunned expression on her face. Possibly her last vision was the blackened holes in the fluffy, white bath towel draped over Maxwell's arm.

Then there was a thunderous roar in Maxwell's ears, like dark, enormous wings flapping inside her head. She couldn't think. She couldn't speak. She couldn't breathe. She sank to the bed and cried uncontrollably.

Once Webster had recovered from shock and wrestled back the

sensation to vomit, he sat down beside her and waited while she blurted out her feelings between giant gulps of breath and tears.

He hugged her close, "It's okay, Doc."

Maxwell thought of her father and how he must have felt after killing her best friend's father. She had never fully considered her father's point of view in that incident. How lonely he must have been; how desolate her estrangement from him must have made him...and had made her. New tears—swallowed instead of shed when she was seventeen—spilled from her eyes.

The sound of feet pounding along the corridor announced the arrival of security personnel and others who heard the shots. Webster reached out with one hand and flipped the wall switch. The illumination reflected in the hanging mirror beside them heightened the red-gold bed covering beneath them.

In Reno, Samuel Ryland received the news that the mine near Bowman Lake had suffered numerous internal explosions. Special Forces under the command of Colonel Alvin Cromwell also had sustained heavy losses, both at the mine and in battles in the surrounding forest. Within thirty minutes, Ryland arrived at the mine via NSA helicopter and was shown into Cromwell's makeshift office at the old lodge.

"Colonel Cromwell, do you think there's anything left underground to find...to help us piece together what in hell was down there that the mine's personnel were ready to die for?"

Cromwell shook his head. "No, what wasn't destroyed in the initial explosions is burned or buried under tons of rock and rubble. It's like Ground Zero down there."

An FBI representative who had arrived minutes ago with his entourage asked, "Colonel, we had reports that Senator Albert

Reinecke and Carson City Police Chief Bud Vigo were in the vicinity of the mine. Do you have any information as to their whereabouts?"

Cromwell shook his head. "Negative at this time."

"What about FBI Special Agent Joseph Falk and BLM's Susan Koski…do you have *any* idea as to the condition of the civilians or those agents?"

"After the explosions, I dispatched a six-man search team that is still somewhere in the field. At last report, the team had encountered heavy small-arms' fire, apparently from some of those civilians you're all so worried about." He ran a finger across his tight upper lip. "I have commenced an air search in the area and more troops are on their way there."

A knock on the office door stopped further conversation as one of Cromwell's men appeared, snapping a crisp salute. "Report from one of the tracking and reconnaissance copters, sir. Three bodies sighted in a heavily wooded area less than 1.6 kilometers from Bowman Lake. T&R are awaiting reinforcements before putting down, sir."

Cromwell sighed. "Soldier, be sure you get this order loud and clear. I want whoever is left in those woods taken alive. We don't know the good guys from the bad in that bunch and I need some answers. I want them all taken alive."

Ryland was on board the next search helicopter. Seated beside the Army pilot, his senses seemed extraordinarily enhanced. He keenly felt the movement of air as it mapped its path around the aircraft. He ran a hand across his bronze forehead and through his thick ebony hair. His eyes, dark gray and solemn as an owl's, scanned the woods of worry below. Where were Falk and Koski? Would he find them before one of Cromwell's other units did? "I want them taken alive," the Colonel had said.

I want them dead, the voice in Ryland's head whispered.

Memories, like strange wind whistling down the long tunnel of time, filled him and an old love of happy predestination burned more brightly than ever in his heart. Since he was a boy in New England he had listened wide-eyed at his grandfather's knee to tales of his great-grandfather. He was an Algonquin chief.

Hearing tales of other elders of the tribe, he took seriously the sobriquet with which his father dubbed him: *Mukuamp.*

In the Algonquian language of the early Massachusetts Indian tribes, the word meant "big man" or "chief." Although he remained Mukuamp in his heart, he legally became Samuel Ryland at age eighteen. The name was unimportant and a convenience he had fingered from the Yellow Pages.

When he attended college in Oklahoma, his introduction to the Plains Indians deepened his kinship with other tribes and pride in his forebears. Some of them still cursed the white man and harbored vengeance in their hearts. They strengthened his resolve to become a twenty-first century leader.

A law degree from Harvard furthered the opportunity for him to envision his long-term goal. From the days the United States Cavalry drove the buffalo, the Comanches, Kiowas, Crows and other tribes from Oklahoma's Southern Plains, Mukuamp's people—for now *all* Native Americans were Mukuamp's people—had been forced to succumb to the realization that their glory days were over. Worse, their culture had lost its ability to evolve.

For years, Mukuamp had schemed and plotted that the greatest moment in their history was yet to be; that the journey to the second golden age of the Native American awaited only the broad eagle's vision and careful silent planning of a truly big man.

For hundreds of years, it seemed beyond his people's reach. Now it would come to pass. It required the singular vision and leadership of a man who was a chief in the bravest, most tenacious and highborn sense of the word.

His grandfather and great-grandfather's words lived only in memory. Mukuamp remembered their curse of the white invaders. He retained the image of a proud past that would come again. Not as it once was, not in the form of fierce, painted, breech-clothed hunter-warriors but as suited, economically, politically, legally and technologically savvy leaders under the administration of a man who would give new meaning to the term *Commander-in-Chief.*

This was not an overreaching statement of Mukuamp's aims. Certainly, in the newly configured world he envisioned, his would be a more powerful position than any *president* ever enjoyed.

It would take time, more time now since the mine complex was lost and the human scaffolding he had carefully constructed with Reinecke, Lovesy, Vigo and the others was deconstructed. As long as his own identity remained protected, however, he could begin again. One did not tear wine from the vine; the rebirth of a nation required ripening.

Chapter 32

The topography was erratic as the three skiers neared the lake; in one moment glacially flat, in the next a hill heaved before them. On the lake, slate gray waves broke into small angry whitecaps and fingers of thin ice crept out from the shore.

Falk, with Koski ahead and Vigo behind him, bent deeply for more thrust and speed, the increasing wind driving him on and stinging his face. For several minutes he was wholly absorbed in the pure act of sailing over the snow, lost in the peaceful surroundings.

Then something impelled him to look back. He caught a glimpse of Vigo disappearing at a confluence of slopes, heading toward the eastern shore.

"Koski!" Falk shouted. When she did not respond, he repeated, "*Koski*," shouting over the wind. This time she heard and circled back.

"Where's—" she started and stopped.

"That's right…he said he's got a cabin up here somewhere." Falk was convinced that Vigo was connected to the lawyers' deaths and that he was at the mine to meet with his co-conspirators regarding some new offensive.

"We're going after him," he said.

"Why?"

"Vigo's dirty."

"No." It was a statement.

"Listen, what else explains the disappearance of the arrow in Carson City…the one Maxwell said was found in a tree and that she placed in the evidence cage? Moreover, Maxwell told me Vigo has access to a helicopter, a helicopter he guards carefully. It's the one that I'm convinced accidentally made the marks on the roof where Sharpe was killed." He paused. "He may even be The Fox."

"Bud Vigo, The Fox?"

"I'll explain later. Let's go."

Following the firefight, Eiker quickly scoured the area and found a terrified Reinecke huddled at the base of a tree, banked in snow.

"Looks like we're all that's left," Eiker said, urging Reinecke through the trees. "I'm saving your arse, senator. I could easily leave you here and let the Army shoot you." He gave the older man an extra shove. "We're due to be picked up by a chopper at four p.m. and I have no intention of missing that flight. So, if you want to stay alive, hustle, old chap."

They hadn't gone far when Eiker heard a low-flying helicopter approaching. He shoved Reinecke toward a rock outcropping and they huddled beneath huge overhanging boulders, not daring to move. Finally, Eiker raised his head cautiously.

"That Army pilot is searching for signs of life, concentrating on the ski tracks we saw."

Once the aircraft passed from view, he shoved Reinecke forward. The senator, who was exhausted and breathing erratically, stumbled and Eiker had to drag him up from his knees. Eiker cursed silently. He must keep this bastard alive long enough to get the last installment on his wages for this bloody gig.

Believing he had lost Falk and Koski, Vigo discarded his skis and raced to his four-room cabin on the lakeshore. Once inside, he went directly to a wall phone and dialed a number. "I'm at my cabin. Pick me up mid-lake as soon as possible."

He hung up and hurried into the bedroom. He kicked aside a woollen rug and lifted several floorboards. He reached down and removed two oilskin packages. Unwrapping one, he uncovered a bolt-action shotgun, the Marlin Model 55 goose gun designed for killing migratory waterfowl at high altitudes. It was a rare but extremely lethal weapon. Vigo loaded the shotgun and scooped up four extra shells, grabbed the second package and hustled out of the cabin and down to the boathouse. Inside, he considered the two-seater Jet Ski he kept there, knowing it was fast.

He figured his chopper to be here in less than fifteen minutes. He had no wish to freeze before it arrived and sitting astride that bucking sport craft in this weather...he thought not. He opened the double wooden doors facing the lake, removed the canvas cover from the outboard motor of his fourteen-foot aluminum fishing boat, slipped the cumbersome package beneath the seat and yanked the outboard motor lanyard three times. The engine sprang to life. Cold wind stung his eyes and nostrils as he steered through the sheer film of ice and out into deeper water.

The original escape plan called for him to fly out of Carson City to a safe house up at Mammoth Lake. Now it had to be Bowman instead of Carson. He didn't like changing plans that increased the chances of fickle fate stepping in. Glancing back at the shore, a split second of curiosity as to what happened to the two agents flickered through his mind. Something told him they would show up.

Falk and Koski broke from the trees just as the sound of an outboard motor kicking over roared in the cold air.

"Shit!" Koski swore, seeing Vigo seated in the stern of his boat and moving out into the lake. "Where are Cromwell's choppers when we need them? They could easily get him from the air…"

"We've got to find a boat and go after him," Falk growled. In the time it took him to finish his sentence, she was gone.

In the boathouse, Falk stared at the sleek blue and white Jet Ski bobbing gently in the water, Koski astride its double banana seat.

"Koski, that's not a boat."

"But it sure as hell can catch that thing Vigo's puttering in."

He had only a second of indecision. "You're right." He grabbed her and pulled her from the seat, straddling it himself. "You stay. I'll go."

"Okay," she said and slid into the seat behind him.

He rolled his eyes and hit the starter. There was a shattering roar as the powerful engine came to life and the machine leapt forward and headed for the open water.

Soon they were a quarter of a mile out on the lake, a white plumed rooster tail gallantly arcing behind them. The openness of the lake conspired with the wind to whip the air from their lungs and Falk's hands tingled with the cold.

He moved his fingers to increase blood circulation. He had to be ready to react when the moment came. Ahead, he saw Vigo's boat, which had a discouraging head start. Notching the throttle wider, he hurled the sport craft across the freezing lake, the bow wave breaking beneath the shark-like nose with the distinct thudding and pounding beat of fiberglass on water.

All of a sudden, Koski was beating on his shoulder and shouting in his ear— "*Behind us! Vigo's chopper!*"

Falk snapped his gaze in the direction she pointed and saw the sheriff's helicopter skimming the surface less than a quarter of a mile behind them. "Hold on!" He yanked hard on the handlebars and the Jet Ski responded in time to allow an arrow to flash past and bury itself in the lake water. He was relieved to realize that this time there was no extra man in the aircraft and no laser-controlled beam to assist the arrow's flight. The odds still were not good. They were unarmed against an arrow-spitting helicopter.

A second arrow flashed from the bird's underbelly, snaking toward them like a serpent's tongue. It embedded itself in the fiberglass hull of the Jet Ski less than an inch from Koski's thigh. Falk pulled to the right in a tight turn, dipping the starboard footrest underwater and causing the nose to lurch upward, nearly bringing the craft to a halt. Then, jamming the throttle wide open, he turned left and hurtled through his own wake.

Vigo was only yards in front of them now but the helicopter skewed into a tight turn and danced in place. Its blades were a wild wash of motion as a rope ladder was lowered toward Vigo's boat, which slowed slightly. He glanced back at the bucking Jet Ski and reached for his goose gun.

"Koski," Falk shouted, "get ready to take over. I'm going alongside. When I jump, pull away at once." She had no chance to reply before Falk powered alongside the fishing boat.

The dangling ladder momentarily diverted Vigo's attention. He was thrown off balance by the boat's rocking in the powerful prop wash from the aircraft's rotors. It was long enough for Falk to throw himself across the few feet separating them. He grabbed Vigo by the leg, the momentum of his leap knocking the police chief down in the boat. Koski pulled away and then throttled down almost to a stop.

Falk took a glancing blow to the right cheek from the barrel of the Marlin 55. He felt himself rock back against the side of the boat, blood running from a gash in his face. Vigo tried to steady the gun to aim, but Falk lashed his right foot out, delivering a scissor kick that caught Vigo's groin. He grabbed himself and screamed in pain.

The helicopter dropped lower; the ladder swung inches in front of Vigo's face. Releasing the gun and grabbing wildly at the rungs, his fingers connected and the pilot immediately started to climb.

Falk scrambled toward the goose gun and scooped it from the floor, his fingers numb with cold, fumbling with the unfamiliar mechanism. The chopper was gaining altitude fast and Vigo, uttering a sound between a rattle and a wheeze, clutched the ladder for dear life, his legs flailing as he desperately tried to ascend by getting a foothold on one of the slippery rungs.

The unsteady boat on the wind-whipped lake was not an ideal platform from which to fire but Falk spread his legs for balance and took careful aim at the helicopter's engine compartment. Steadying the 36-inch, full-choke barrel of the Marlin, he fired. Quickly working the bolt and sliding the second round into the chamber, he took a fast aim and pulled the trigger. The shot hit the engine. Grabbing extra shells from the floor, he got off one more shot before losing his balance and nearly toppling into the lake.

Vigo grimly hung onto the ladder as flames billowed from beneath the engine cowling, licking downward, driven by the thrust of the down draft from the aircraft's blades. The yellow flames licked at Vigo's hands as he twisted from side to side in an effort to escape the searing heat. Falk righted himself and took careful aim at the man dangling from the chopper, sighting in on his neck. Nevertheless, this kill was not to be his.

When flames suddenly met fuel, Vigo's helicopter exploded into a fireball, erupting with a vast thunderclap of searing heat felt by Falk and Koski two hundred feet below. Killed instantly by exploding debris, Vigo dropped, his fingers clutching scraps of the ladder as he fell, legs flapping wildly in space.

The shattered remains of the copter hung in midair for a few seconds before it dropped, slamming into the lake. It boiled and bubbled on the surface then sank from sight, trailing steam and smoke and leaving only an oil slick and jetsam in its wake.

Koski eased the Jet Ski alongside the aluminum boat. "Your face...you're bleeding!"

Falk swiped at the blood. "Superficial, head to shore." He moved to the rear seat of the fishing boat and pulled the outboard to life. It was on the way back to the boathouse that he noticed an oilskin package jutting from beneath one of the seats.

Back inside the boathouse, Falk secured the open craft, reached under the seat and removed the oilskin covering from the second package, revealing a bow, four laser-guided arrows and a handheld laser guidance system.

"Wow," Koski gasped, "the whole enchilada."

Falk had the laser system working within minutes, aiming the red dot on the inside wall of the boathouse. "Aim the dot at the target... and the arrow hones in on the dot," he purred. "Fantastic weapon but it takes two to tango with this."

"Nothing wrong with that, Joe." She could not remember when she began to call him by his first name; it just happened.

Falk refolded the covering over the equipment and glanced around the interior. "We'll just leave it in here for the time being." He placed the bundle on a shelf near the door and they hurried toward the cabin.

As he walked, Falk pondered what he knew. Only one piece of the puzzle remained and it would not be as simple as fitting the last piece of a jigsaw into a remaining void.

Eiker and Reinecke kept a screen of trees between them and Vigo's cabin as they approached the boathouse.

"Don't make a sound," Eiker hissed. He and the senator had seen the chopper go down in flames, watched the man and woman return the Jet Ski and fishing boat to the boathouse and enter the cabin. "We'll take the fishing boat." Eiker held the side of the boat as Reinecke gingerly stepped in. "Here." He handed two paddles to Reinecke. "We'll paddle out a way before starting the outboard. Might as well have as much of a head start as possible."

Moving to the Jet Ski, he pulled the key from the ignition and dropped it into the lake. Snapping open the engine compartment, he reached in and ripped out a handful of electrical wiring, totally dismantling the ignition system. He returned to the boat and climbed in, released the lines, took one of the paddles and pushed out into the lake.

"Paddle," he ordered but soon took over himself, seeing Reinecke's strength failing. When he judged that they were far enough from the cabin, he pulled the outboard to life and steered eastward, slowly increasing speed.

Chapter 33

"You must be exhausted," Falk said to Koski, once he checked out the cabin. "I'll make a call and get us out of here." The cabin was small and comfortably furnished in a style somewhere between shabby chic and early New England. The living room had an old pot-belly stove.

Falk went to the antique wall phone but hesitated. "Damn! I'm not sure who we can trust at BLM...or the Bureau for that matter. I'll try Ryland." He dug into his shirt pocket and extracted a folded piece of paper. Lovesy had given them three numbers for Ryland. Falk chose the cell number, waiting as the old rotary dial slowly returned after each digit.

Koski shivered noticeably, eyeing the stove. "I think I'll fire up this relic." She took newspaper and kindling from a large version of a Vermont maple sugar bucket. She stuffed them into the stove, struck a wooden match and touched the flame to the edge of the paper. She added the kindling, adjusted the damper on the stovepipe and rubbed her palms together as if to hurry the heat.

Ryland answered on the first ring.

"Agent Koski and I are in a cabin on the east shore of Bowman Lake," Falk said after identifying himself. "The cabin's owned by Chief Bud Vigo of the Carson City—"

"Yes, I know of it," Ryland interrupted. "I'm in an Army chopper nearby."

"Good. Look, I'm not sure who we can trust at BLM Reno anymore or who I should contact at the Bureau—"

"No one," Ryland quickly put in over the static on the line. "I'll take care of all calls. Stay where you are. We'll be there in a few minutes."

After he hung up, Falk turned to Koski, who was placing a log on the fire. "Ryland's on his way. He'll notify the Bureau."

"What'll we do next?" She turned her back to the stove. "Is this case closed?"

"Not by a long shot." He paced the floor, frowning darkly. "I've worked out a rough what and why scenario about the case but I don't have a "who" yet."

"But I thought Vigo was The Fox and if—"

He stopped at the window and looked out at the lake. "I've failed. The mastermind is still out there."

"No!" When he turned, she shot him a chastising glance and added an aside. "Friends don't let friends go on guilt trips." She slowly twirled back to the stove, staring at the fire through the door's tempered glass window. "Maybe Webster, Maxwell and Spade have come up with something." She sighed. "I wonder about them." Turning again, she looked at him. "I wonder about *us, too*."

He sank into a large, low swivel rocker with tan and white plaid upholstery and honey-toned wood. The cabin was warming up and he noticed a blush on Koski's cheeks. "*What* do you wonder?" he asked.

She casually moved a few steps closer to the rocker. "After all the excitement of this assignment, what could ever possibly get our adrenaline flowing again?"

Looking at her, he wondered if his eyes gave away the longing in his soul. He held out his hand. "*I'll* get your adrenaline flowing."

She took his hand then slipped onto his lap and slid her arms around his neck. He thought about how she handled herself in the crises they had been through. "I like the way you get angry instead of being afraid," he said softly into her ear.

She nuzzled her nose against his neck "I like the way you get afraid instead of being angry." She immediately pulled back and faced him. "Only *kidding*!"

He kissed her, a sweet, lingering kiss at first but her lips parted beneath his own and a rush of warmth went through his body…Then he heard the thwoping of rotors. "Ryland," he said with a sigh as he gently pulled away.

"Damn!" Koski whispered, still holding his eyes. They rose and as they started for the door she said, "I'd like a rain check on whatever was about to happen back there."

"Mmmm…" he purred and touched her hand. "You got it."

When they opened the door, the helicopter had already put down in the only open space in the area beyond a dense palisade of birches. Ryland had deplaned and approached the cabin, offering his hand. "Samuel Ryland."

Koski's greeting was half-hearted. She shook his hand.

Falk nodded. "Thanks for coming for us," he said as he turned back into the room. "I'll bank that fire and we'll be with you in a sec."

Ryland walked past them into the cabin, stomping snow from his boots. "Oh, no rush."

Koski cried, "The chopper— It's leaving!"

The cabin door was still open and Falk looked out just as the aircraft lifted off. "What—" he began but Ryland waved away their concerns.

"Not to worry. He was low on fuel when I got your call. I told him I'd wait here with you while he refueled. He'll be back within the hour."

Falk closed the door. "That the only bird available?"

"Apparently so," Ryland said as he lowered into a straight-back chair. "This man isn't going to be easy to track. He's a well-trained pro."

Koski sank into the swivel rocker and added, "And a cold-blooded killer."

It was Ryland's turn to nod. "You have the United States Army to thank for giving you the opportunity to escape from that English mercenary."

"You know about him?" Falk asked.

Ryland shrugged. "It depends on what you mean by 'know about.'"

"You said 'English mercenary.' I assumed that if you knew he was English and a mercenary you'd had some contact with him."

"No, no." He stretched, as if feeling the warmth of the fire. "I must have picked that up in a briefing."

Koski swiveled slightly toward Ryland. "Have you received any word on Webster, Maxwell and Spade?"

"I inquired about them several hours ago. They're fine."

"Really!"

He smiled at her almost childlike curiosity. "Really," he replied. "Spade is at home and Webster and Maxwell are safe and recuperating in a secured environment. Webster's expected to recover totally from the concussion he sustained."

Under the flattering light of Koski's attention, he briefly outlined the incident of Lester Carter's death following his luncheon with Ryland and Maxwell at Harrah's and Maxwell's relocation to Top Gun.

As Ryland spoke, it occurred to Falk the extent to which this man had been there for Falk's team—and, in the process, privy to at least some of the entire team's movements.

"You've been a regular Johnny-on-the-spot for them," Falk said when Ryland paused.

"You might say that." His modesty was polished.

"And you, a man probably constantly in demand at NSA headquarters at Fort Meade…privy to top-level security information… on call to the president himself no doubt…" He paused, watching Ryland's face and then went on. "When I stop to think about it, it's amazing that Koski and I are fortunate to have the privilege of your… magnanimity." He lingered on that last word and felt Koski turn the lighthouse of her eyes in his direction.

Ryland got up and moved away from the stove, his heretofore perfectly maintained composure slipping slightly. "I'm not sure I understand your point, Falk."

When he had watched Ryland deplane and walk toward the cabin, it was obvious to Falk that the man was of Native American descent. Now he noticed how dark and slick his hair was. Falk recalled the old trapper he had shared a fish dinner with in the woods years ago and the description the trapper gave of the person he heard on the phone in the mine's parking lot.

That recollection spurred Falk on.

"Don't you see the irony of it, Ryland? A man highly placed in national security. A man so powerful that even the Nevada Mafia would probably kiss his ring. A man with access to instant transportation to hop around the country at will; in fact, a man in

charge of overseeing the investigation into the lawyers' deaths…
Should such a man turn out to be the very brains behind those
killings…well, you see where I'm going with this…"

Falk stood up, wanting the advantage of being on his feet.

Koski didn't move or speak.

Ryland compressed his lips then released and licked them. "I
don't like what you're insinuating, Falk."

"Oh, I'm not insinuating. To insinuate is to suggest indirectly. I
thought I was frankly laying out the foundation for a plan to ultimately
take over the United States from within."

A muscle rippled along Ryland's jaw and his dark gray eyes
flared.

"Take over?" Koski said almost inaudibly.

"Take over," Falk repeated firmly, "big time." Cocking his head
slightly, he continued to look directly into Ryland's eyes. He
remembered something Tom Stewart had said at their meeting in the
motel with the flickering neon sign.

It was Stewart's oblique reference to his and Cerberus' part in this
investigation. Cerberus' responsibility was to be "acutely aware of the
balance of domestic power and any possible shift in that power."
Stewart, therefore, must have known—or at least had a hunch—about
a grand plan although he had no idea at the time that it was *Ryland's*
plan.

"We don't want to be surprised by an economic earthquake,"
Stewart had said and added, "You may find it difficult to imagine a
full-scale Indian uprising in this country in the twenty-first century,
Joe, but I believe it's a distinct possibility."

Now Falk realized the phenomenal proportions of the earthquake
Stewart feared and Ryland had in mind.

"Let's see if I've got it right," Falk began. "I've been informed that there are approximately three million Native Americans in North America, hardly enough to take over a nation of better than 280 million. It's certainly not enough to take over in the traditional sense of that word or even in the sense that the events of September 11, 2001, envisioned."

He paused and turned his head but not his eyes to his partner. "I'm sure you've guessed, Koski, this new threat is not only about how many Native Americans there are and how many casinos they own but about the land on which those casinos are located. They're located on Indian reservations, of course; reservations that belong to the Indian nations. In addition, Indian nations are *sovereign* nations—technically, independent nations within the United States.

"Think about it, Koski. If, through vastly extended gambling and the dollars it creates, the tribes were to be *truly* unified—under a determined, powerful, intelligent and charismatic leader—they would be able to operate as the independent nations they are."

His head turned back to Ryland. "Abetted by lawyers of all races whose loyalties are moot so long as the financial remunerations are sufficient. These independent nations could make their own laws… mint their own money…organize and train their own militia…"

He paused to assess Ryland's reaction, which evidenced that Falk was indeed on the right track before he went on. "The United States as we know it may find itself surrounded by wealthy, independent Indian nations.

"Other state citizens couldn't even enter, say, without visas. These nations could trade with whomever they wished…import and export goods with foreign countries at their discretion, despite regulations and embargoes set up by our present government to the contrary. They will be able to generate their own gross national product into the billions." He glanced in Koski's direction. "You can see the disastrous ramifications."

Koski did not move, stunned by the chilling potential. "That would rip America apart," she whispered. "*Worse than* the situation created in the Balkans back in the 1990s. The federal government couldn't do anything about it."

"Nothing," Falk replied. "These nations could choose as allies various miscreant countries of the world that will leap at the opportunity to send their troops, requested by the tribes, to protect and serve their interests. Imagine Chinese, Iranian or Korean troops on our soil." He paused again, getting confirmation from Ryland's silent, smoldering look. "How am I doing, Ryland?"

Ryland's demeanor switched to a pretense of indignant consternation. "It's your theory, Falk."

"That's not the whole of it," Falk continued. "For years public records have proved that millions of dollars appropriated by the federal government for the tribes every year never trickled down to the reservations for which they were intended. Under this new federation, as more Native Americans come out of law schools and more money is available to them, suits will be brought against the federal government for unlawful disbursement of funds.

"I suspect that the class action suits would dwarf those brought against the tobacco companies and nearly bankrupt the government. What was left of the United States would be strangled in many ways. Lawyers working for the tribes have already taught them how to protect and sell their water rights to towns and cities who once took their water for granted. The American public doesn't even realize that the takeover has begun."

"But," Koski said, looking for a positive aspect, "these scenarios only make sense if the tribes were *empowered*, infused with the big bucks more casinos would generate. The campaign we've seen— killing the lawyers who are working *against* the tribes—would have the opposite effect and turn the public against the American Indians, resulting in *less* support for their gambling and the tribes in general."

"To say that demonstrates your gross ignorance of the weakened American psyche," Ryland growled. He suddenly seemed puffed with pride, willing to participate in spelling out the details of his plan. He was eager for his two companions to understand the grandeur of the strategy he continued to see as achievable and the tactics involved in that achievement. "Are you not aware that the liberalization of America begun in the '60s was completed in the late '90s and continues today, despite the surge of traditionalism that was sparked after September 11? It is a common joke in other countries that when an American sees a badly beaten man lying in the gutter, he doesn't say, 'We need to find the person who did this and punish him.' They say, 'We need to find the person who did this; *that* person needs help.'

"This perverse form of reverse psychology will work mightily for my people. At the conclusion of this campaign, when it is proven that Native Americans were not to blame, when they are shown as the innocent victims of hate crimes planned to make them look bad, public empathy for them will rise to new heights...a bump in the polls, so to speak. New laws will be put into place to protect their civil rights. My people will enjoy more freedom than ever before."

"*My people,*" Koski said softly as she got up and walked to Falk's side. "Of course..."

"Meet Mukuwamp, Koski," Falk said. "Would-be sachem of the Algonquin Indian tribe, owner of the Colonial Mine, a.k.a. The Fox."

Ryland scoffed. "The Fox, a silly sobriquet my associates hung on me." His dark gray eyes narrowed. "How did you uncover my tribal name?"

"ESP," Falk replied. "I also have friends in Covert Transmissions. I was born in Connecticut; we had our share of Algonquin Indians. I went to school with one, in fact, and remembered that Mukuwamp means "Chief.""

Ryland straightened and his head rose defiantly, his vision momentarily lost in the space between himself and the ceiling. "The Sovereign Commonwealth of Native Americans," he pronounced. Lowering his gaze to Falk, he continued to interpret his vision. "One nation, under Mukuwamp, free to establish its own justice, ensure its own domestic tranquillity, provide for its own common defense…with liberty and justice for all Native Americans."

A sliver of ice ran down Falk's spine. Suddenly he thought about the Army chopper that had brought Ryland and wondered if it would return. He had no ready weapon. There was a chance that Ryland didn't have one either. He wanted to keep him talking until someone arrived who did.

"So, it's all pretty clear now, right, Koski?" Falk said. When she was profoundly silent, he went on. "Abraham Lincoln's words were to be prophetic, 'If America ever falls it will be from within.' You had to love the prospect, Ryland. You would ultimately take the country back from those who stole it from you."

Falk sighed and shook his head. "Not only was my team a farce, meant to evidence that something was being done, even as we were being prevented from doing it, but also this whole thing about making the Indians seem guilty was a smoke screen to eventually *help* them, to lure already perverse public opinion to your will."

"We're professionals, Falk," Ryland said matter-of-factly. "We all know that now and then someone has to sacrifice. Like in baseball, not everyone is given the signal to hit a home run; sometimes somebody has to bunt."

"And the weekend militia members at the mine also were just pawns in your game. They never dreamed their maneuvers meant anything, didn't know that you meant to eventually build them up into a true fighting force. Their vision probably didn't go beyond the equation that more casinos equal more money equals more rights. They're not farsighted enough to envision their new wealth being used to reconfigure the entire United States of America."

"Few of my people are farsighted enough," Ryland scoffed. "In fact, I expect my plan will meet with passionate resistance among all the tribes but no matter. They'll come around once I make them aware of the big, attainable picture."

Falk shook his head. "Getting the Nevada gaming people involved was good. They'd be more than happy to make the Indians and the prospect of more of their gambling establishments look threatening. However, even they didn't grasp the whole concept, did they? Their limited sights were probably set on keeping Nevada's coffers full. You alone were the brain trust, pumping out individual components, never disclosing to one exactly what the other's part or the final outcome would be."

Ryland seemed comfortable now—too comfortable—as if he had a trump card and could afford to reveal more details of his scheme. "Except for Villachi," he said. "He knew that nothing can stop the expansion of Indian gambling all over the country so he wisely decided to opt for a piece of the action."

Falk rasped, "And Reinecke?"

"The worst kind of thief, who sees more money for the tribes only as more money and power for himself."

"Bud Vigo's part was to do the actual killing," Koski interjected, "with arrows projected from his helicopter." Her husky voice grew scratchy in extreme anger. "You're nothing more than another terrorist."

Ryland snorted. "Yes, well, Vigo was the perfect grass—a man with one foot in the police department and the other in the underworld. Useful but in terms of evolution, I placed Vigo one step behind orangutans." His twisted smile faded but no readable emotion took its place. "Speaking of killing, I understand from Cromwell that you killed Vigo."

"Not really," Koski responded, imaging Vigo hanging from the rungs of the helicopter's ladder as the aircraft above him exploded. She added venomously, "Although we gladly would have."

"I assume you orchestrated Lovesy's death," Falk queried. "Why?"

"He was a weak link on the verge of falling apart." Ryland glanced around the room, suddenly impatient with further conversation.

"One more question," Falk said, a new rise in anger tightening his throat. "My Bureau Chief Lester Carter also was my friend and a man who I doubt ever harmed you. Why kill him?"

Ryland's vision flickered to the floor then back. His voice carried a tenor of regret.

"He was my friend, too, that hot-headed English son of a bitch!" He looked away, shaking his head. "I called the meeting at the mine for the express purpose of discussing how best to terminate his services."

"Eiker," Falk said with vehemence, "the Limey gun for hire. But *why* did he kill Carter?"

"As we saw," Koski put in, referencing the unarmed soldier at the mine entrance on the hillside, "that bastard doesn't need a reason to kill people."

"He and Carter had a history," Ryland offered. "Some time around the attacks of 9/11 Carter apparently thwarted some mischief Eiker had planned for Hoover Dam. Apparently, Eiker just decided it was payback time."

"It figures," Falk growled.

This brief moment of near camaraderie, in which all three individuals knew a common enemy, caused Falk to momentarily drop his mental guardedness. That he had no ready weapon did not mean he had no defense against one should it be produced; heightened mental alertness might help him spontaneously devise an effective strategy. Ryland's hand shot into his jacket and came out with a .38 caliber, blue-steel, snub-nosed Smith and Wesson.

Falk nodded regrettably. "I should have figured you for a gun." His hand slowly reached out and tucked Koski behind him. "But not a woman's gun," he finished.

Ryland was unfazed by what was obviously meant to be a denigrating remark. "It'll serve the purpose."

"Don't be a fool, Ryland. The Army chopper will be back any minute."

"By the time it is, you'll both be in the past tense." He moved toward the door, his back to it. "Eiker—pain in the ass though he is—can be handy. Even as we speak he's directing our pick-up aircraft here."

"But you said the Army chopper would be back," Koski insisted, stepping from behind Falk, her cheeks scarlet with anger.

"I lied." A subtle, almost playful grin rippled across his lips. "I needed to be sure Eiker's copter could pick me up without being challenged so I sent the pilot away."

"Well," Falk said with acerbity, "at least your plan for the great Sovereign Commonwealth of Native Americans has suffered a fatal blow. Too many of the dominoes have fallen and there are still people like Reinecke and others who, to save their own asses, will bring you down."

"No, this has only been a temporary setback. Even if all the present plans were to be exposed and abandoned—which is highly unlikely—I have here the only two people who could and would expose me. If I were to be eliminated, young warriors who are now making their way through law schools will one day take up the standard. They will see that my labor of creating a true Indian nation comes to fruition." He waved his .38 toward the door, "Hands on your heads, outside."

Falk's mind raced as they walked out the door and toward the boathouse. Maybe when he and Koski didn't return with the pilot, Cromwell would figure something was wrong and send another aircraft. Maybe one of the choppers out searching for Eiker and Reinecke would come this way. Maybe—what was he thinking? He knew better than to hang his hopes on maybes.

Eiker spotted the small, fast-moving Bell 205 skimming the lake's surface. His recovery team was running right on schedule. He headed the fishing boat into shore and up onto a narrow beach, jumped out and shouted for Reinecke to follow. The helicopter sank earthward, raising a squall of snow. Eiker bolted for it then stopped. Reinecke barely moved. He gasped for breath and clutched his chest as he stumbled toward the aircraft.

Eiker cursed and grabbed him, pulling him aboard with the help of the co-pilot. As the Bell rocked and ascended on a bearing toward Vigo's cabin, the senator slumped to the floor and leaned back against the fuselage.

"This guy we're picking up had better be ready," the pilot shouted over his shoulder. "We've got another storm *and* the Army to consider."

Scanning the sky for any sign of pursuit aircraft, Eiker sighed and leaned back; all clear. His contract was almost fulfilled. He'd be glad to put this assignment behind him. Glancing across at Reinecke, he saw the senator's head slump on his chest; his lips were flabby, agape and tinged in blue. Eiker knew the signs. The exertion had been too much for a man accustomed to a soft lifestyle. Could Eiker resuscitate him if his heart gave out?

That was too much bloody bother. The Brit champed furiously on his gum. Would he collect his final payment if he didn't have this trophy? Why not? He had performed well. Without the last installment due him, he had enough to retire nicely but he wanted it. He could insist that the situation was beyond his control, that the senator died of natural causes, which would not be altogether false. He decided to risk it.

"Open up," he ordered the co-pilot. Reaching under Reinecke's arms, Eiker dragged him to the door as the other man, mechanically following orders, unlocked and opened it. A blast of freezing air took his breath away.

"Look at it this way," Eiker said to Reinecke's ashen face, whose eyes were like half dollars now, facing two deaths, "I'm saving your family the expense of hiring a school of lawyers to defend you." He shoved the limp but resisting body out, watched it quiver downward and thump into the center of the lake. He yanked the door shut.

Chapter 34

"Open the door," Ryland commanded. Falk slowly pulled the boathouse door open and waited. Ryland nodded, "Inside, you, too, Agent Koski."

Once inside the boathouse, Falk saw that the fishing boat was gone and the Jet Ski's cowling was open, exposing frayed remains of ripped out wiring.

"Characteristically thorough," Ryland said, "that's Eiker's style. He wanted to be sure he didn't have a tail when he went to meet the copter at the rendezvous point."

As he trained the revolver on them with his right hand, he smashed the left side of his fist against an ordinary looking wallboard. A spring door snapped open to reveal a slender, vertical cabinet in the wall. Falk's sense of frustration notched up when he saw Ryland extract an AK-47 from its groove in the cabinet, checking to confirm it was loaded.

"I've made use of Vigo's little vacation spot in the past, unbeknownst to him, of course." He took two extra magazines from the cabinet and stuffed them in his jacket pockets. "My absentee host was equally unaware of certain precautions I took..." He paused and raised his eyebrows at Falk. "Why so surprised? I'm an NSA agent." He slung the weapon across his shoulder. "Face the lake, Falk. Keep your hands on your head."

Falk looked down at the icy water a couple of feet below the inside dock and felt the irony of sweat in the stubble of hair on his upper lip.

"Kneel," Ryland barked.

Falk slowly eased to his knees, aware that Ryland was watching him closely. Good, it might allow his attentiveness to Koski to waver, in which case she might find an opening—

Then, as if reading Falk's mind, she did. A sudden lurch to the right, a duck and she was a blur as she turned and slammed a sweep kick that dislodged Ryland's right kneecap with the crunch only distressed bone can produce.

Ryland wailed in pain and went down on his left knee. He had the strength and presence of mind, however, to retain his hold on both weapons.

Reacting instinctively, hoping to catch the man off balance before he could fire, Falk lunged forward, ramming a shoulder into him with sufficient force to knock him back toward the door. Ryland fired the gun as it slipped from his hand and fell into the lake, the bullet missing Koski by inches. In the split second in which Falk halted to assure himself that Koski wasn't hurt, Ryland scrambled from the boathouse, retaining the AK-47 that dangled from his arm.

Falk was at the door in a flash, prepared to pursue Ryland. Instead, he shouted, "*Down!*" and quickly back-pedalled, slamming the door shut and flinging his body sideways to avoid a succession of shattering blasts that signaled Ryland had recovered control of his Kalashnikov.

Chunks of wood blew inward as the door was riddled with bullets. Falk rolled back toward the prone Koski, bullets seeming to sense him, to etch his shape as they raked the building. His eyes desperately swept the interior for cover but there was none. "*Over the edge*," he shouted and they both dropped into the freezing lake water, clutching the dock, as Ryland continued to blast the boathouse. Bullets ricocheted off metal tackle boxes, cans and bottles, exploding shelves and thudding into the far wall.

"He'll run out of ammo soon," Koski said through chattering teeth.

"Not soon enough. He took two extra magazines, remember."

"Shit!" They were silent for several seconds. Finally Koski whispered, "He stopped."

"Could be reloading, I'm going to try to see where he is. Stay put." Pulling up, he raised his head over the edge of the dock and took a fast look around. "Jesus! The walls look like Swiss cheese."

"You can't go up there," Koski warned. "He'll see you through the bullet holes."

"Chance I'll have to take." He pulled his body over the edge of the dock and, propelling himself on his elbows, slithered toward the door, his body leaving a wet trail across the floor. The silence reinforced his courage. "I'm going to open the door just a crack," he whispered. "Remember, you stay there."

"Okay but I'm about to freeze to death."

Raising his body to a crouch, Falk moved to the right of the door and slowly eased the battered exit open an inch and then two.

Nothing. No violent retort followed his tentative movements. He thought how a cowboy from the Old West would have removed his hat and slid it into the open space to draw any potential fire and pinpoint his enemy's location.

Falk didn't have a hat but he had gloves and an old broom stood in the corner behind him. He stuck a glove on the broomstick and used it to force the door open several more inches, pulling his body back to the wall. Still no response.

He glanced around the interior once more, searching for anything he could use as a weapon. His vision fell on a shelf and the oilskin package he had found in the boat and placed there earlier. At the time, he wasn't sure why he felt compelled to hide it there; some instinct he didn't understand but for which he now was grateful. He seized on it as his next strategy.

Turning to call to Koski, he discovered she was already there, drenched and shivering with the cold, crawling toward him. "I can't see him," Falk said, "but I have an idea." He unwrapped the bow, arrow and laser equipment and tested the laser, shining the red dot on the back of the Jet Ski for a second before snapping it off.

There was no way he could do this on his own. It would take the two of them to pull it off. Koski was sodden and cold. Was she up to it? In that second of doubt, his mind instantaneously rewound through the many occasions in the past few days when she outperformed any agent he had ever known, and he put uncertainty away forever.

"We're going hunting," he said. "Since you were on the archery team, you take the bow and a couple of arrows. I'll handle the laser. Remember, you don't have to hit the target by careful aim. Shooting in the general direction will do as long as I place the laser beam on the target. We'll have to be quick. The element of surprise is all we've got against the AK-47."

She nodded. "First we have to find the bastard."

Suddenly Falk put a finger to his lips and pointed upward. Her eyes flickered to the roof and she listened intently. There was the unmistakable sound of someone limping across the snow-covered wood shakes. "He's crossing the boathouse to the wide entrance facing the lake."

Falk whispered, "A flanking maneuver; he plans to surprise us from behind." He handed her the bow and two arrows. "If we hurry, we can get out." Easing the door open slightly, he took one quick look around. "There," he whispered, indicating a fir tree twenty yards away. "Go!"

Koski bolted through the snow with Falk at her heels. They dove into the snowdrift at the base of the fir. From this vantage point, Falk had a clear view of Ryland, who didn't see them as he hobbled across the roof, his attempt at furtiveness made almost comic by his lumbering gait.

"Notch up one of those babies, Koski," Falk said and she quickly strung an arrow and held the bow in readiness. Activating the laser device, Falk projected a red dot up the side of the boathouse, dancing it in Ryland's direction. Another second and he would have his mark in his sights.

Then Ryland slipped and fell. In one second he was a target, in the next, a flashing blur in a cloud of snow that dropped from sight on the opposite side of the building.

Falk snapped off the laser. "Son of a bitch!" Ryland may have broken a leg or been otherwise injured, or was he still able to play the most dangerous game?

"Koski, go back to the boathouse, opposite to where he fell. If he's not hurt and comes around the building, I'll make sure he sees me. When he does, I'll put the bead on him and you take him out."

Like Falk, Koski was tired and rightfully uneasy, considering the disparity of weapons between them but she nodded without question and took off.

259

The laser device was similar in shape to that of a light sporting rifle with a telescopic sight. Falk had little understanding of laser technology beyond knowing that most were battery-powered.

Amplified light created in the form of a beacon shot through a crystal to emit an intense, direct light beam. Falk didn't need to understand the device; only make it work. He waited until Koski took up her position, then he edged from behind the tree and eased toward the building, using what cover he could.

A burst of automatic gunfire abruptly splintered the branches above his head. Falk dove to the ground hard and rolled in the snow, a volley of bullets coming at him in a wide spray. Ryland had survived his fall and was alert enough to spot Falk before being seen—so much for the element of surprise.

When there was a pause in the gunfire, Falk started to inch his head around the tree trunk that sheltered him. Again, bullets splintered limbs and showered him with pine needles. He needed Ryland to show himself. Koski needed her target. He saw her, crouched beside the boathouse wall, opposite Ryland's position. Falk cursed silently. Pinned down this way, he couldn't simply step out and draw Ryland's fire; death would be the inevitable result of that.

His sodden snowsuit was crusted with ice. Immobility increased his sense of cold and threatened to numb his mind. He desperately sought an answer. At first, the drone of a helicopter in the distance did not register on a conscious level. When it did, Falk knew that *it* was his answer.

By the sound of its engine, he knew it wasn't Army but a smaller aircraft, the one meant for Ryland's rendezvous. Ryland would have to make a run for his transportation out of here. Falk eased his head slightly around the tree for another look and all hell broke loose.

A blizzard of bullets split the side of the tree inches above Falk's head, ripping free a splinter of wood eight inches long and sending it plunging deep into his left bicep. No sensation at all, he thought. Then numbness gave way to fiery, agonizing pain that pumped through his entire arm and the laser device slipped to the ground.

Gritting his teeth, he reached across with his right hand and yanked the dagger-like shard from his flesh. Somewhere deep in his consciousness there was a sense of relief. The jagged, wooden missile had struck bone but didn't break it.

Sound signaled that the chopper was overhead. Ryland *must* show himself. Falk looked up. It was Eiker all right, the shock of red, unruly hair plainly visible in the plane, back to collect his superior. Ignoring his wound, Falk retrieved the laser with his good hand…

Ryland was running, half dragging the leg Koski had dropkicked earlier. He made for the clearing behind the stand of birches where the chopper was about to put down.

Knowing Koski waited with the bow and arrow, needing the guiding beam that only he could provide, Falk lifted the laser with his right arm, resting the barrel against the side of the tree for support. The laser dot bounced across the clearing, the red pinpoint seeking its mark. Exhausted and cold, Falk fought for the calm determination he needed. Concentrate…

Ryland was one hundred feet from the chopper. Then fifty… twenty…ten…

Steady the laser…Falk leaned against the tree, his motor skills not attending the command of the neurons that fired in his brain. *Concentrate! A deep breath…Zero in on the objective*…He could almost hear the fast arrhythmic beat of Ryland's heart as the man prepared to climb into the aircraft. *Steady…Hold the dot steady between his shoulder blades…Now shoot, Koski, shoot!*

The arrow flashed across the clearing like a heat-seeking missile, thudding squarely into its target. Its impact rocked Ryland, piercing his heart and taking portions of that organ with it on its journey through the front of his chest. He managed to stay on his feet for a few seconds before his knees folded and he dropped to the ground. The Fox died bleeding out, like any other hunted animal.

Falk slumped against the tree but not before he glimpsed Eiker, saw the Englishman yank the chopper door shut and order the pilot out of the area.

"Damn!" Falk cursed. Eiker no longer had a dog in this fight; he simply wanted to get away. Falk had a score to settle with the mercenary that went beyond the cold-blooded murder of the young soldier back at the mine entrance and the two others he killed on the trail. A man like that, who killed with impunity, was the antithesis of the very essence of Falk's ideals.

The practice of killing for killing's sake bred weakness in humankind. Men like Rodney Eiker had a part in killing humanity itself. Falk did not know why, how or when but he knew that his and Eiker's paths would cross again. Falk looked forward to that meeting.

Then Koski was kneeling beside him, assessing the extent of the wound in his arm.

"Oh, God," she said at sight of the flow of blood. Inverting one of her gloves, she pressed it hard against the jagged gash in his flesh and it stuck. "We need—" She quickly unzipped the front of her drenched snowsuit and reached inside toward her right side, beneath her sweater. Using her right hand to push her left elbow farther in, she reached the clasp she sought, then withdrew her hand and a black lace bra.

"This'll do," she said with an exaggerated swagger in her voice as she fashioned the attractive tourniquet around his arm, tucking the "C" cups in at the edges.

Falk looked from his extraordinary Florence Nightingale to the darkening sky. No more search planes could fly over the isolated area this day.

He struggled to his feet and leaned against Koski, his attention caught by the sudden sound of a pack of whining engines. First there was movement beyond the trees. Koski's eyes followed his gaze as the growl grew louder. Then half a dozen snowmobiles burst forth from the woods, snarling in their direction.

Falk had no idea if these white-suited visitors were friend or foe but it didn't matter. He and Koski were through running for today. He took her hand as the lead machine slowed to a stop nearby. The man slid to his feet and removed his helmet.

"Colonel Cromwell!" Koski exclaimed.

Falk never imagined he would be happy to see the crusty old bastard again. "To what do we owe this pleasure, Colonel?"

Cromwell's lips turned up into the quirky grin Falk had witnessed earlier. "You two were like bees in my bonnet, so to speak," he said, and ran a finger across his upper lip. "I missed you."

Wincing at the sight of the wound in Falk's arm, he ordered one of his men to break out the first aid kit and brandy. "I was concerned when the chopper with Ryland came back without him or you. One of my men reported smoke from the cabin's chimney, which we were told was vacant." He nodded toward the snowmobiles. "We were losing the light so we had to resort to using these monsters—"

"Excuse me, sir," a young soldier returning from the clearing by the birches said. "It's Mr. Ryland, sir. He's dead."

Cromwell's forehead creased in several places. "What in hell happened, Falk?"

Falk shook his head. "It's a long story, Colonel." He wondered if Cromwell—or anyone—would believe Ryland's ominous plot when Falk relayed the details. If not, as Mukuwamp had said, another warrior would take up the banner…the threat was still out there.

He watched the soldiers lift Ryland's body and drape it over one of the mobile units. "You got him, Koski," he said, turning to her.

She shrugged and bobbed her head, as if to amiably take issue with his remark. "I got him…you got him…we got him…"

Glancing at the black lace tourniquet, which had been removed in favor of a more traditional one and displayed for all to see, Cromwell shrugged and said, "Whatever works."

Chapter 35

Two days later Koski drove to a dinner engagement at Alex Spade's home. Falk was seated beside her with his left arm in a sling. Approaching vehicles flashed past, light snow reflecting in the glare of their headlights.

Koski said with a sigh, "About the Tribes…what happens now?"

"The lawyers take over, reducing life to the vernacular of their trade. As Indian gambling continues to increase in California, lawyers on both sides will work together to ensure that California *and* Nevada continue to profit." He checked his watch and switched on the radio. "I nearly forgot…the president is supposed to be speaking to the states' governors and the nation."

"In a further development on the domestic front," the distinctive voice said, *"I'm happy to report that a home-grown terrorist plot to overtake the government of the state of Nevada by killing lawyers and creating economic chaos was thwarted this week."*

"Overtake the government of the state of *Nevada*!" Koski said, incredulous. "They're watering this down to a *local* problem!"

Falk gently shushed her as the president continued.

"To those Native Americans who believe that, as a race, they were unjustly targeted or accused in the attorneys' deaths, I state my regret. I want to reiterate what cannot be stressed enough: We are all

Americans, any American who persecutes or discriminates against another American based on race, religion, age or gender is committing a crime and they will be dealt with accordingly.

"Finally, I have appointed a blue-ribbon committee to thoroughly investigate the allegations that monies allocated to the Native American Trust Fund have been misappropriated."

Falk angrily switched off the radio. "They're not making it a *local* problem. They're not making it *anyone's* problem."

Koski seethed, "They're just sweeping it under the rug. I don't believe it."

"I suppose they figure there's no sense stirring up the Tribes who, by Ryland's own admission, didn't know about his plan. Left alone, they'll probably go along as they are for years. They're in the catbird seat and don't know it."

"What do you mean?"

"The individual members of the Tribes would probably be happy just running the new gaming establishments and raking in the big bucks. But if…when…another Ryland comes along and sees that army of fat cat casino owners sitting there, ready to be introduced to another grand plan for "economic chaos," who knows what will happen."

"The American public has the right to know about Ryland's plot," Koski insisted. "It was aimed at the heart of our republic. People should *know* that."

"The president probably thinks they can't take it and he's right. Since the War on Terrorism began they've heard nothing but bad economic news, along with anthrax, possible dirty bombs and other terrorist alerts. Maybe Americans have reached a saturation point where they just can't handle more bad news."

"That's the point at which we become even more vulnerable to enemy attack."

He smiled and flexed his left arm in its sling, attempting a more comfortable position. "Not exactly," he said pointedly, lightening the conversation. "There are always those of us who get pissed off instead of afraid. Right, Koski?"

Her solemn expression turned playful, too. "Right," she said graciously and signaled, veering into Spade's driveway.

Falk thought of Tom Stewart and Cerberus. Like a sort of early-warning system, their wakeful diligence would ensure that new threats to the country were swiftly recognized and dealt with. Were he to take the time to explore it, Falk would have to admit that one slightly disquieting aspect of Stewart's part in this nagged at him.

If Stewart initially saw the potential for the Commonwealth of Indian states that Ryland envisioned, and it seemed now that he must have, did he also feel that Falk and his team could be set up…perhaps killed? No, he was being absurd. In the future, he would revert to focusing only on the positive aspects of his revered organization.

The American president's image, viewed by direct satellite broadcast, faded from the flat-screen plasma television set in Eiker's suite at the Grosvenor Hotel in London. Eiker lounged back in a leather chair. He slowly swirled a glass of warm brandy, reached for the remote and lowered the volume, at the same time that the phone rang. He picked it up and heard a soft but firm American voice.

"My name is Tom Stewart. I understand you're a highly professional mercenary."

About the Author

A. G. Hayes studied television writing at UCLA. He has published short fiction, including *Cover Up, Not a Penny Pincher, Home, Payment in Full, Small Wonder* and *Guided through a Mine Field*, and written scripts for CBS TV and other television production companies. He lives in the Sierra Nevada Foothills and spends his time writing and traveling to nearly every part of the world. He has used personal experiences gained during service with the British intelligence in Eastern Europe and the Middle East to enrich the characters of his protagonist teams.

If you enjoyed *Who's Killing All the Lawyers?*, consider these other fine books from Savant Books and Publications:

A Whale's Tale by Daniel S. Janik
Tropic of California by R. Page Kaufman
The Village Curtain by Tony Tame
Dare to Love in Oz by William Maltese
The Interzone by Tatsuyuki Kobayashi
Today I Am a Man by Larry Rodness
The Bahrain Conspiracy by Bentley Gates
Called Home by Gloria Schumann
Kanaka Blues by Mike Farris
First Breath edited by Z. M. Oliver
Poor Rich by Jean Blasiar
The Jumper Chronicles by W. C. Peever
William Maltese's Flicker by William Maltese
My Unborn Child by Orest Stocco
Last Song of the Whales by Four Arrows
Perilous Panacea by Ronald Klueh
Falling but Fulfilled by Zachary M. Oliver
Mythical Voyage by Robin Ymer
Hello, Norma Jean by Sue Dolleris
Richer by Jean Blasiar
Manifest Intent by Mike Farris
Charlie No Face by David B. Seaburn
Number One Bestseller by Brian Morley
My Two Wives and Three Husbands by S. Stanley Gordon
In Dire Straits by Jim Currie
Wretched Land by Mila Komarnisky
Chan Kim by Ilan Herman

Soon to be Released:

Ammon's Horn by G. Amati
Wavelengths edited by Z. M. Oliver
In the Himalayan Nights by Anoop Chandola
Blood Money by Scott Mastro
Random Views of Asia from the Mid-Pacific by William Sharp
Almost Paradise by Laurie Hanan

http://www.savantbooksandpublications.com

www.ingramcontent.com/pod-product-compliance
Lightning Source LLC
Chambersburg PA
CBHW071129260626

47162CB00003B/723